A Prequel

A MOM WITH BLUE FEATHERS

CORINNA TURNER

ALSO BY CORINNA TURNER:

I AM MARGARET series
For older teens and up

Brothers *(A Prequel Novella)* *
1: I Am Margaret*
2: The Three Most Wanted*
3: Liberation*
4: Bane's Eyes*
5: Margo's Diary*
6: The Siege of Reginald Hill*
7: A Saint in the Family
'The Underappreciated Virtues of Rusty Old Bicycles' *(Prequel short story) Also found in the anthology:* Secrets: Visible & Invisible*

I Am Margaret: The Play *(Adapted by Fiorella de Maria)*

UNSPARKED series
For tweens and up

Main Series:
1: Please Don't Feed the Dinosaurs*
2: A Truly Raptor-ous Welcome*
3: PANIC!*
4: Farmgirls Die in Cages*
5: Wild Life*
6: A Right Rex Rodeo*
7: FEAR
8: A Different Kind of Camouflage
9: A Different Kind of Freedom
10: What's Done is Done
11: Weigh the Odds
12: A Nest of Piranha'saurs†

Prequels:
BREACH!*
A Mom With Blue Feathers
A Very Jurassic Christmas*

Short Stories (ebook only):
'Liam and the Hunters of Lee'Vi'
'A Truly Clawful Christmas'*
'A Very Jurassic Lent'
Also available as a paperback:
Three Clawsome Tales*

FRIENDS IN HIGH PLACES series
For tweens and up

1: The Boy Who Knew (Carlo Acutis)*
2: Old Men Don't Walk to Egypt (Saint Joseph)*
3: Child, Unwanted (Margaret of Castello)*
4: A Lion for a Tomb (Ignatius of Antioch)
5: The Higher You Go (Pier Giorgio Frassati)†

Do Carpenter's Dream of Wooden Sheep? *(Spin-off, comes between 1 & 2)*

1: El Chico Que Lo Sabia (Spanish)
1: Il Ragazzo Che Sapeva (Italian)

YESTERDAY & TOMORROW series
For adults and mature teens only
Someday: A Novella*
1: Tomorrow's Dead†

OTHER WORKS

For teens and up
Elfling*

'The Most Expensive Alley Cat in London' (Elfling *prequel short story*)

For tweens and up
Mandy Lamb & The Full Moon*
The Wolf, The Lamb, and The Air Balloon (Mandy Lamb *novella*)

For adults and new adults
Three Last Things *or* The Hounding of Carl Jarrold, Soulless Assassin*
A Changing of the Guard
The Raven & The Yew†

† Coming Soon
*** Awarded the Catholic Writers Guild**
Seal of Approval

CONTENTS

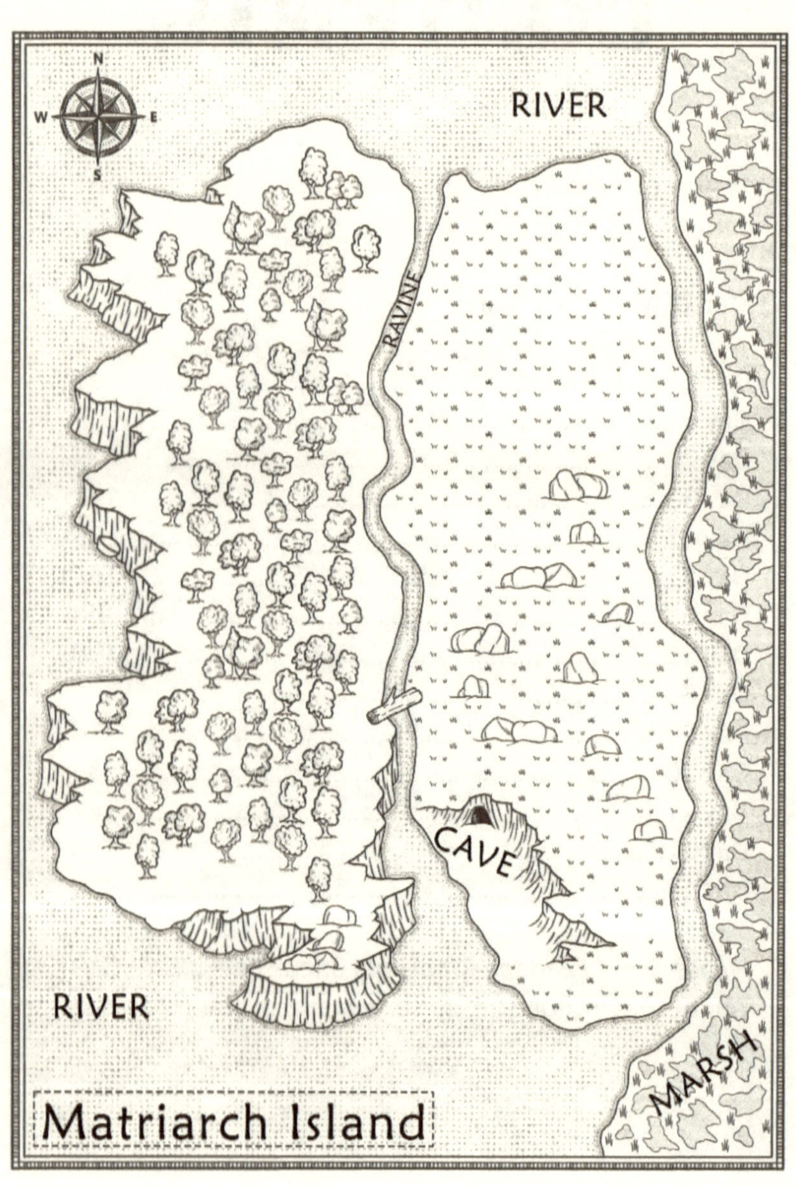

N
W E
S
RIVER
RAVINE
RIVER
CAVE
MARSH
Matriarch Island

DAY 2

TIME: 7 YEARS BEFORE THE MAIN UNSPARKED SERIES.

JOSHUA

Feet away, the fully-grown Dakotaraptor—as tall as Dad and many times longer—stands looking right at me. My heart pounds, *thud, thud, thud, thud,* each beat so hard it hurts, and a strange ringing fills my ears as I stare at my death. I wanna run for the cliff, but the raptor will be on me in one bound. My body's shaking, and I'm furious with myself, 'cause only little kids move when there's a predator around.

The raptor raises her muzzle, sniffing...about to spring? For a moment I'm afraid I'm gonna wet myself, even though I'm eleven. Or just run away, screaming like an idiot.

But I can hear what Dad said to me, once. *Someday, Josh, there might come a time when it's over, and there ain't nothing that will save you. Then there's only one choice left—whether to take it like a man.*

When Dad imagines this moment, that's what I want him to picture. Me taking it like a man.

And I want it to be true.

I'm not gonna run. I'm not gonna scrabble at the

cliff like a panicked puppy while the raptor drags me down from behind.

I stand straight and look her in the eye—and wait.

DAY 1

ISAIAH

"There are plenty of fish!"

Zech has only just given the all-clear, and it feels like my hand's barely left the door control, but Josh is already down by the stream, peering into the rippling water.

"Look, Dad! Trout, whitefish, sauger…catfish, see?"

His ten-year-old voice isn't too loud, despite his excitement. His Uncle Z's on watch in the Habitat Vehicle's turret, of course, rifle in hand, but it's always better not to draw attention. We'd rather be outside fishing and enjoying the September sun than sitting in the HabVi waiting for a prowling carni'saur to clear off.

"Well, don't catch them all before I get my turn." My big brother's voice comes over my earpiece, and Josh's. Josh and I have switched off the audio between our two, since we'll be outside together.

"We'll never catch them *all!*" Josh tells Zech, still staring into the water. "There're so many this year."

"Guess they had a good summer," I say.

Glancing around, I admire the strategic terrain again. We're surrounded on three sides by cliffs, crags, and boulders that make a decent deterrent for large carni'saurs. The small river or mountain stream—it's between the two, size wise—is just deep and fast enough to create a bit of a barrier between us and the long stretch of grass and vegetation on the other side. Near-as-never-mind our own private beach. We can set the motion sensors to cover the cliffs and boulders, and concentrate mostly on surveilling that open land across from us. Sweet.

I drop from the HabVi's side door, leaving it open in case we need to make a quick retreat at some point, and head down the slope, carrying my fishing pole, gear, and a cooler with a few snacks and drinks. Finding a comfortable spot to settle on the bank's rather dry grass, I make sure the cooler's stable, and start laying out my fishing gear.

By the time I'm ready to cast, Josh has already kicked his boots off, waded out into the shallows, and taken up a position on a flat rock, his thin, sleek fishing spear held ready.

"Sure you don't wanna use a pole?" I tease him. "It's so much more restful."

"And boring!" *Plop!* The spear flashes down into the stream and emerges with a flapping fish on the end. Josh gives the spear a sharp flick, with an extra little twist to free the fish from the barb. *Splat* — the fish lands on the bank nearby, splashing me.

"Hey!"

Josh snickers. "Sorry! Come on, slow poke, or I'll catch more than you!"

I roll my eyes. Even Zech, who's way more competitive than me, don't pretend to be able to out-fish my son. Josh is like a heron with that spear of his.

I cast, place the pole into its holder and settle back on the bank in the sun, watching Josh — *plop-splat* — fishing with an efficiency I can't hope to match. Still, no need to worry about catching enough to justify the trip to this remote location. Zech and I can simply relax, and Josh will fill the fish-locker for us and enjoy every minute of it.

Plop-splat.

He's eleven tomorrow. How is that even possible? Seems no time since I were carrying him, gurgling happily, in a sling on my front. Or that he were crawling around my feet on days like this, chirping back to any bird or 'saur nearby.

Plop-splat.

Eleven. He's still a child — just. He's already so sensible and level-headed. Only a few more years, now, and he'll be a man, pretty-much. And he'll be a good one. Still, it's so hard to imagine. My little

Joshua...

Despite the approaching fall, it's warm in the sun today, as the hot summer still refuses to yield its grip. I could happily take a nap, but Zech or no Zech, I'm not doing that while Josh is out-vehicle with me. I don't have to stay on high alert, but I do have to stay awake...

Plop-splat.

A huge trout cascades me in water as it splashes down on the bank.

"Aw, come on, Josh!"

"You looked like you were nodding off!"

"Were not. That's one fine fish, though. That will do for dinner."

"Don't I get to pick?" says Josh. "If Christmas and Easter start at nightfall, then by dinner-time it's my birthday too, right?"

Zech snorts from my earpiece.

I shrug. "Well, I guess you could argue it that way, little lawyer. Your birthday being a special occasion and all. Yeah, you can pick."

"Okay. But not until it's time to cook. I might catch a better one by then!"

"You might, at that. You are unbelievable with that spear of yours."

JOSHUA

I shrug Dad's praise away and turn back to the teeming water. Why do he and Uncle Z make such a big thing about my spear-fishing? Anyone could do it, right? You just watch, and you can guess which way they're gonna go and then...

Plop.

I flick the fish onto the bank—*splat*—a little further from Dad, this time. It's funny when they splash him, but if he gets too soggy he'll wanna go back into the 'Vi. Even with the strong sun, there's a slight nip of fall in the air, biting at my bare feet. Some years it rains on my birthday, but tomorrow...I glance at the sky. Yeah, unless some'at changes a lot by this evening, tomorrow we'll still have sun! We can fish and chill out all day.

*Ooo, look at that one...*I track a plump trout until...*yes...*

Plop. Got'ya. I flick it to shore. *Splat.*

"I still think we shoulda tried the ice rink again," says Uncle Z in my ear, obviously talking to Dad.

I shoot a glare at the turret, then turn back to the water and try to ignore them.

"He don't wanna go to a city-rink." Dad's voice gets a slight edge to it, like it always does when they're arguing about how best to deal with my...problem. "He don't wanna go in-city, period."

"Yeah, but he's gotta, ain't he? Sometimes. Why not

practice getting him to leave the 'Vi for some'at fun?"

"Because it ain't fun for him!" snaps Dad. "I'm not torturing him for his birthday treat!"

"He's gotta learn to cope with—"

"I've already said he's going with me or you to the store and the shop *every* time we go in-city from now on, ain't I? He's old enough now people won't look twice, even if we are clearly hunters. Now give it a rest and keep your eyes open. It's his birthday, for Saint Des's sake. Almost."

Uncle Z shuts up at last and I stare into the water, trying to concentrate. But I miss my next thrust.

What did Uncle Z have to bring that up for? I hate cities so much.

It didn't used to matter. Dad and Uncle Z never used to even *let* me leave the 'Vi—not that I wanted to. Only after dark. Then I were allowed to venture out with them and join the other hunters around the firepit or grill or whatever the 'Vi-park had for a gathering place. Never in daylight.

I didn't rightly understand why, 'til they took five-year-old me to that Father Morris to arrange a baptism—a just-to-make-sure baptism, 'cause Dad had already done it shortly after I were born. They thought I were old enough by then that the city-priest wouldn't freak out when he realized I live in the HabVi all the time, the way the social workers did when I were a baby. But, boy, did he. The priest and Dad ended up having a tug of war over me right there in the church parking lot—I were crying, all the adults were shouting—sick shudders still run through my belly at the memory.

Dad and Uncle Z ran away—literally ran—carrying me, leaving that Father Morris screaming after them that he were gonna call...someone or other, and they would...some'at or other, but it boiled down to taking me away from Dad and locking me up in-city.

We left behind a load of rubber on the pavement of the 'Vi-park and a ton of expensive gear that were being serviced in the shop, and crossed the border into Yoming State only a few hours later. Didn't come back to Exception State until I were seven, though we like it better here. By then Dad and Uncle Z weren't so worried. I could go outside in the 'Vi-park, any time. Lots of hunters start taking their kids on short hunting trips from about seven onwards. But we ain't never been back to *that* city. And even *now* we don't go nowhere where someone might figure out that I live in the 'Vi full-time.

It were when I were seven that I saw that amazing video of people ice-skating—just flying over the ice— so Dad and Uncle Z took me to a rink for my birthday. Almost all 'Vi-parks are right on the outskirts of the city, just inside the fence, and I hadn't left one since I were five. That were the last time we dared go to church—and we always went to the closest one, Christmas and Easter only.

I'd never wanted to go further into no city, but when I did, to go to the rink, I found I actually couldn't stand it *at all*. Felt like the roof were gonna fall on me. Like the place were about to chew me up and eat me. Like I couldn't breathe, trapped there among all those buildings and people and artificial scents and sounds.

I guess it were only then that Dad and Uncle Z realized there were some'at wrong with me. They've been arguing about how to fix it ever since. Uncle Z prefers a tougher approach, thinks I should learn to grin and bear it. Dad's more understanding.

It's so not what I wanna think about on my almost-birthday. Thanks for nothing, Uncle Z!

Plop. I miss another thrust.

"Come have a drink, Josh," calls Dad. "You've already been at it a while."

Yeah, there's quite a heap of fish. I should gut them and get them into the freeze-drier.

I splash to shore and put my spear beside Dad's useless fishing pole, resting there in its mount. He offers me a canteen, but I shake my head.

"I'm gonna take care of these first."

He smiles. "Ah, you're Mr. Responsible, you are. You're right, though. Let's get them done."

ISAIAH

Josh squats on the bank on the other side of the pile of fish, pulls out his belt knife and gets to work—guts into a biodegradable starch bag I've taken from my gear, clean fish into a second. I draw my own hunting knife and do the same. We don't want no carni'saur to show up, following the growing scent of fish blood, nor do we want his fine catch to spoil in the sun.

"These are excellent fish."

"Yeah." He don't look up from his work, his knife flashing swiftly over a silvery whitefish.

Zech's upset him, bringing up his city-phobia in his usual insensitive way. I think a swearword at my brother, up there in the turret. He don't seem to get that this ain't just some little dislike Josh has. I can't watch my son going white and clammy and gasping for breath and think that he just needs to *try harder*. No. He needs very small doses, build up gradually.

Zech's just worried, I guess. I mean, I am, too. But why did Zech have to bring it up *today*?

I toss the final filet into the clean fish bag. "There. Well, that's a good start. Good job, Josh."

Josh smiles, and before I can think about getting up, he's grabbed one bag in each hand and bounded up the riverbank to the 'Vi. It looms 'bout sixty feet away, towering above us with its steel window shutters, huge wheels, and massive ground clearance, the full observation turret sticking up from the middle of the roof. The light armor glints in the sun. Well, light, compared to a tank. Even so, the cliff and the mountain range rising behind it dwarf our happy home.

Josh hasn't had much of a growth spurt yet, and the floor is still above his head, but he springs up at the doorway without pausing, one foot landing precisely in one foothold, the other in the second, and with a vaulting leap, he's inside, his hands never touching down. I hear the clang of the freeze-dryer's door closing, then the low roar of the incinerator as he drops the bag of fish guts to its fiery fate. And then he's leaping down from the doorway and racing to join me again, arriving beside me in a puff of sandy dust.

"Want a drink now?"

"Yeah!"

I hand him the bottle and he drinks thirstily. "Thanks, Dad! Caught anything yet?"

"Nah. Not with you stirring the water up all the time."

"You're not even trying, admit it," says Zech.

I ignore him. So does Josh.

"What, so now I'm getting the silent treatment?"

Josh looks round at the turret and makes a rude gesture, though not so rude I'd have to punish him for it. Yeah, Zech's really upset him.

"It's just 'cause he cares, y'know," I say softly.

"Well, mebbe he could *not care* until my birthday's over. That'd be good. Can we stop talking about it?"

"Oh, Josh, your Uncle Z and I won't always be here forever, y'know. One day you'll *have* to be able to do stuff in-city by yourself—"

"Dad? Seriously?" Josh's wail cuts me off.

"Ah, sorry, Josh. I won't mention it again. Hey, come 'ere." I put an arm around him and draw him in for a hug. He lets me, but without the enthusiasm he'd once have shown. It's the same now when we have a carni'saur or dangerous herbi'saur in the rear pen and I have him sleep in with me in the 'master bedroom' for extra safety. He complies, 'cause we raised him obedient, wouldn't be safe no other way. But he don't do it excited at the novelty, no more, just grudgingly, obviously feeling it a slight to his approaching manhood. Heck, he's growing up so fast. But he accepts the hug, and after a moment even leans into it for a while. Then he's on his feet, grabbing his spear and heading back to his fishing rock.

Plop-splat.

By the time Josh has deposited his second catch of fish in the 'Vi, the sun is so strong that he gleefully strips off his shorts and T-shirt and starts rolling down the bank into the river—*splash*—over and over, with much giggling and laughter and satisfaction.

No, he's not quite grown-up yet. We've got a year

or two more.

When I see him so completely at home in his natural environment, so confident and radiant in his love for the wilderness, I don't regret how I raised him. No city kid is this happy. No city kid will have the career fulfillment my son's gonna have. I guess you can't have both, right? Josh is wilderness-bred and he can't cope with the city. But drop some city-people down in the wilderness, and they'd hyperventilate fast enough, and not think there were nothing *wrong* because of it. So can Zech really say there's some'at *wrong* with Josh?

Josh just needs to be able to cope *enough*. And he will. We'll get there. But if Zech brings it up again this trip, I'm gonna stuff pebbles in his sleeping bag. If Josh don't get to it first.

If he went for pebbles, that is. That one time, after what Zech did to Rudy the velociraptor, Josh crept into his cab-bedroom at two in the morning, went right up to his ear, then let rip a full-volume Utahraptor "found some prey" call. Scared Zech half to death. Scared him so bad his sense of humor suffered a complete failure, and Josh ran and shut himself in the turret until Zech calmed down enough to see the funny side.

But Josh were only six then—and Zech's slept with his door locked ever since.

JOSHUA

"What are you thinking about?" Dad asks after I've lain on the bank for a while, drying off.

"Rudy the raptor," I say. More or less truthfully. Mebbe I could roar like a T. rex, *really* loud...

"You are, huh?" I don't fool him, because after a moment, he adds, "Revenge is bad, y'know that. Saint Des don't like it. Nor Momma Mary. Nor God. He *really* don't like it."

I sit up again, avoiding Dad's eyes. "I know."

"Then stop thinking about, ah, Rudy, 'kay?"

I hang my head. "Yeah. 'Kay."

I mean, Uncle Z *does* care. It's just thinking about the city puts my insides into a tangle, and I weren't expecting to have to feel like that for the whole of this trip. Why does he have to be so...so…

No, I don't wanna think about it no more.

I pull my shorts and t-shirt back on. I'm just reaching for my spear, to go catch some more fish, when some'at on the far bank snags my attention.

After I watch for a moment, a long, thin neck, with a small, bird-like head, appears over the top of a bush.

I tilt my head back and warble a musical call.

Dad looks around. "Huh? What's out there? Ornithomimus, is it? Oh yeah, there it is."

The bird-like head cocks this way and that, peering in our direction.

I eye the sleek neck. "I think it's a *golden* ornithomimus, Dad! See the feathers..."

I call again. This time, the herbi'saur calls back, stepping out from behind the bush. Yep, golden feathers all over, blazing in the midday sun.

Dad whistles, very softly. "Whew, look'it that."

"Zoos pay good money for those, y'know," says Uncle Z.

"It got awful close, Zech," says Dad. "You asleep up there?"

"I've been watching it for fifteen minutes, but I never heard of no one et by an ornithomimus—they ain't even got teeth—and I thought no one were talking to me. How about we try to catch it?"

Dad sees my face fall. "We're on vacation, Zech, remember? Fishing and lazing, right? If it's still around when we're ready to go, sure. Until then, it's just pretty scenery, okay?"

Uncle Z gives an exaggerated sigh, but don't insist, saying nothing more. It's not that I'd mind trying to catch it, normally. I love fine animals, and Uncle Z's always talking about "bills to pay." But we *are* on vacation, right? The moment we start going after that critter, it's just a normal day.

I call again, more loudly. The orni calls back, a challenging note entering its voice.

"Hold your horses, Josh," says Dad. "Don't lure it

over here. They're territorial, remember, and 'kick like an orni' is a saying for a reason, y'know that."

I sigh—Dad never wants me to make friends with nothing much larger than I am—but I give up my conversation with the orni. It stalks back and forth for a few minutes, making me think of the ostrich bird I saw in a video once. That ostrich reminded me a lot of an orni, except it didn't have a long tail or wing-arms.

"I can see why zoos like 'em," I say, as the plumage glints and shimmers.

"Oh, it's not just the feathers," says Dad. "You know they're endangered, right? They're one of those breeds that have never held their own well in the wild."

"Why not? Normal ornis are everywhere. Real successful."

"Yes, but this ain't a natural breed. Y'know, an *original* breed—well, as original as any of 'em turned out by the time the scientists had messed around with them. And when, later, they bred those beautiful gold feathers into the species, they bred some important stuff out. But they're so pretty, people are keen to capture 'em and breed them in controlled conditions to keep the species alive."

"They don't breed well in the wild, right?"

"Exactly. They're hopeless at nesting and taking care of their young. Site their nests badly, don't guard them well enough, abandon the chicks, half the time. Useless mothers."

I think about that for a moment. "So...they're like my mom, then?"

ISAIAH

Josh's quiet question makes me look at him, sharply. "Well, that's...that ain't really a fair comparison. The golden ornis just don't have the instincts no more. They can't help it. 'Cause, y'know, we sometimes *say* an animal loves its young, but it ain't true. It's all instinct. You can't, like, genuinely love without making a conscious choice to put everything on the line for the other person and, well, only humans can do that."

Josh's silence deepens and, belatedly, I wish I could bite out my tongue. In my attempt to be fair to the ornis and educate Josh, I've just told him...

"So, my mom," he says at last, "*chose* not to love me."

I've always been completely open with Josh about his mom. Whenever he asked a question about her, I answered it. Mebbe city-folk would be horrified that I told him at the age of four that she hadn't wanted him, and by the time he were six he knew she'd tried to kill him, and knew by the age of seven that she only gave birth in the end because I handed over every penny of my savings. But I were determined he grow up knowing and not building fantasies about what might have happened, only to have some terrible, identity-up-ending shock waiting for him when he were older.

I sigh. But there's no getting around the truth. "Yeah. That's what it boils down to."

"But why did she want me dead?" he asks very softly.

I put out my arm and gather him to my side, heedless of whether the movement spooks the rare herbi'saur. "Oh, Josh, she didn't really want *you* dead. She didn't recognize you were there at all. I guess that were the biggest problem. She thought you were just cells."

"I *am* cells." He frowns up at me, brow creasing.

"So am I. But, I meant, she thought 'cause you were just very small, you didn't count. That you weren't really there yet."

"But if I weren't there, she wouldn't have been worrying about it at all."

I sigh again. Josh is still too young to grasp this very unscientific viewpoint. "I don't think she'd have wanted to hurt you if she coulda held you in her hands, Josh."

"But she coulda once I were born. And she still didn't want me."

"Didn't wanna raise you, no, but she wouldn't have *hurt* you, then." Heck, these conversations don't get no easier. We've taught him all about how humans are like raptors and should mate for life and everything, and I'm still waiting for him to ask *so why weren't you married to my mom?* The fact he hasn't makes me wonder if he's asked his Uncle Z—and exactly what his Uncle Z told him. The truth is ugly. I guess I'm worried my son will pity me—or be disgusted. Or, worst of all, hate himself because of what his mother did.

"Josh, I'm so glad she didn't wanna raise you," I blurt. "Because if she had, I wouldn't've got to do it. You know that, right?"

His forehead wrinkles again. "Uh, know what?"

"That...that I'm so glad you exist."

His face clears. "Oh, yeah, I know *that*."

No, he don't hate himself. He don't secretly think I couldn't really want him. I'm just being paranoid.

"Dad?" Josh sounds tense, like he's about to ask some'at real important.

Uh-oh. "Yeah?"

"Do...do all women act like that?"

"Like...what?" It comes out awful cautious, but I can't help it. "Bad mothers?"

"Yeah. And...stuff." His eyes slide away from mine. Yeah, Zech told him, didn't he? That I were too drunk to make a real decision and she weren't, but she did what she wanted anyway. Well, it's probably for the best.

"No, of course not. Most women ain't bad mothers and hardly any of them act...like *that*. Same as most men don't act like that. You just get the odd dud egg."

Josh looks awful relieved. "Why've you and Uncle Z never found mates, then?"

"Wives," I correct. "Well, it ain't that easy to find women who wanna marry hunters, Josh. 'Specially if you don't have a camp. Mebbe one day."

Even harder when you spend years not daring to venture in-city for a day longer than necessary or even to stop at farms. But I'm not mentioning that. Josh may be the reason why, but I don't regret it. I feel bad for Zech, though. He coulda been married with kids of his own, if I hadn't been so stupid. He says he don't regret it neither—wouldn't swap Josh for a wife—but...I still feel guilty, sometimes.

Still, it ain't like either of us are old or decrepit. I'm only twenty-nine and Zech's thirty-two. Mebbe now we don't have to worry so much about people seeing Josh and trying to take him away from us, we'll meet more ladies.

"If Uncle Z mated...got married...I'd have an Aunty Z, right? But if you got married I'd have an...um...?"

"A step-mom. But she could be, kinda, your proper mom, if you liked her. Since you don't have one."

Josh slides down to lie on the bank and stare at the blue sky. "That'd be nice."

How much does he miss having a mom? He's never given no sign that he thinks the subject worth more than the occasional thought, but...at his thoughtful face, unease gnaws at me.

Thankfully, after contemplating the step-mom idea for only a short time, he sits up again, looking for the orni, which he clearly finds far more interesting. His wistful expression as his eyes follow it makes me feel mean. But he don't call to it again, and I don't relent and tell him he can. If anything, Josh is almost too bold, when it comes to his natural environment. An orni may count as a fairly small 'saur, but it ain't some'at for a ten-year-old to mess around with, 'least, not unless it's well secured in a pen.

"Blue..." I tense as Zech speaks suddenly—so does Josh. "...sky today, ain't it?"

"Zech!" I throw a glare at the turret. Zech and I go to all this trouble teaching Josh to never, ever, *ever* cry wolf and now *Zech's* pranking us!

"What?" Zech puts on an innocent voice that fools neither of us.

There are three alert words, and they're all colors: Red, Green, and Blue. Red is most serious, Blue least. If Zech cried Blue for real, we'd have got up, picked up our gear, and headed briskly back to the 'Vi. Only once we were moving would Zech tell us why. Move first, information second. If he'd cried Green, we'd have grabbed the gear real fast and run. Red, heaven forbid, means drop absolutely *anything*, leave *everything*, and sprint.

Mebbe Zech's trying to distract Josh from the orni. Or mebbe he's still miffed that we got so angry with him. Or mebbe he were trying to rescue me from any continuation of the awkward conversation. Mebbe all three.

False alarm, anyway. We don't have to go in-'Vi.

Josh sprawls on the bank again, basking like a lizard, but soon he's up and grabbing his spear, all energy. The orni retreats fifty feet when he springs back onto his flat rock, but seems fairly unconcerned. This is such a wild region, they probably don't have much experience with people.

I'm quite happy to go on lying in the sun, watching Josh fish.

"You gonna get your harmonica out tonight, Zech?" I ask at last, just to show he's forgiven, 'cause I don't really need to ask. He always gets his harmonica out when we're on vacation.

"I guess I might be persuaded." Which is what he always says.

Silence falls again, broken only by the river and the occasional distant warble from the golden orni. And a regular *plop-splat* from our little heron.

Before long I'm getting drowsy again. I sit up and take a look in the cooler. Oh yeah, I threw in that pack of city-bought fruit bars, for a treat.

"Wanna fruit bar, Josh?"

Josh don't look around. Having tossed a trout longer than my lower leg onto the bank a few minutes ago, he's clearly found some'at else of particular interest already. "Uh, later?"

Grinning, I extract a bar for myself, rip it open, and take a bite.

"Got'ya!" Josh's triumphant cry draws my gaze back to him. He's pinning a huge fish to the rock, one foot on its tail, as he gets a firm hold of it with his hands. He draws the spear out, and with another quick jab, finishes it off. "Look, Dad! *This* one's for dinner!" He hefts the monster fish triumphantly.

"*RED!*" Zech's voice cracks in my ear like a whip and he is *not* fooling.

I drop the fruit bar and shoot to my feet as Josh— *thank God, good boy!*—lets go of his fish at once. He leaps to the bank, dropping his precious spear and heading on up the slope without pausing. I start to run too, catching up to him in a few strides.

"There's some'at coming downstream!" Zech's voice is tense. "Water— Get Josh inside..." His voice rises, panicked. "No, the tree! Get to the tree! Grab

Josh, hold onto him!"

There's only one tree of significance nearby, a stubby, gnarled willow. I swerve towards it, glancing to the side to check Josh is following, but he's already changed direction. I glimpse upriver, but it's only as I face front again and carry on sprinting that my mind makes sense of what I saw. A wave—fierce like the storm waves we saw that one time we took Josh to the sea—is roaring down on us.

Zech's right. There's no time to reach the 'Vi.

JOSHUA

Dad reaches the tree just ahead of me. He wraps one arm and both legs around the little trunk, anchoring himself firmly, then reaches out toward me.

Water's roaring up behind me, fast, but I don't turn to look. I pound my feet against the ground as fast as I can, trying to cover the last few feet super-quick.

Almost there...

Dad's hand clamps around my wrist, and he hauls me toward him. He's gonna pull me up against the trunk and pin me there. Another step and I'll—

The water hits from behind like a charging triceratops, knocking my legs from under me. Dad's hand tightens around my wrist so hard a squeak of pain escapes me...but it's not enough. The force of the water drags my wrist through his fingers—he manages to grip my hand, just—but it's fish-slimy and the next second it slides free.

"*JOSH!*"

I glimpse his horrified face—then I'm being tossed and spun and whirled in the water like a piece of driftwood as I'm carried away.

ISAIAH

"JOSH!" I'm yelling as loud as I can with the water pounding the breath out of me, but it's no good. He's *gone*. For a moment pure panic paralyzes me. *Josh...*

I've gotta go after him!

But even as I start to ease my grip on the tree's trunk, I become aware of a voice bellowing in my ear.

"ISAIAH! *Hold on!* Hold onto the tree! Can you hear me? Hold on! Do not let go! You can help Josh best by *holding on*, do you understand? Just hold on tight and as soon as it's over we can drive downriver and get Josh. Just *hold on*, okay?"

Zech repeats himself, over and over, until the panic eases enough for me to grasp that he's right. The temptation to throw myself into the surging water dies away. "Okay, okay, Zech," I gasp, finally. "I'm holding...*bleugh*...on." Spitting water from my mouth, I crane my neck, trying to look over my shoulder. Is it me or is it still getting deeper? It were half-way up my chest when it snatched Josh, now it's up to my neck.

Very carefully, still hanging on as tightly as I can, I begin to inch my way up the tree, letting the water buoy me upwards. Finally I'm able to climb above the waterline, sitting on a just-about-thick-enough branch and clinging to the trunk 'cause the branch is bending under me.

"Zech," I gasp. "Josh is gone..."

"I know. I know. Just hang on until it's safe to get back to the 'Vi, and we'll go find him, okay?" Zech's voice is unusually strained.

I stare at the surging water below me. Huge tangles of grass and branches float past. Entire logs. A drowned mountain goat. Followed by a drowned Dakotaraptor. A juvenile. Already almost as tall as me and several times longer from nose to tailtip. Mebbe it didn't run fast enough when the pack matriarch sounded the alarm. I shudder. Josh is barely larger than the goat. Can he even survive the turbulent water? The thought that he might already be floating silently along, as limp and still as those animals...

"I shoulda gone after him! I shoulda—"

"Don't talk nonsense," snaps Zech. "You think you coulda caught up with him, even found him, in *that*? It wouldn't have helped *at all*. Just hold on and keep it together, okay? It won't be long before this dies down.

Flash floods don't last long."

"Where the heck did it come from?" My voice comes out high, with a faint hysterical note. "This don't look like no flash flood zone!"

"I guess somewhere further up into the mountains the weather's broken and a storm's dropping one heck of a lotta rain. Some places flood regular and can be avoided, but you can get a flash flood on pretty much any river like this, once in a blue moon. We got unlucky."

Unlucky. It's too mild a word.

Josh...

O God, Saint Des, Momma Mary, Mom, please, please, please look after him!

JOSHUA

I try to swim, but the water's so rough, tossing me this way and that, I can barely tread water enough to keep my head up. *Eugh!* As a wave smacks over my head, I inhale water and choke, trying frantically to snatch breaths in between coughing and spluttering and more waves.

I gotta get to the bank! So I *gotta* swim...

Desperately, I strike out again, but it's hopeless. The storm surge tosses me around like a fallen leaf.

The next time I'm spun around, I glimpse high

ravine walls on both sides. Getting to the edge of the river won't do no good right now. Too dangerous. Okay, so I need to tread water. Save energy. Let the current carry me through this gorge to somewhere with low banks where I can climb out.

If I don't drown first. I inhale more water as the river dunks me under the surface again—I come up, coughing and choking. *Saint Des, help!* I'm too small...

I whizz past a rock, peeping up above the flood. The current carries me clear of it, but I start trying to see ahead, afraid I might smash into the next one—but there's nothing I can do about it. I've got no control over my direction at all. Half the time I'm facing backwards, half the time I—*glurk*—I go under again, just managing not to breathe in more water. How long can I survive this?

Trapped in this narrow channel, the water's showing no sign of losing any force. It's like being carried along by a...dunno, an inter-city bullet train?

Agh! The river dunks me again, and I inhale far too much water, struggling to stay afloat as I cough, fighting for air as I frantically try to clear my chest. When will this gorge end? If I don't get outta this, I'm gonna drown.

Saint Des? God? Help me!

Smack! Something strikes me hard on the back of

the head and the next moment it's riding over me, pushing me down under the surface. I kick upwards, but my reaching hands strike against some'at rough and solid...a great knotted tangle of branches and grasses has forced me underwater, and I'm trapped beneath it. Pulling myself along, I kick as hard as I can, trying to reach the back of it. *Ah, I need to breathe!* There weren't enough air in my half-waterlogged lungs when I went under. *Please, where's the surface? Air, air...*

My groping hands break above the water and with a final effort, I grab at the branches one last time and pull myself upwards...

...Only to come to a halt as my t-shirt snags on some'at. No! I twist and pull as hard as I can, but I'm still caught. No, why won't it just *rip*? I pull again, but my chest burns and dark spots are spreading over my vision, hiding the tangle of wood just in front of my nose. It won't come free and I'm out of oxygen and strength and everything.

I'll have to...have to slip out of it... That's what I have to do... Feebly, I reach for the hem of my t-shirt and try to lift it, but my arm's heavy as lead and blackness is swallowing everything...

ISAIAH

"I think the water's dropping." I peer down at the trunk of the tree. I can definitely see more of it now—I think.

"Yeah, I reckon so, but stay put for now. If you move too soon and get swept away, it ain't gonna help Josh."

"It would if I found him."

"Yeah? With no rifle or nothing? Some help."

"A grown man with a hefty stick and some'at solid at his back has at least a *chance* of fending off a pack of little velociraptors, say."

"Yeah, great, one single species you could—just mebbe—protect him from. But you'd probably get washed up in a different place, and there'd be no one then to provide cover while I were driving around looking for the two of you. And you know how dangerous that could be, when I found you."

"Josh knows better than to break cover until receiving the all-clear. And I'm certainly not gonna do a stupid thing like that."

"Yeah? Well, I'd say not, but some very experienced hunters have been so overcome with relief at the sight of a 'Vi they've forgotten all their training, let alone a ten-year-old boy, so I'd just as soon have you up in the turret when we find him, to be on the safe side. Doncha think?"

He's right, of course. I think Josh is too level-headed to make that mistake. But after hours of stress and fear and danger, people do stupid things. I can help Josh best by not getting myself swept downriver. That'll just leave Zech with two people to look for, all by his lonesome.

But is Josh even alive?

At that thought, all the rational arguments fly away again like thistledown.

I shoulda gone after him. I shoulda...

JOSHUA

The surging water pushes me sharply sideways, and suddenly I'm free. With my last scrap of strength, I pull myself upward...then my face breaks the surface and air rushes into my heaving lungs. Oxygen!

For long moments I can only cling tightly to the tangle of driftwood that almost drowned me and draw deep breaths of air into my aching chest. But finally, another smack from the wild river almost tears me from my...makeshift raft? Weakly, kicking my legs and pulling with my arms, I inch my way up onto it on my belly, like an alligator. It's large enough to hold me, just. Suddenly, being small is an advantage.

I lay my head down on the hard branches and lie there, shivering with cold, shock, and exhaustion as my mind tries to catch up. I guess this is a flash flood? Didn't look like the place for one, or Dad and Uncle Z wouldn't have stopped there. How far downriver am I gonna end up? Well, Dad and Uncle Z will be along right-quick to get me. Once I make it to shore—I try not to think *if* as I watch the water heaving and swirling, inches from my nose—*once* I make it to shore, I just need to keep my head and follow the survival plan. They'll soon come.

Yes, that's what I need to do. I try to run through the Things To Do as soon as I'm on dry land, but my thoughts are slow and heavy. I'll think about that later. Right now I'm just gonna...just gonna lie here...and enjoy the air...

ISAIAH

I look at the sky and check my watch. Heck, I've been up this tree for almost an hour. I glance up at the sky again, at the sun. Only an hour past noon, but with fall well on the way, the nights are drawing in. At this rate, how far downriver will we have time to get before dark?

On the other hand, waves still lap around the 'Vi, and we'd be wise to wait until the water's dropped before trying to drive off, in case we dig ourselves into the bank when it's at its very softest and have to waste even more time getting out.

I sigh heavily.

"Patience, Isaiah," says my big bro, making me wanna throw some'at at him. "More complications—and that means delays—come from haste in these situations than anything else, you know that."

I shoot a glare over my shoulder towards his silhouette, up there in the turret.

But he *is* right. Still...

"Show me a man who can be patient when his child has been swept away into a wilderness crawling with deadly predators, and you'll have found a saint!"

"Josh is smart, Isaiah. He knows what to do."

"He's ten years old, Zech! Even a pack of little velociraptors could take him down in about thirty seconds, and you know it!"

Silence from Zech. Because he does know it. He's just trying to keep me calm, is all.

Yeah, good luck with *that*, big bro.

JOSHUA

Nearby, I hear a velociraptor call: *Found some prey.*

Huh? Did I fall asleep? Or just into a daze? How much time has passed?

Well, I'm safe out here on my raft.

Hang on... I'm not moving anymore. The river still

laps all around me, but my little snag-raft is motionless as dry land.

Dry land... *Then*... I lie motionless, listening hard. Where is that raptor, and what's it found?

The weight of my hunting knife still pulls on my belt, but it'll be no help against even one velociraptor. It'd have to get far too close. A sturdy branch would be better. Will any of the branches in my 'raft' come loose easily? But they're probably really well lodged, and I don't dare move enough to find out.

More excited raptor calls. *Prey! Prey!*

They're being very noisy about it, though. So they've found carrion. Or what they take for carrion...

Every muscle in my body screws itself up, tighter and tighter, as I wait to hear footsteps splashing toward me.

Nothing. More happy raptor chatter. The sounds of meat tearing. Guess they've found some actual carrion. They're awful close, though. How long before they find me, too?

Slowly, I open my eyes, squinting against the light, and take in what I can see without moving my head. Okay, my raft is grounded on a wide area of flat rock. Water still trickles past between me and the shore, but it's probably less'n half a foot deep. From the faster rush of water from downstream, behind me, the shallows must end only a short distance away, spilling the shallow water back into a narrower, deeper channel.

The sounds of raptor-feasting are coming from about in line with the top of my head. I'm gonna have to move to see. Very slowly, I tilt my head up, straining to get a look. A feather suddenly whirls down in front of my eyes, and I barely keep from jerking away. It settles on a branch near my nose. A...golden?...feather. Bloodstained.

I move my head a fraction more and finally get a look at the raptor pack. Yes, they're gathered around the sodden, bedraggled remains of the golden ornithomimus. Guess the flood swept it away too. Well, it's saved me from the velociraptors— temporarily. How am I gonna get out of here?

I could wait, I guess—hope they eat their fill and clear off. But the chances of them not roaming around a bit more before they go are very slim. And every minute I wait increases the chances that some'at bigger and nastier—or more numerous—will show up, drawn to the smell of blood. Then, even if that don't get me, the velociraptors will be prowling around looking for a replacement meal.

No, far too risky to wait. Dad and I put on ScentBlock gel earlier to reduce the chances of our morning being disturbed, but most of it has probably washed off by now, and from the stinging, aching patch on the back of my head, my skin's broken there. And I see other cuts on my hands. As far as scent is concerned, I'm totally compromised. If I weren't downwind of them, they'd have noticed me already.

The pack are feeding busily, tearing off strips of meat and gulping them down. They've come out in the heat of the day to check for carrion while a lotta the larger carni'saurs are safely asleep in the sun. No fewer than twenty-one of them. Normal for this time of year in so wild an area. I count eight full-grown females and seven adult males, along with six young juveniles, this year's chicks. Probably several more hatched out in spring, and by the time the winter's over there may be only one or two of these left. But right now, they've still got six of their young 'uns. Nice for the pack, bad for me.

But they're distracted at the moment, so this is probably my very best chance to get away. How, though? Everywhere is open, the flat rock the river runs over extending on either side. I'm stiff and sore and tired. There is absolutely no way I can tip-toe—or splish-splash—my way out of sight without them noticing me.

I turn my head a bit further, slowly, carefully turning onto my belly to get a better look to the other side—and put myself in a better position to get up quick, if I need to.

A sudden eruption of snarls and hisses sends me motionless again. The smallest, scrawniest adult male is backing away from the carcass, having clearly offended its senior pack members in some way. Uh-oh. It's gonna look around for a safer meal, I bet. Can't get much safer than a small unarmed human, right?

The scruffy one is only the size of a spaniel, but it's sharp-toothed and ferocious. More to the point, the instant it finds me, the whole pack will be over here like a flash, and the other adults are all wolf-sized. I turn my head slightly and finish looking around.

Ugh. There's only one option. The last thing in the world I wanna do, right now, and it's a long shot whether I can even make it.

I eye my raft, trying to spot a solid branch that might be loose. Mebbe...that one. Slowly, stealthily, I shift my hands until I can grip it and pull, applying all the muscle control I can to avoid it coming free in a sudden jolt. Yes, it's shifting. A good yank from an upright position and it should come out.

I ease up a little, checking distances. Okay. It's do-able. Mebbe.

Saint Des, help?

I start to slide quietly off the back of the raft, still holding onto my chosen branch. Ooh, yeah, I'm awful stiff. Are my muscles gonna work?

I've got both feet under me in the shallow water

when the lone raptor's head turns sharply towards me. The next second it's coming with bouncy, lightning-fast strides.

Showtime!

I straighten, letting rip the loudest T. rex roar I can muster from my weary lungs. As the raptor skids to a halt, almost falling on its tail in fear that it's just made a terrible mistake, I heave on my branch.

Yes! It comes free.

With another roar—the pack's heads are all up, turned our way, anything to make them hesitate even a millisecond!—I turn and sprint downriver. It takes me closer to the carcass, worst luck, but...

The lone raptor's recovered. I hear the rapid *splash-splash-splash* of its footfalls as it comes after me again. Not scared enough of a T. rex my size that looks and smells so like a human.

Run, Josh, run!

Splash-splash-splash-splash...behind me.

Ah, I'm not gonna make it...

Splashsplashsplashsplash...and leap...

I spin around, using my turn to add extra power as I swing the stick with all my strength.

Smack. The stick collides with the raptor's head, knocking it from the air and sending it sprawling in the shallows, stunned or unconscious. But the pack are halfway to me, coming full-speed.

Roaring savagely, I hurl the branch at them, making them scatter, then turn and *sprint*.

ISAIAH

"I'm giving it ten more minutes, Zech, then I'm trying to get back to you, okay?"

The water's still lapping around the very base of the 'Vi, but the flow is gentler now.

"You be careful, Isaiah. We can't even drive off yet. You might as well wait."

"Easy for you to say. You think this is a comfortable position?" The least of my worries, right now, but my hands and my butt are numb and aching.

"So climb a bit lower and sit in that fork."

Huh. Zech's right. The water's dropped that much. I climb down and settle myself into the slightly wider, more comfortable perch. Then I sit there and stare malevolently at the water below me.

Drop! Come on, drop! Drop, you evil liquid, drop!

JOSHUA

My bare feet skid and slide on the smooth, slimy riverbed, but I keep running.

Run, Josh!

My chest burns. I can't get enough air after all that

drowning earlier...

Run!

Almost there! Almost!

The splashing behind me is getting closer, closer, closer, *closer*...

There!

The rock drops, shelving steeply in a kind of stepped waterfall. No way can I keep my balance running down that. I dive, arms first, like going down a very bumpy and uncomfortable slide, my hands clawing at the rocks, trying to gain traction, to pull me faster, elbows scraping, knees banging. A raptor's coming down behind me—*splash-splash-splash*—springing lightly on its lethal-clawed feet. I fight for every bit of speed I can get as I bump-bump-bump-bump-bump—nearly there...hot raptor breath tickles my heels...

Splash!

I'm in the water. My head goes under. Deep water? Yes, I can't touch the bottom. Deep and fast. By the time I claw my way to the surface I'm already some distance from where several raptors now cluster on the rocks, staring after me and hissing in angry disappointment. Yeah, the current has me. After earlier, I'm not sure drowning is quicker or nicer than being eaten, but right now it's far less definite.

The river's still running very high, from the look of

the banks, but the force of the flood has eased and it's flowing more normally. It could still drown me or batter me to death in its rapids, but mebbe I'll be able to get out before we come to any.

I'm gonna stay in here for a while, though. Let it take me out of the velociraptors' territory. I wouldn't put it past them to follow along the bank.

Mebbe not, though. They've got that poor orni, after all. And they *were* a little worried whether they were chasing a human or a very small rex. Poor suckers. Most humans can't imitate 'saurs as well as me, I dunno why not. Dad counts as a pretty good mimic, but Uncle Z and I can always tell it's him. I've always been able to fool them—and the critters themselves. No harder than human talk, to me. I don't see what's so difficult.

I tread water as gently as I can, to save energy. My limbs feel heavy, my muscles twinging every time I move them. I'm still gasping for breath. How long *can* I stay in the river, raptors or no? The water's so cold, I'm shivering already. To think only...I glance up at the sky...only a few hours ago I were rolling in here for fun. I can't wait to get out, now.

Shame I threw my stick away. I shoulda kept it. Woulda provided me with a little buoyancy. But again I remember the feel of that hot raptor breath on my heels and shudder. No, if I hadn't thrown the stick and delayed them that millisecond, they'd have had me. It were that close.

I try to keep an eye on the banks, try to keep my ears open too, though that's hard with the sound of water all around me. No sign of the pack. Not surprising. That were a nice, big, fresh orni. Their matriarch's obviously too smart to chase after me and risk some'at else eating it while they're gone. Still, I'd like to get just a little further away.

But I'm *so* tired. No, I'm gonna have to get out, whether I'm still in their territory or not.

Hey! *There...* I've just floated alongside quite a decent-sized chunk of log. I grab hold of it and...yes, it's enough to hold me up. Ah, that's better.

I lie on my back, my arms hugging the log to my chest, and let myself float. That's more like it. I'll just get clear of the pack, and then I'll climb ashore. After all, every bit of extra distance means longer before Dad and Uncle Z can reach me.

Right this moment, are they closing the 'Vi's shutters to be ready for travel and pulling away? Or is the water still too high? They'll be on their way real soon, I bet. I peer up at the sun. It's quite a while after noon, already. I fell asleep on my raft, I guess. Or passed out. I musta been on it for an hour, easily, floating along — or stationary, snagged in the shallows. How far have I come? Impossible to tell, but too far for them to reach me before nightfall, most likely. Not following search procedures.

I need to den up in sight of the river, so they'll find me first time, no problem. It'll just take them a while to get this far.

Huh. They'll know the storm surge coulda carried me a real long way, but all the same...if it were a full hour on that raft... I'd better get out very soon.

I start kicking, trying to move closer to the banks. Ugh, I'm so tired. Mebbe I'll just have to float along until I get washed ashore. Nah, rapids. And distance. I *gotta* get out!

I glimpse a flat, muddy beach not far ahead. *There.* I kick as hard as I possibly can. Cold, shaking, and aching, I don't dare let go of the log and try to swim the distance.

I'm getting there. Getting there...

The river catches me in an eddy and pushes me the last little way, and suddenly solid, motionless ground presses up along the length of my tired body. Heck, I could just lie here in these sun-warmed shallows and sleep. But a deadly little breeze ruffles my hair, carrying blood scent away from me.

I have to move.

ISAIAH

A matted snarl of branches bumps against the trunk, jerking me from the unthinking daze I've sunk into. Is...? Yes, the flow has slowed still more. Right, I'm gonna go back to the 'Vi. I twist around, my eyes scanning the area as I check for danger.

"You're all clear," says Zech, in my ear. "Mebbe it's time to make a move."

"That's what I'm thinking."

I shimmy down the trunk, keeping a careful hold of it as I slide into the water. But it's only thigh deep now, its force nothing I can't move against. I let go of the tree and take a step, my eyes fixing on the 'Vi. Huh, the water still hasn't dropped that much. I still can't see the—

Urgh! My chest constricts in horror, and I lurch forward at a stiff run, splashing my way up the bank. "Zech!" My voice comes out strangled. "Zech, the *'Vi!*"

"What's wrong?" Zech's voice is sharp. "What's the matter?"

"The 'Vi! The *'Vi!*" I can't find words, so deep is my dismay. All I can do is wave my arms like a madman and stumble onwards. "The 'Vi, Zech!"

I stagger right up to the vehicle, a few wavelets still lapping around my feet, which sink to the ankles the instant I stand still. "*Zech! O God...*" My groan is more appeal than cussing.

Zech's given up on getting a reply from me, 'cause a moment later he's there in the doorway, rifle in hand, jaw dropping in equal dismay as the door hisses open. He spits a cuss word, a bad one.

Yeah. The vehicle's sunk so deep into the sandy soil he can step straight out onto the squelchy bank — and does so, coming to stand beside me and stare at the catastrophe.

"Sheesh," he hisses. "We're sunk clear to our *belly*. What the heck..." He bends and grabs a handful of wet soil and lets it run between his fingers. "It's more sand than anything. I guess it took up all the water like a sponge and became virtually liquid. The weight of the 'Vi just pressed all the sand-water out from underneath and down it went. Heck, I've never seen a 'Vi this deeply bogged outside of an actual marsh."

I wanna *wail*, "Zech, what are we gonna do?" but I clamp my teeth together. *Keep it together, Isaiah. Keep it together for Josh!* "Well, we've gotta get it out," I say instead, trying to keep the quaver from my voice.

"Heck, yeah," says Zech. But after a moment he hesitates, dragging his booted feet out of the ooze and stepping back into the solid doorway. "Isaiah, I know you don't wanna hear this, but I think we'll have to wait for morning. The bank will have drained by then."

"*Morning*, we can't—"

"How can we pull it out when there ain't no solid

ground to pull it onto, Isaiah?" Zech speaks very firmly. "It's gonna be a difficult job as it is, but until the bank firms up again, it's simply not possible. Come inside, let's get a hot meal into you, then we'll turn out the lockers and get all the recovery gear located and organized and checked over, make sure everything's completely ready for a quick start tomorrow, 'kay?"

The disappointment in my chest pounds with my heartbeat, like a physical ache, and I can't help checking my watch. This is gonna cost us, what, six whole hours of traveling time? Six more hours before we can find Josh. Six more hours alone in the wilderness for my little boy.

No, far more than six. Even if the 'Vi comes out easily, it's gonna be a several hour recovery job in the morning. And if it don't—

Nausea strikes my stomach so viciously I have to swallow hard, afraid I'm actually gonna hurl. Zech steps back out into the muck and grabs my arm, steering me inside. "Come on, Isaiah. Wet clothes off, in the shower, get warm and dry. I'll cook some'at. You'll be no use to Josh or to me with a stinking cold. *Come on.*"

I let him tow me inside. I'm clammy and shaking, this latest shock combining badly with several hours of exposure up that tree. I wanna insist we get to work *right now*, pull ourselves out, *right now*, without delay, but Zech's right. It's simply not *possible*. We have to wait.

Hold on, Josh. Hold on.

JOSHUA

First of all, I lie still for a few moments, listening, looking, scenting the air, alert for any sign that a creature other than myself is nearby.

Nothing.

I sit up and scoop up a handful of mud, sniffing it. It's not great stuff, very little odor and not very sticky, but I smear it over my face, rub it into my hair, roll in it to cake my t-shirt and shorts, attempt to make it stick to my bare legs. My bare, cut legs. My elbows and knees are skinned, as well. I've got far too many cuts. My absolute first priority is to find a good sappy tree. I can worry about better scentCam after that.

Hang on! My hand flies to my ear, searching. Yep, my earpiece is gone, snatched by the wild water. Oh well. I'd be totally out of range here, anyway, though it woulda been useful to talk to the 'Vi when Dad and Uncle Z came to get me.

I go up the sloping mud beach on all fours and peep over the lip. Repeat the waiting and looking and listening and scenting. Though I don't wait as long as I normally would. I've *gotta* find a sappy tree, fast!

No sign of danger, though. Or even anything that a predator might be stalking. I eye the landscape. I've been washed far enough downstream that the river now runs through wide, flat valleys, with plenty of space to either side before it gets steep.

My heart leaps as I spot a promising tree silhouette in the far distance.

Crouching and crawling to take full advantage of cover—though mostly just crouching 'cause of the need for speed—I start to move, stopping to check for danger every time new ground opens up to my view.

It's quiet, though. The sun, thank God, remains high enough and strong enough that a majority of creatures are relaxing. I spook a jackrabbit that's crept out to feed for this very reason, and slip past a few birds in a tree without disturbing them, but hot, lazy silence hangs over the landscape. All the better for me.

Finally, I reach the sappy tree. After a particularly thorough check for danger—I'm about to make a racket, after all—I draw my hunting knife and, reversing the blade, use the saw to cut off a modest-sized branch. Then, I carefully clean and sheath the precious knife and retrace my steps to the river. I gotta be quick—but I gotta be careful!

Eventually—or what feels like eventually—I'm back on the riverbank with my little sappy log. Reluctantly, I get back into the shallows and wash my legs and feet, my arms and hands, and most particularly the back of my head, where — *ouch* — I have by far the worst wound. That's where my 'raft' ran me down. It bleeds after I wash it, but I just keep rinsing it over and over until it's both clotted and blood-free.

After sitting in the sun for a few minutes to get good and dry, I draw my knife again and slice through the log's bark to reach the gummy sap. Then it's just a matter of coating every wound or cut with the stuff and waiting for it to set as much as it's gonna any time soon. A dusting of dry powdery soil from higher up the beach to reduce the stickiness, and my wounds are tended.

I reapply a layer of mud all over before sniffing at the largest cut on the back of my arm, testing the scents. No, I don't think it's just wistful thinking, I really can't smell nothing but sap and mud. Carni'saurs have way better noses, of course, but to scent blood now, I reckon one would have to be so close that I'd be done for anyway. So that's one thing I can stop worrying about.

It only takes a quick inspection of the muddy beach to confirm that this is not where I wanna hang around for Dad and Uncle Z. The easy, open access to the water is clearly well used by herbi'saurs and carni'saurs both. I don't wanna be anywhere near here at dusk when the herbi'saurs come to drink and the carni'saurs come to prey on them. I need to mark the spot, though, so they know where I climbed outta the river. I use a sharp stone to gouge a big arrow on a rock, pointing to the river where I climbed out, and wedge some large sticks and things around the area as well. No, they shouldn't miss that. Not if they're actually foot patrolling, which they will be if they don't find me with an initial drive-by.

My next priority is definitely to find the safest spot I can to wait. No question, I'd class my status as 'confident.' There are three statuses in this situation: 'confident,' 'indeterminate,' and 'poor.' You decide which you are, and then you know what to do. 'Confident' means you're sure someone knows roughly where you are and is coming to get you soon. 'Indeterminate' means you think you've got a chance of rescue but you ain't completely certain. And 'poor' means you're fairly sure no one's coming for you.

Only if your status is 'poor' do you try to hike to safety. You're, like, fifty times more likely to be discovered—and eaten—if you're moving around. 'Course, if no one's coming, that's what you gotta do, tough jerky.

If you're confident, you just find the very safest place you can to den up, and you leave it only once or twice a day to drink—and do the necessary—and for nothing else. You don't worry about food unless you absolutely have to. You just stay put and wait.

If you're 'indeterminate' you den up for a few days to give rescue a chance to arrive, but you pay more attention to food—to keeping yourself in good condition—in case you have to downgrade yourself to 'poor' and take that hike.

But I'm definitely a 'confident.' Dad and Uncle Z will be along for me—though probably not until some-time tomorrow morning, the distance they gotta cover. I just need to hole up somewhere in sight of the river. I've still got quite a few hours of daylight left to find a good place. Though, the quicker I get myself tucked away, the better.

Returning to the water's edge, I slide the narrow filtration straw out from the seam of my knife sheath, carefully slipping the wire loop over my finger before bending to drink. Dehydration a some'at I can't afford, 'cause I'll start making stupid decisions. When I've drunk my fill, I equally carefully put the straw away again. Straw and mirror, that's what hunters carry in their knife sheaths, and I've got my handy cord in my belt. The chances of getting separated from your 'Vi are so low, it's not worth carting more of a survival kit.

That done, I collect my precious sappy branch—loosening my belt so I can tuck it through at the small of my back to keep it out of the way—and set off up-river, crouching and crawling again, making like a cautious deer.

I've gotta find more effective scentCam, as well as a good hidey-hole. And fast. The heat of the day is starting to fade, and all sorts of creatures will soon be out and about to graze and hunt. Thin-skinned, hornless, juicy little morsels like me should make themselves scarce, like that jackrabbit will have done.

He's already got his burrow picked out. Unlike me.

Noises from behind an outcrop to the left... I drop quietly into a patch of long grass and lie still, listening hard. A herd of triceratops? Sounds like. Rising, I creep silently up the rocks on my bare feet to a place where I can peer through to the other side.

Yep, triceratops. The closest ones are grazing just on the other side of these rocks, with the rest of the herd spread out across an open area of grass and shrub. Huge, horned, and armored, the healthy adults—easily as long as the 'Vi—have no fear of any carni'saur smaller than a T. rex, a very aggressive allosaur, or a large pack of highly motivated Utahraptors. Is there any way I could get myself into the middle of the herd and benefit from their protection? My gaze darts over the open ground, but there's nothing solid I could shelter in except a flimsy old log. The herd will probably move on before dark, anyway. It's not that late yet.

A triceratops crushes the end section of the log to

powdered wood under one big foot—without even noticing. Yeah. Mebbe not. The protection would be more dangerous than the predators. And I'd better not hang around here. I'd make a nice snack for anything checking around the edge of the herd for young, sick, or injured targets.

I climb carefully down from the outcrop, check that my log is secure, and go on my slow, careful way. Soon I'm passing over a long expanse of exposed riverbank. Animals could come down to the water anywhere here to drink. Scrub and bushes provide some cover as I creep along, but they'll provide no protection from a large herbi'saur blundering through—areas of crushed undergrowth prove that, as if I had any doubt—and certainly no shelter from predators. I have to keep moving.

The sun drops steadily through the sky as I continue my cautious trek. Heck, it will be going dark soon. Am I really gonna have to just fight my way into the thickest, tallest patch of scrub I can find, and hope I survive the dusk and dawn arrival of thirsty herbi'saurs at the water? Of course, the one thing more dangerous than denning up in this poor cover would be to still be moving around at dusk.

I shoot another glance at the sun and try to move faster, straining all my senses to make up for my speed, though they're already kinda-sorta aching from being on high alert for so long. This flat ground can't go on forever. If I can just find another outcrop, even the smallest crack or overhang would be better than a bush, especially if it were off the ground. Or even a good-sized tree. I scan the skyline again. Trees ain't good when it comes to keeping warm, though.

What I really want is a deep crack or small cave. Some'at that would exclude most predators simply on the grounds of size, with a narrow enough opening that, with the help of a good stick, it could be defended from velociraptors. With a climbable tree nearby, preferably, in case of piranha'saurs. 'Cause a shoal of those little nippers will overwhelm you in any cave you can fit into. They climb well, of course, but if you keep knocking them down with enough force, they'll usually give up and go away.

Right now I'd settle for a crack *or* a tree. Never mind both. Just one or the other. The light's turning warm and golden. Coughs, grunts, and calls reach my ears as the land stirs to life around me. Evening's coming far too fast.

Hang on. I pause for a breather, shading my eyes from the low sun as I peer ahead. Yes, there's rougher ground, up ahead! Now mebbe I can find somewhere to hide. Quickly.

I'm about to step forward when a scuffing sound and low breathing from behind a particularly large patch of bushes freezes all my muscles. I drop on my belly into the grass and creep forward, inch by painstaking inch, until I can glimpse...

I go flat on my stomach and lie motionless. A fully-grown male allosaur is having a dust bath in a well-used depression. Just my luck! Allosaurs, with their leathery hide and only a small feathery display crest on their head, take only a fraction of the number of dust baths that all-over-feathered 'saurs take.

On second thought...would I rather an entire pack of raptors were enjoying the dust? Yeah, a single allosaur is much safer. Kinda.

I lie very still and quiet, waiting for him to finish up and clear off. But he takes his time, twisting onto his back, his huge tail thrashing, little forelimbs stretching luxuriously as he rubs his backbone in the dirt. It would be either cute or funny, if I were watching from the safety of the 'Vi. With eighteen feet of thin air between us instead of half an inch of steel plates...not so cute.

Finally he hauls himself to his feet, shakes himself so hard I press my nose into my arm to prevent the drifting dust from making me sneeze, then stomps to the water's edge to drink. That done, he shakes again and plods off. I sit up and watch from the shelter of a bush, not letting him out of my sight until I'm quite sure he's actually *gone*, rather than simply taken up an ambush position nearby, ready for the herbi'saurs' dusk water run.

But no, he's gone. I'd better get past the dust bowl quickly, before the next critter turns up to use it.

Hang on… Fresh allosaur dung. Oh yes! That's better than this useless river mud. Not much is bigger and meaner than an allosaur. I coat myself liberally in his unintended gift.

Heck, it stinks.

Good.

The light is turning to evening so fast now that I more scamper than creep the rest of the way to the rougher ground, stopping only to pick up a particularly sturdy stick. Herbi'saurs call to one another as herds begin to move riverwards. And I don't just need to find a den, I need to find scentCam bedding too, for maximum safety overnight—and maximum warmth.

Still, I feel a little safer with the dung hiding my scent.

The gently rising and falling terrain right beside the river soon turns into rocky outcrops, and I circle each one, studying them. The wind-and-water-worn limestone is very smooth, worst luck. Not much shelter. If all else fails I could sleep right on top of one, I suppose. Cold, but safer than nothing.

Finally I spot a promising opening halfway up a steep rocky slope. The ground shows no signs of occupation but it's hard rock, no chance of proper tracks. Dung lies here and there along all these narrow, frequently used paths between the outcrops, herbi'saur and carni'saur and even a little mammal; no way to tell if any of it relates to the cave or not. Scooping up a sharp jagged rock and clutching my stick in my other hand, I move to the most sheltered position from which I can chuck the rock through the cave opening.

Clack-clatter.

If there's some'at already in residence, better to find out before I'm inside a cave with it. I wait, peeping and listening. Nothing stirs, so I grab another couple of missiles and inch up the slope, my bare feet silent against the rock. I near the hole, listening. Nothing. I chuck another rock in, hard, hearing it crack into the rear wall. The mouth is wider than ideal, but it's not a very big ca—

Some'at almost as large as me—with far too many teeth—bursts out, snarling.

ISAIAH

I stare through the window into the darkness, my hands clenching and unclenching helplessly. Night, and we've yet to stir one inch after Josh. It's like being trapped in a nightmare.

Well, it won't seem like night to Josh, yet. Merely dusk. But looking out from the safety of the well-lit 'Vi, it's as good as night, now.

Recovery gear lies all over the living area, neatly lined up and in the best possible order we could put it in, blocks and tackles and extra winch cables and heavy chains. A stack of traction boards. Zech's busy cooking two steaks over the stovetop, one of which I'm quite sure he's gonna force me to eat. Right now he shoulda been mixing up one of his nice desserts while I helped Josh lift that monster fish outta the oven. Zech would complain that the fish woulda tasted nicer fried, and Josh and I would roll our eyes at one another...

I swallow hard and turn my gaze to the table, but there's nothing left to do. And I mean, nothing. After obeying Zech by taking a shower and forcing down some lunch, we sorted the gear. Then I just sat and compulsively loaded magazines, new or old, filling every last one we possess. The last thing we want is to run out of ammo at some crucial moment tomorrow. Then I cleaned every firearm in the gun cabinet, including the rex gun and piranha'saur scatter gun. Everything except Zech's main rifle, which it woulda been rude to touch.

Now there's nothing for me to do. It's dark—almost—and I can't stop thinking about Josh. Where is he? Has he found a good place to shelter? Safe? Well, as safe as is possible. Warm? He must be so hungry. And frightened. He must wonder why we ain't come to get him yet.

What if he weren't even carried that far and he's just a mile or two downriver? I coulda *walked* to him. Mebbe I shoulda gone to check...mebbe we both should. Only, if we got et, who'd go rescue Josh tomorrow?

"Steaks are ready. Can you clear that stuff?" Zech jerks his head at our cleaned, oiled, immaculate arsenal.

Glad of a task, however small, I put the guns away again. But as I place the last one inside, I glimpse the pair of neatly wrapped birthday presents nestled in the bottom of the gun cabinet—the best hiding place, since Josh usually has no need to open it, having his own rifle with him in the 'Vi. I've kept myself together all afternoon, kept busy, concentrated on practical things that will help Josh, but now… I don't even have time to hide away in my bunk. All I can do is drop into the nearest chair and bury my face in my arms as the sobs rip from me.

I hear the clang of Zech moving the pan off the stovetop, then a scuffing as he draws another chair alongside me—then his hairy arms drop around me. He don't say nothing, he just holds me tight. Real tight. His breathing feels shuddery, and I've got a feeling he's trying not to cry too.

He don't say nothing for a long, long time. As those choking sobs finally ease a little, it's me who speaks first, though my words come out as a barely intelligible keening. "Why didn't I hold onto him tighter, Zech? Why didn't I hold onto him?"

He grips me even harder for a moment, shakes me slightly. "Don't say that, Isaiah. You and Josh did everything right, the water were just too strong. Didn't you hear him yelp as you were trying to hang on? Any tighter and you'd have crushed his wrist."

"Better broken bones than..." I can't finish.

"It ain't your fault, Isaiah. It ain't no one's fault. We'll find him tomorrow."

But then he goes back to saying nothing. 'Cause he knows as well as I do that we can hunt as thoroughly as we like, work as hard as we can, get the 'Vi out of the mud in world-record-breaking time, but if Josh has already been lying limp, sodden, and still, on some bank somewhere, for *hours*, what good will it do?

JOSHUA

I snarl like the allosaur whose scent I'm borrowing, keeping it low and menacing, and the critter skids to a halt, head lowering, tail swishing as it shifts its rump nervously from side to side. Heck, it's a deinonychus.

Larger than a velociraptor, but smaller than a Dakotaraptor, with a similar killing claw but a distinctive domed head, the only good thing about them is that they live in single pairs with only a year's worth of chicks, rather than larger packs. Small mercies, when a single one is more than enough to do me in.

This one, though...only coming up to my shoulder, instead of to my head as an adult would, its distinctive juvenile plumage still covers a few tufts of nestling down. And it's scared of unfamiliar me. Yeah, let's keep it that way!

With another really mean snarl—but a quiet one, 'cause I don't know where the parents are—I hurl the rock, hitting it smack on the nose. As it yelps and jumps back, I wave my stick and lunge as though to attack, growling. Screeching in terror, it dives back into the cave, catching me across the face with its long tail. The second it's inside, I'm running full-tilt down the slope, fighting to keep my footing. Somehow I reach the bottom in one piece, and keep sprinting. For all I know, the parents are asleep in the cave. Unlikely, after my rock-chucking, but they won't be far away. And as soon as they realize some'at attacked their chick, they'll be trying to track the intruder down.

Will little deinonychuses attempt to chase an allosaur from their territory? Probably, after this.

They'd be hugely outmatched, except there would be at least three of them up against one allosaur. It's the sort of situation that would normally involve a lotta snarling and exchange of insults, but little contact. The allosaur wouldn't be fast enough to catch his irate hecklers, and eventually it would probably just get fed up with the hassling and clear off to quieter pastures.

Unfortunately, I'm not actually an allosaur, so if they catch me it'll go rather different.

If I keep running blindly like this, though, I'll probably blunder into some'at else. I've gotta put some sort of barrier between me and the angry parents so I can proceed with caution again. I eye the river. Heck, am I getting sick of that river. And I really don't wanna wash off my precious dung. On the other hand, right now a family of angry deinons are tracking an allosaur, so mebbe I'm better off without it.

The river's wide, here, shallow and slow moving. The far bank looks easy enough to climb up. I pause, undecided, until a distant screech from behind has me wading right in. I'm able to wade all the way across, in fact. The deinons could swim it, but chances are they won't. Rivers like this are usually natural territorial borders. I scramble up the bank, pausing only for a quick roll in the mud, then get outta sight behind some thick bushes, watching the opposite shore.

I'm not a moment too soon. Two adult deinons

appear, a male running just behind a larger female, followed by a female juvenile and last of all, hanging back nervously, my friend from the cave. They're obviously following my scent, 'cause they stop at the edge of the river and sniff around here and there for a while. Their feathers are the usual deinon cream and beige, the male sporting elaborate patterns in his ruff, though only in those two colors, unlike raptors. Elaborate enough to have won him a big, sleek, healthy-looking female, anyway. The male and female juveniles look strong and well-fed, too. I'd be happy for them if I weren't in such danger of contributing to their well-fedness.

When the adults stop sniffing and stare across the river, I don't even breathe until they look away again, though I'm almost certain they can't see me through the undergrowth. With some disgruntled chatter from the parents and a bit of snapping and snarling between the two juveniles, they turn and disappear back toward their den.

I finally let my breath out. At least now I can continue knowing that they didn't decide to cross after me. Pausing only for a more thorough application of mud, I head along the bank. I need to cross back sometime, 'cause that's the side Dad and Uncle Z are mostly likely to show up on, terrain permitting, but I'd rather get a bit further upstream first, and if I find somewhere on this bank, I'm definitely stopping over here tonight.

I hurry onward, almost running, though the risk of walking into an ambush is rising by the minute as the light drains from the sky. I'm a heck of a lot smaller than the sort of herbi'saur most predators would be hoping to catch, but they won't object to a juicy little appetizer.

An 'armadillion'—or ankylosaur as the scientists would say—is drinking from the river, four tons of armored scales with a massive balled club on the end of its tail. I skirt around it. Short-sighted and dim-witted, it don't notice me—fortunately. A flock of small herbi'saurs scatters at my approach, bolting in all directions.

Panic balls in my belly, creeps up my throat. A tree? A large bush? Another outcrop to sleep on? But the riverbank is flat here, open, even the bushes are too small to consider.

Saint Des, help! I've *gotta* get settled!

I've not gone much further when the river broadens out even more. Oh great. It's getting harder and harder to cross. Still, it'll come together again. Hopefully not too far upriver. We're still too high in the mountains for it to stay this size for long. And right now I'm more worried about reaching tomorrow alive.

When I spy trees and dirt and cliffs rearing up in

the middle of that wider river, I stop cursing it at once. An island? Looks very like one. Now that would be as safe a place as I can hope to find.

About a hundred feet of river flow between me and it, but not too fast. There's even what looks like a deep overhanging bank high up on the closest shore. With the sun nearing the horizon, that overhanging bank looks mighty attractive. There's undergrowth on the island for scentCam bedding. And trees, some probably climbable.

Yeah, I wanna get over there.

With effort, I control the hysterically relieved urge to just leap into the river and reach my—hopefully—safe place as fast as I can. Sluggish flow or not, I'm wary of the river after the events of today. Especially since I ain't eaten since breakfast and I'm totally exhausted.

Quickly, I chuck a small stick in, watching where it goes. The stick travels downstream fast enough it woulda missed the island by a considerable distance had it been me, swimming towards it, sluggish flow or not, so I walk upstream quite a bit further before repeating the experiment. And then upstream a little more, just to be sure. After the third stick, I hunt out a log large enough to, if not completely hold me up, at least provide me with plenty of buoyancy. Then I return to the bank and finally dare to lower myself from the bank into the water, clutching my log, gasping in shock at the water's cold. My sappy branch also provides me with a little extra flotation, but, heck, I'd better try and be quick crossing. I've had far too many immersions today. Dad made sure years ago that I understood how efficiently cold water sucks the energy out of you.

Clutching my log, I kick hard, keeping myself moving across the river as it carries me along. The water's calm, unlike earlier, and soon I'm pulling myself up onto a rocky shore, panting with cold, effort, and relief.

I sit for a few minutes, shivering and dripping, before I can muster the energy to scramble up that steep rocky almost-cliff, but once I make it to the top I hurry eagerly back toward where I saw that overhang. There could be critters on here with me—assuming it actually is an island and not just a funny-shaped promontory from the other bank—and I ought to proceed with due caution until I've at least had a chance to scout around, but twilight is settling over everything, and I ain't got a moment to waste.

Here! I recognize an ash tree and hurry to the edge of what is virtually a cliff, lying flat to hang my head over the edge and look. Yes! There's been a collapse quite recently, and a stony, earthy cavity remains, the roof held up by the roots of those plants still clinging on. Not a great hidey-hole, 'cause it might easily collapse again, but it looks stable enough at the moment, and I'm desperate.

Bedding, then. Quickly. I hurry around the surrounding area, inspecting bushes. The first species is poisonous, the second thorny. The third would be fine to handle briefly, but not sleep touching—I'd be covered in hives by morning. The fourth is safe, but not that strongly scented. The fifth...ah, good. Safe and very pungent.

I cut as much as I can carry and lug it over. Go back for another load. I'm so cold. My legs wobble under me. All my muscles feel like jello. I fetch two more armloads, then take a break by climbing down and transferring what I've already cut into my make-shift den. But climbing up again almost finishes me off. I stagger to the bush and cut more, heave it back. Return to the bush again. I'm swaying as I walk. Halfway back, a wave of limb-wringing tiredness overwhelms me, and I just sit down on the ground like I've been shot, curling over my armful of branches. I could sleep right here...

No. No... Somehow, I shake myself back to full consciousness. No, I've nearly got everything ready. I just need to pee and get a drink. Oh heck. Why didn't I drink before coming up here? Scrap that plan, then. Dehydration risk or no dehydration risk, I can't walk back down to the river tonight. I'm literally gonna be crawling soon.

I abandon the heap of bedding long enough to totter just about far enough from my den to do the necessary, then I stagger back through the fading light and somehow manage to pick it up again and stumble 'home.' I leave a litter of fallen branches behind me, but can't go back for them. I almost topple off the cliff climbing back under the overhang as it is, and painstakingly transferring the last of the bedding to my nook leaves my head swimming. I need to get horizontal and rest.

Survival rules actually state that if you're confident of a quick rescue it's better to simply stay awake until it arrives. Yeah, nice theory.

I pick out the worst of the stones by feel, since it's now too dark under my overhang to see, and spread out a thin layer of undergrowth for a bed. I ain't gathered enough, so I'll keep most of it to cover myself with. And then...ah, I'm able to lie down in this lovely bumpy bed and arrange the rest of the bedding over me, laying it across me, feet to head—never length-ways, where it would simply tumble off, leaving me exposed to predators' noses and the elements.

Soon, the last heap is arranged over my head, and I'm all tucked in for the night. Heavenly. Fresh air filters through, but I'm starting to warm up already.

The overpowering smell of fresh cut foliage is more welcome than any scent I can imagine. Well, except mebbe the aroma of a bacon sandwich. *Any* kinda sandwich. Heck, a slice of bread. *Moldy* bread. Now that I'm lying still and not moving around, it's much harder to ignore the ache in my empty stomach.

I noticed a few possibly climbable trees, but no edible plants. Hopefully I can last until the 'Vi arrives tomorrow. But I do need to move to the other side of the island—if it is an island—to see what's what and find a den on that side, if I can. If I see anything edible in passing, I'll grab some.

I rest my head on my sappy log and close my eyes. No carni'saur's gonna be interested in a small muddy object hidden under a mound of greenery over the barely accessible rim of an almost-cliff. And if they are, that's just too bad.

Saint Des, please watch over me. Watch over Dad and Unc... Uncle Zzzzzzz...

ISAIAH

I lie on my back in my over-cab berth, staring into the blackness and longing for morning—or sleep. Neither will be coming no time soon. Zech went on about how we should both get a good night's sleep, but I can't hear him snoring beneath me, and if I can't hear him snoring, he ain't sleeping.

The events of the day go through my mind over and over again. The flood. Josh's wrist in mine...sliding...his hand, slimy...slipping from mine. Could I have held on any tighter? Does he feel like I failed him? *I* feel like I failed him. To hold on, that were all I had to do.

Frustration boiling over, I slam my fist into the bottom of my berth so hard it makes a *thud* even through the mattress. To just. *Thud.* Hold. *Thud.* On. *Thud.*

"Go to *sleep*, Isaiah!" A faint voice comes up through the floor.

Hypocrite. I know I didn't wake you.

But I stop my pounding.

DAY 2

JOSHUA

Rustling. Sniffing. I come awake with a jolt, heart pounding, skin prickling, ears straining. There's some'at alive moving very close to my head.

I draw breath through my nose as silently as I can, searching for a scent-clue. Carni'saur? That distinctive dry whiff. Hard to tell what species through the stench of the foliage. How big? How many teeth?

Some'at moves around some more—tiny feet moving soil and stones. My stomach clenches up. Piranha'saur? There's never just one. How fast can I get outta here and to a tree? Can I even climb one in the dark before they pull me down and overwhelm me?

It's tugging on the branches over my face. Nibbling sounds. It's *eating* the leaves? Piranha'saurs are completely carnivorous, at least if they've any choice at all.

Another sniff, followed by a small, squeaky whistle, and I relax, relief pouring through me.

Rodento'saur. Omnivorous, same size as a piranha'saur, only feathered. Much larger head and jaw and capable of inflicting a worse bite—but they're solitary hunters. When it comes to having 'em inside their fences, farmers either love it or hate it, 'cause the tough little critters will take down chickens and even rabbits—but also rats. But a human toddler would be too big, let alone me. Not that it won't sample my nose too, if it gets that far uninterrupted.

It tugs on my bedding again. Can't have that. It can go get its own veggies!

I turn my head toward it and hiss like a peeved velociraptor, then grin into the darkness as I hear the sudden scuffing as it jerks back. *Patter-patter-patter*—it scurries away along the overhung shelf. Ah. I bet I'm camped right on its normal run. Like the rodents they're named after, rodento'saurs prefer to move around undercover as much as possible.

Sorry, little brother. I'll be out of your hair tomorrow.

I yawn. My side aches from the hard stony ground. As quietly as I can, I shift my position, then worm a hand up to check the branches over my head; tug them back into position. I'm not very warm—I shoulda had a much thicker layer than this. I were just so tired.

Nothing I can do. How long did I sleep? I've got that deceptively alert, well-rested feeling that comes after several hours of very deep sleep, but whether I've had three or five hours I don't know. I peer through my bedding, trying to glimpse the stars, but the over-hang blocks too much of the view. My gut tells me it were probably closer to three hours than five, worst luck. That's nowhere near enough. Not after the day I've had. I need to settle off again or I'll be a zombie tomorrow. Josh the zombie'saur.

I close my eyes and try to feel sleepy, but I'm wide awake. If only there were some light, I could get up right now and go look for food.

No, food cannot be my priority. Making sure I'm in the right place to signal to the 'Vi when it passes tomorrow comes before anything. But right now I gotta *sleep*.

Since I *can't* seem to sleep, now seems like a good time to pray. 'Cause y'know, I could use all the help I can get.

Yeah, Saint Des, please help. I'm only ten, you know. And that's quite young to be out here, I guess.

I pray the first few bits of Saint Des's chaplet then get distracted...

Hey, or am I eleven? I might be eleven, Saint Des! If it's after midnight. But I still need your help!

I don't have a set of beads to pray on, so I'll hafta use my fingers. I start with the Big Bead Prayer.

"From T. rex's jaws,

from raptor's claws,

from life indoors,

from all our flaws,

deliver us, O Lord.

And smile upon us,

Mother mild."

Dad's got that picture of that pretty lady in blue, my Momma Mary in Heaven, so it's never seemed to matter much that I ain't got no mom. What's it like, though, having a mom around? Like, visibly? Do they tell you y'have to clean your rifle before you can start watching the raptors on the drone cam? 'Cause Dad does that, anyways...

Huh, I'm supposed to be doing a chaplet. I tap my thumb for the first small bead. "Jesus, I trust in you..."

ISAIAH

"...Jesus, I trust in you. Jesus, I trust in you. Jesus, I trust in you..." If I can't sleep, at least I can do the one thing I can do for Josh right now. Mom's rosary, so smooth and well-thumbed, slides through my fingers. It's our special rosary that we hang beside our photo frame and only use occasionally, but I brought it up to bed with me 'cause this is bigger than anything I've ever prayed about in my life—at least since Josh were born.

"...Jesus, I trust in you. Jesus..."

Tomorrow we'll get the 'Vi out as soon as it's light, and we'll head downstream as fast as we can. Josh will have done everything right, 'cause he's a smart kid, and he'll be waiting for us, safe and well. I try to fix my thoughts on this version of the future, to fill my mind with it.

But that little voice keeps whispering. Whispering that even if he got out of the river alive, there's a world of difference between survival theory and putting it into practice on the ground. He's ten, for pity's sake! I check my watch. Eleven. He's eleven. Oh God, please let him be eleven? But grown hunters struggle to survive the difficulties inevitably produced by the gulf between theory and reality. How's Josh supposed to cope?

Better, mebbe, suggests another little voice. He's too young to be over-fixated on 'how it ought to go.' He'll just get on and deal.

Oh God, let that be so, too!

"...Jesus, I trust in you. Jesus..."

JOSHUA

When I open my eyes, a thin strip of dark gray sky is visible against the black curve of the overhang. Dawn is on the way. Finally. I did fall asleep after a couple of chaplets and get what I'd guess to be another hour or two of deeper sleep. Since then I've been dozing on and off. I'm trying not to make a racket tossing and turning to ease my ever-growing aches and pains. Every time I dig my fingers through my thin bed and tear out one sharp rock, another two seem to rise to take its place.

I'm chilled through by now. Well, no surprise—I knew I didn't have enough bedding.

 And I'm so thirsty. Not to mention hungry. And I really need to pee. Yep, I'm so looking forward to it getting light.

I ought to stay put until an hour or two after dawn, though, when the herbi'saurs will have been and gone at the water's edge. But it's not even dawn yet, so that will be *hours*.

I didn't see any evidence of large grazers—or large anything—last night, anyway. Not likely to be, on an island.

Okay, so I don't know yet that it is an island. But whatever it is, I'm on the wrong side of it. If Dad and Uncle Z were almost all the way here yesterday, and decide to set off again at dawn—which they sure will—assuming I'd have taken up my position yesterday... heck, I don't wanna miss them. Yeah, I'm gonna get moving as soon as it's light enough to see. Get a drink and head over to the other side, check things out, find a good spot. But I force myself to stay put for now.

Finally, I can see fairly well, and only then—after a long, careful listen—do I peep over the top. There's plenty of wildlife, but none large enough to concern me. A squirrel chitters in the undergrowth, and rabbits nibble busily at the grass on the exposed area right beside the cliff. A few birds stir in the trees. Even as I watch, the small feathery form of a rodento'saur—my friend from last night?—drops down from a tree with a bird in its mouth, sending the rabbits bounding away down their holes.

I scramble up and start moving. A small, feathery tail whisks away as I spook the rodento'saur again. I could certainly believe this were an island, from the number of small mammals.

The river flows below, wet and delicious, drawing me. All the same, I make myself move slowly and cautiously as I search for a place where I can get down to the shore. But soon I'm sucking sweet river water through my straw. The coldness hits my stomach like an ice-hammer, rapidly taking me from chilled to violently shivering. My clothes are still a little damp from last night. Not enough bedding.

My hand drifts to the crucifix hanging on its leather cord around my neck, which happens to be made of firesteel. One more, secret, survival tool. No. Fire is a total last resort. Only if lost in midwinter, with snow on the ground—or at death's door from exposure at any other time—would you light a fire, and even then not until you had no other choice. Carni'saurs are wary of fire, like any critters, but the more curious ones will come along to take a cautious peep. A lotta them are so large that to keep an impressive enough fire burning to actually scare 'em, you'd spend all your time *away* from the fire, gathering fuel. One guess how that's likely to end.

I'm gonna walk fast to the other side of my island. Not ideal for stealth, but it will warm me up, and it'll be safer than a fire. And it'll get me over there quicker. I'm terrified of missing Dad and Uncle Z!

I have to stop several times as I scramble back up from the river, panting, my muscles like the water I've just been gulping. I'm too hungry. Mebbe if this is an island, I can leave my new den — once I've found one — and hunt around near it for food.

No, that's silly. I should just hunker down and wait. Dad and Uncle Z will probably be here by noon. However exhausting yesterday were, I can wait that long, right?

I strain my eyes and ears and nose as I stride through the wooded belt that stands between me and the river's far bank, but detect nothing other than small mammals and birds. I hear the rodento'saur — or another one — calling a little way away. No sight or sound of nothing larger.

It would be fun to catch the rodo and try to tame it. They're harder to domesticate than piranha'saurs, but if you can manage it they make better pets, 'cause they'll be nice to all humans, instead of just the person who feeds them. Uncle Z says that's why city-boys prefer piranha'saurs, 'cause they're one-boy pets and it makes their owners feel special, but Dad says taming rodento'saurs just takes too long, so pet shops ain't interested. Plus, some'at about their name putting off the parents who'll be forking out the cash.

I've always wanted one, though, but we don't see 'em often. After all, we go to so much trouble making sure the 'Vi don't smell of nothing they'd like to eat. But imagine Dad's and Uncle Z's expressions if I strolled up to the 'Vi with my new pet under my arm...

Reluctantly, I shake the daydream from my mind. *Concentrate, Josh!*

The walk takes probably less than two minutes, and I've barely warmed up when I see the trees thinning ahead. Guess it were stupid to expect more, in a river this small. I slow my pace and advance more cautiously, not wanting to stumble out into the open—or off another cliff. This side also has a barer area between the wood and the...cliff? Trees clearly tend to topple over the edge, leaving open ground. After checking for danger, I cross and look down. Yeah, it's easily climbable right here, but definitely counts as a full-blown cliff.

The river runs at the bottom of the cliff, shallowly, over rock. Perfect spear-fishing conditions, a lot like where we were parked up. In fact, I can see the silvery glint of the fish from here. My mouth fills with saliva, and I force myself to finish looking around.

Upstream, the curve of the island is visible in the distance, disappearing out of sight. Downstream...

Oh heck.

It ain't an island.

ISAIAH

"Coffee's ready." Zech's voice and a sharp rap on my door snatch me awake. I blink groggily. Guess I finally slept. I don't get even a moment's blessed forgetfulness, though. My brain can't have switched off completely.

I'm out of my sleeping bag, grabbing my rifle—and Mom's rosary—and climbing down right away. I hang the rosary back beside the picture frame—right now showing Josh with a juvenile Snappy the piranha'saur perched on his shoulder—and immediately peer out the window. Steel gray sky. If we were outside and our eyes were adjusted, it would seem like daylight, near enough. I'm glad Zech woke me. By the time we scarf down a bite or two, it'll be light enough to work.

I do feel a bit more optimistic, after a little sleep. Josh knows what he's doing. He should be waiting for us.

Just so long as he made it out of the river in the first place...

JOSHUA

I frown as I take in the details, then I scan the rest of the landscape carefully. Actually...it kinda is an island, geo...graph...ically, I guess. But it ain't one practically. The wide shallow river runs into a fissure that splits where I am from the land on the other side. And the fissure looks like it must run clear to the other end, making it—technically—an island.

But even from here I can see one fallen tree lying across the narrow gap, one place where the bank has collapsed across, and another where a boulder is wedged firmly in place. All spots where carni'saurs up to the size of a Utahraptor—the largest raptor species that loom above a grown man's head—could cross. Some'at a bit bigger like an allosaur would need a pretty strong motivation to attempt the necessary balancing act.

On the other side...the higher area is fairly open ground, and lower down, a short cliff half encircles a flat rocky area beside the shallows where the ravine begins. But on the other side of all that...it looks, from here, as though there's another river channel, wide, and probably not that deep, though likely deeper than the shallows below me. And beyond that...marsh. Marsh, stretching, as best I can judge, from beyond where the island starts clear to the other end of it. The island's probably causing the marsh, somehow.

Yeah, so it's not so bad. Altogether, I reckon this is, practically speaking, as good as an island. Raptors or deinons would need a good reason to cross that. They don't like getting their feathers wet and muddy. They're not aquatic like the herbivorous duckosaurs grazing in the marsh. And then they'd have to cross that deeper channel. Which looks slow enough that they could, easily enough, but again, they won't swim for their dinner unless they have to. Once across that, they could get onto my island no problem at all, sure—but only if they'd already made it the rest of the way.

So, actually, this is a great place to wait. I take a good look at the distant terrain, or as good as I can without a scope, then lie on my tummy to peer down the cliff and prod at the rock. Yeah, if I climb a little way down, I can hack a big X into the soft limestone. The straight white lines will show up a long ways away. Dad and Uncle Z should see it just before they turn inland to go around the marsh. I'd better do that first.

I head upstream, to see if I can put my marker closer to where they'll be, but the cliff gets steeper and steeper, so I head back to the shallow inlet. Coming from this direction, I spot a cave at the back of that flat, rocky hollow, but after a moment's excitement, I realize it's too big for me. A Dakotaraptor could walk in or a Utahraptor squeeze in.

Hmm. I move to the place over the shallows again and study the flat hollow as carefully as I can from this distance. It's rocky, so it would be hard to make out tracks even if I were down there. But there's no sign of dung, and some'at's been breaking open rotten logs and prying stones from the earthy banks at the upstream end, hunting insects. That's the sort of thing rodento'saurs do—or small mammals.

It would be a silly location for any good sized predator, anyway. Having to cross the river channel and the whole marsh to reach a decent hunting ground? Nah. But I know Dad and Uncle Z would expect me to look. Well, I've looked.

Now I'm looking at those fish again and my mouth's watering worse than before. No. I have to carve my marker and find a den. The den's probably unnecessary, considering, but—"Nature don't forgive complacency, Josh." How many times have I heard that?

Pulling my sappy log from my belt, I put it down on the grass, then I get a good grip on some straggling roots with one hand, and a rock with the other, and swing my legs over the cliff. It's an easy climb, but I don't go far. Just to the nearest good-sized flat area, as close to the top as possible for maximum visibility.

I wince as I draw my carefully-honed, well-kept knife, but ya gotta do what ya gotta do. I'm at least able to use the back of the blade, which don't matter so much. The fish scraper at the front don't need to be sharp, and the saw blade ain't touching the rock.

The cliff surface is nice and soft and cuts easily, but the 'Vi's gonna be so far away. This had better be big. I mark from one corner of the flat section clear to the other, going on two yards. By the time I've hacked a broad line all the way, my hands are shaking, soft rock or no soft rock. Stubbornly, I mark out the other line and carry on. I can't stay on this nice safe island unless I can let them know I'm here. The cross is more important than anything.

Huh, that sounds like some'at Saint Des would say.

I'm getting blisters. I wanna stop so bad. No, I *can't*. They could drive into sight any moment, and a full X is far harder for the eye to dismiss as natural than a mere three-quarter X. If I finish this, they won't miss it, and I can stay here and be safe. Otherwise I have to cross the marsh and find a position over there. Back in the deinons' territory, for all I know. And every other species of carni'saur.

Saint Des, I dedi...dedi...cate this cross to you. Just please help me finish it!

I stop to cut a strip from my t-shirt and bind my hands. Bleeding blisters ain't a good idea. A nice strong whiff of human blood might tempt some carni'saur to make the journey over here, making this all totally pointless.

Ah, that's better. With my hand bound, I make better progress for a while. Still, my palm and fingers are searing and burning as I painstakingly, and increasingly weakly, chip out the last few inches.

Thank God. It's done.

I lean back slightly, trying to take in the overall effect. The white gouges blaze in the morning light against the age-darkened golden stone. They will *not* miss that. I can find a den and relax until they arrive.

Well, once I've climbed back up this cliff. *Ow.*

Tiredly—and painfully—I ease my way back to the top. There, I sit down and unbind my hand to inspect the blisters. Most have burst, despite the binding, though they're only weeping fluid, they're not far enough gone to bleed, so that ain't so bad. I hack at my sappy log and coat them with sap. Great. Sticky-sticky hands. Once it's dried some, I rub loose soil onto them so I won't stick to every dang thing I touch.

It's nice sitting here. Tempting to just flop here and wait. But: "Nature don't forgive complacency, Josh."

Groaning, trying to ignore the silver glint of the fish below, I drag myself to my feet and stumble upriver, looking for a den. After trudging all the way to the tip of the island, it's clear there's not much choice, and nothing perfect. I'm starting to wonder if the people who wrote the survival rules have ever actually tried to find one of their so-called 'ideal safe places' themselves. *Pah.*

This one is just a crack under a tall flat rock that sticks out from the earth at a funny angle, leaving a gap between it and the earth. I can lie at the back and pile scentCam in front of me, making the chances of anything smelling me real small. But it offers little protection. Even an allosaur could stick its head under and grab me. A T. rex's head would be too big, but if I met a T. rex on this little island I'd die of shock anyway.

But it does have a clear view of the upstream end of the marsh, the place where the 'Vi is most likely to appear. So, seeing how safe this island is, mebbe it is kinda ideal. Enough.

I need to cut some bedding...but first, I head along to the fissure and take a look at the nearest crossing points. I expect with such a long distance, they'll signal me to stay put and one of them will come and get me while the other provides as much cover as they can—boy, are they gonna butt heads over who does which!—but still, I'd better know how best to get over there.

The log is solid enough, not too rotten, and probably the best route. The cliff-fall looks unstable and the boulder would be a bit chancy to cross. The log is fine. No need to look any further away. I walk across it and back again, just to be sure. I'm just stepping back off it when some'at catches my eye. I drop to my knees, peering at a small patch of bare shadowed ground half under the log. Is it...? I reach out, tracing the indents with my fingers, letting myself feel what I can barely see.

Yes... My breath hisses out in dismay, and my heart rate kicks up. It's a raptor pugmark. And not even a velociraptor, it's a Dakotaraptor. I feel the shape again, estimating size and weight. Full-grown male. But...this is an old footprint. Very old. I tap the rock-hard surface of the dirt. Yeah, this is a place where water collects in the winter. The raptor stepped in it when it were halfway through drying out in the spring, which has left the pugmark preserved perfectly all summer.

Using my hands more than my eyes, I run my fingers over the surrounding ground, feeling what's under the grass. Eventually, my fingertips make out the shape of another pugmark. Female. Full-grown. Yep, a Dakotaraptor pack has been here.

Well, that makes sense. I can understand a local pack crossing to the island once or twice in the winter to make a sweep for the sort of small game they'd turn up their noses at in summer. Makes total sense. But they won't be coming over here now. I don't need to worry.

All the same, I head under the trees and search the small-game trails nearest to the log bridge, checking for fresh tracks. But there's nothing. No raptors are gonna be swimming over here in summertime. All the same, I'm glad I've found a den to hide in. Even knowing it'll be a few months before they're likely to venture this way again, the island don't feel quite so safe no more.

I have another pee, well away from my den, then cut a big stack of foliage and pile it at the mouth of the crack. Sliding into the back, I pull the bedding closer. I'd warmed up a little while hacking at the cliff, but I'm shivering again already. I leave a good gap in the bedding at the head end, though, so I can see out clearly. Then I lie, shaking and aching, watching for a silvery glint of Hab'Vi armor, a flash of light off a windshield, or the blaze and smoke of a flare.

I'm sure I didn't miss them yesterday, so it must've taken them quite a while to work their way downriver. But they'll be here before lunchtime.

Lunch...

Ah, no. I ain't gonna think about lunch.

ISAIAH

Straightening, I wipe sweat from my brow and glare up at the blazing noonday sun, managing to merely think the swearwords I'd like to say, and only 'cause I so don't want Saint Des upset with me right now.

"How's it going?" Zech speaks from my earpiece.

"It's gonna take a while longer."

"How far down have you got?"

I stare at the muddy, oozing hole beside the front wheel. I can't believe the ground's still this wet when it were so bone dry up here before the flood. It's 'cause the river level's risen so much, of course. Still, Zech and I were both dismayed when we saw how little it had drained overnight. This spongy sand-soil is sucking water up from the now-closer river, instead of letting it all drain back out. It's no longer like sand-soup, but it's still sloppy. Hitching the front recovery winch to the tree we'd parked in line with—just in case of rain making the ground slippery—we almost ripped the tree out by the roots. We never planned on it having to raise the entire weight of the 'Vi, just give it a little help.

Since drilling into one of those rocky outcrops and in-setting rings will take ages, it seemed best to just dig the 'Vi out. A hole in front of each wheel, insert a traction board, bit of help from the winch—we stopped before we actually ripped the tree up, of course—and it should have come out.

That were the theory. I've been digging for two hours and...

"'Bout three quarters of a foot."

"What? Isaiah! If it's that bad, what're you wasting the energy for? Come back in and wait for it to drain some more."

"Wasting?" I snap. "Josh is—"

"Oh, don't give me a hard time, Isaiah! You know as well as I do that it's filling as fast as you're digging, if that's all you've managed in the time. Come inside and save your energy. Or better yet, start drilling bolts into that rock, in case it don't drain fast."

If we go down the bolt route, we'll be lucky to be making a second attempt before early evening...

"No! I'm not trying hard enough!" Desperately, I dig the spade into the soft ground, heave up a massive scoopful, toss it aside. Do the same again. And again. And again...

I don't stop until the side door hisses open and Zech steps out, grabbing the spade and pausing its swing as he stares grimly into the pathetic hole.

"Isaiah, stop! It ain't working. We gotta drill the bolts in. That or wait. But we may as well start drilling while we wait. If it drains before we're done, who cares; it's only some sweat and bolts, right?"

Trembling, I let him take the spade from my aching hands. He's right. I know he's right. But accepting it means accepting that some time tomorrow morning is now the earliest we can hope to reach Josh. He'll have been out there almost *two days*.

Oh God in heaven, two days? He's eleven. Please?

Even my prayers aren't making much sense. I'm

close to breaking down again. Can't have that. I blink, swallow hard, and take some deep breaths.

"Let's get the bolts and drill." I manage to keep my voice steady, just about.

But Zech grabs my wrist and turns my hand over. "No, first I'm gonna take care of these blisters. You shoulda stopped—or fetched your gloves."

I bite my tongue on another round of argument, letting him tug me back into the 'Vi. The quicker he gets my hands patched up, the quicker I can get back to work.

JOSHUA

The sun blazes down outside, heating the day to summer-like temperatures, but hungry me shivers in my shady hideout and damp clothes. A tell-tale hue in the sky suggests that summer may finally end tonight, and with a heck of a storm. Well, I should be snug back inside the 'Vi by then, right?

I may not feel very warm, but I'm getting awful thirsty. It's been hours since I had my morning drink. But I don't wanna go out unnecessarily. Dad and Uncle Z will be here soon. And if they don't come, I shouldn't venture out again until taking a final pre-dusk drink before settling down for the night.

But they'll be here before then. *Right, Saint Des?*

I can't keep thinking about water.

Or food. Definitely not about food.

Fish.

No.

Silver fish, swimming...

No!

I've gotta stay put.

I've gotta think about some'at else. I should...try and think how I could trap a rodento'saur, since there are plenty on this island. I could at least figure it out in my head. What sort of trap would work? Piranha'saurs are super easy to trap for the pet trade. You just find a shoal, then chuck some meat in the rear pen and drop the lower ramp-door. And in they flow, like water. Close door. Job done. Yeah, they're greedy, nosy, and too bold for their own good, oftentimes.

Rodento'saurs are much shyer. You'd have to leave your ramp down so long that some'at much larger might well come along to check out the blood smell. A good cage trap would be best, but I don't have one. Some sort of simple snare might work, if I were right there watching and could rescue the critter before it strangled itself.

Dad and Uncle Z used a cage trap to catch Rudy the velociraptor. They didn't catch him for the fun of it, of course, it were for my rex training. T. rex only pay attention to moving prey, so my dad and uncle started teaching me to stay still when I were real tiny. They'd set movement sensors, and if I could sit—or later stand—for a certain amount of time without triggering them, I'd get a reward. But it's too easy staying still when you're safe in the 'Vi and there's no T. rex sniffing around your head.

So, once I got real good at it, they caught a little piranha'saur and let it hop around me on a leash. Uncle Z even let it graze me once or twice, so I wouldn't feel so safe that it defeated the whole point—though Dad weren't too happy about that. "Better a scratch now than a rex biting his head off later," Uncle Z would say, unmoved. Me, I were real proud of my little wounds— since I hadn't moved.

Rudy the velociraptor were the next level. He were always muzzled and had his killing claws capped, of course. But even a muzzled raptor breathing in your face is harder to ignore than an itsy-bitsy piranha'saur. Then, finally, Uncle Z got him out of the rear pen one day when Dad were asleep and had me sit still while Rudy prowled around me on the leash unmuzzled. I didn't move an inch, so Uncle Z called it graduation day. Dad called *him* several other things, later.

Rudy had already calmed down a bit by graduation day, so Dad and Uncle Z figured to keep him a little longer, till he were zoo-tame, and sell him. Dad would put Rudy's muzzle on and stroke him to speed the process along. Once Rudy stopped lashing out with his wing-claws, he'd let me pet him too. Dad and I even started to teach him to do a few tricks. I guess that were when he became more of a pet, instead of a live asset— at least for the two of us...

Ah, Rudy. Such sleek, charcoal grey feathers, with their white and black dappling. The rich purple of his ruff. His bright, intelligent eyes...

Rudy arches his neck, hissing contentedly as I scratch his itchy spots. His sharp gaze fixes on my hand when I finally take it away and reach into my pocket for a treat.

"Shake, Rudy."

He lifts his right wing-arm at once, holding it out. I take his wing-claw and shake solemnly, crooning like an approving senior raptor, then reach out with my other hand to slip the treat through the bars of his muzzle. He crunches it up, then butts his bare, leathery face against my chest, begging for more.

"He's getting super-tame, now," I giggle, burying both hands in his ruff and stroking vigorously.

"Yeah, though he sure likes you best," says Dad, from where he crouches beside me. "I guess you speak his language."

"What should we teach him next?"

"Dunno." Dad sounds hesitant. "He don't need to know any of this stuff for the zoo, y'know. No keeper's ever gonna go near him. They just don't want him throwing himself at

the fences trying to get at them—or cowering away from them, come to that, and upsetting the city-folk by seeming scared. Either looks bad. He ain't gonna do neither, now."

"No, but he likes learning stuff. Let's teach him to sit and stay. That's useful, right?"

"Well…" I can tell Dad's tempted. "They ain't never gonna get in the pen with him until he's muzzled, but I guess it wouldn't do no harm."

It's hard to believe they'd need a muzzle soon. Rudy's so friendly. Dad insists on putting it on each time, though, and checking the caps on his killing claws, before letting me come in.

Rudy's now rubbing his head against my shoulder, arching his neck, trying to wear me down.

"No, Rudy," I tell him. "You've gotta do a bit of school, first. You're only a juvenile still, after all." Like me! Though I always talk like I'm dominant to him—which he still ain't totally convinced about. Thinks I'm rather small and skinny, I guess. We're about the same size, standing, if he lifts his head high, but he's two or three times my length from nose to the tip of his tail, if I lay down.

He chatters at me, so I chatter a response. Back and forth we go for a while, like he's trying to trick me into saying some'at non-velociraptor. But I don't, and he understands every sound I make.

"Breakfast."

Dad starts slightly as Uncle Z's voice suddenly comes

from the pen doorway, and I jump a little, too. Whoops. I thought Uncle Z were still in bed. How long has he been standing there?

Dad looks uneasy as he chases me out of the pen before whipping off Rudy's muzzle and sliding out himself. But Uncle Z don't say nothing. I guess he didn't see Rudy doing the tricks, or don't care as much as Dad thought he would. Dom...est...ick...ate...ing raptors is illegal, I do know that. I mean, I'm six, right! But that's not what we're doing, Dad says. We're just zoo-taming him. That's allowed.

I wish we didn't have to sell him, though. It'd be so nice if we could keep him. But only the army is allowed to keep trained guard velociraptors long-term. And they're all imprinted on their trainer at birth. Rudy's bonding with us so well, though. Especially me. 'Cause I talk to him properly. I bet we could tame him enough.

But Dad says he's gotta go to the zoo. Next time we're in-city. That'll be several months yet, though, 'cause we never go in-city more often than absolutely necessary, thank God. So we'll have Rudy a little longer.

When the breakfast's cleared away, Dad picks up his hand-pad. "Okay, reading time, Josh."

"Okey-dokey." Good. Better than math. And I wanna know what happens next in the book.

Uncle Z plunks down in front of the console and jabs a finger at the ceiling. "I need to concentrate on this. Take it up to the turret, would'ya?"

He must be doing the mysterious 'accounts.' Or "evil life-math lessons for adults," as Dad calls them. They always make Uncle Z cranky. And the sun's shining. The turret is definitely the place to be. I shoot up the ladder and have all the windows open by the time Dad climbs up. He shuts the hatch behind him to keep the sound in. The fresh spring air fills the turret with outdoor-smell.

When Dad's settled himself in a chair, I scramble onto his lap. He groans dramatically. "One of these days you're gonna squash me flatter than a pancake."

"Ain't happened yet," I say, propping my bare feet on the console and squirming until he can put his arm around me and hold the hand-pad in front of us both. "Let's read!"

"Okay." He switches it on. "You first, then."

My turn to groan, 'cause the story's great but the words are a lot harder than the last book. I start, but I've only stumbled through a page when there's a shot from below. I stare at the hatch, puzzled. I thought Uncle Z were doing accounts. And that sounded like a safety round, the kind that don't go through walls. Why's he even got those in his clip right now?

Dad's gone rigid under me. "Zech, you rat!" he whispers, sending a chill up my spine.

What's going on? I jump off his lap and grab the hatch, swing it up.

"Josh, wait!" Dad reaches for me, which makes me even more certain I wanna know what's going on.

I dodge his lunge by leaping onto the ladder. I slide down it, bare feet clamped to the sides. As I land lightly at the bottom, I look around. What...? Uncle Z's standing in the doorway of the rear pen, holding his rifle. What the—? What's he doing?

My chest is so tight it hurts. I dash forward just as Dad comes sliding down after me. I slip under Uncle Z's arm, half shoving him aside.

Rudy lies crumpled on the pen floor, dead still. His wing arms are flung out limply, his neck flopped back at an awkward angle.

"NO!"

I throw myself down beside him, lifting his head in my hands. But I don't need to see the round, bloody hole in his forehead. I knew the moment I saw him lying there like that.

"No!" I clutch helplessly at his soft feathers, the last of his nestling-down fluffy under the adult growth. "No... Rudy..." I croon softly to him in raptor-talk, but of course he don't answer.

I hear Dad call Zech some'at Saint Des wouldn't approve of as he peers into the pen behind me. "What the heck, Zechariah? We coulda discussed it!"

"Ain't nothing to discuss, Isaiah. It's done."

"It sure as heck is!" Dad calls him another bad name.

"You'll get over it."

"Yeah? Sure, I will. But what about Josh? Did you think about that?"

I spring to my feet and spin around. "What did you do?" I yell, though I don't need to ask. "Why? Why did you do that?" I throw myself at him, hitting him as hard as I can, over and over, with my puny fists. "I hate you! I hate you! Why did you do that? I'll hate you forever! I hate you..."

"Hey, Josh..." Dad plucks me away from Uncle Z, and I'm too small and weak to escape. "Hey, now. Don't say that. Don't say that, now... Shhhhh..."

"I mean it! I hate him! Why'd he kill Rudy? Rudy never did nothing to him! Rudy were my friend!"

"Yeah, so you clearly thought." Uncle Z's voice is flat. "And that's why he had to go."

"I'll hate you forever!"

"Fine. Hate me forever. Better than that thing ripping your throat out at some point in the next few months."

"That thing were my friend!"

"He weren't your friend, Josh! How many times have we told you, raptors think everyone is either pack, predator, or prey. They'll only for certain-sure take you as pack if they've imprinted on you. Which Rudy sure hadn't. Sooner or later, you'd have gotten careless, and he'd have treated you like raptors treat anything that ain't pack—he'd have attacked you. Come on, you're six, you must understand that?"

Twisting in Dad's grip, I fling out my legs as far as they'll go and manage to land a solid kick on Uncle Z's leg. "I HATE you! I hate you!" I pull every bad name I've ever heard from my memory and launch them at him in turn.

"I'm sorry you're upset, cub," he says, when I have to draw breath. "But I ain't sorry I shot the raptor. Your life's worth more to me than its is, any day. So call me whatever names you like."

I come awake with a jolt, shivering. It's only partly the nightmare. I'm so cold.

Poor Rudy. I did like him a lot. I paid Uncle Z back that very night—made him all but wet himself, I gave him such a scare. He were so mad. I had to hide in the turret until Dad got him calmed down. Then Dad came up and did some'at really weird. Well, it seemed weird, then. He apologized to me. Said it weren't Uncle Z's fault about Rudy, it were his. That he shoulda never let me get so fond of him. That he shoulda never started teaching him tricks. That Uncle Z had done the right thing.

That made me mad at the time, though eventually after a long talk about revenge and why it's horrible, I went down and we all kinda made-up over a midnight snack. Well, two AM snack.

But Dad *were* right, of course. Uncle Z too. I've known that for years. Rudy weren't imprinted on neither of us, and sooner or later one of us woulda left off the muzzle. And mebbe that woulda been okay once or twice. But we could only ever be predators or prey, to Rudy, and sooner or later, one of us woulda gotten hurt. Hard to find a case when someone kept an unimprinted pet raptor and it didn't end badly. But...deep down, I guess I still find it a little hard to believe that Rudy woulda hurt me. And that's why Uncle Z shot him.

I missed Rudy for a long time. Uncle Z gave me Snappy the Piranha'saur when I got a bit older, and I did love having him to train and look after, but he weren't smart like Rudy.

Heck, I gotta stop thinking about Rudy. I feel so down, now. Cold and hungry and tired and...

Argh, no, were I asleep? I were asleep, weren't I? I couldn't have missed them, could I? No, I'd have heard the flares and the horn. I'd have woken up, right? But they'd be a long way away...

I peer out past the scentCam, my eyes searching the far landscape. Nothing. No 'Vi. No distant glint of metal and glass. Just that herd of medium-sized duckosaurs wading in the marsh on their long scaly legs, scooping up waterweed with the long claws on their skinny arms. I weren't asleep long, right? I check the sun. No, it's not moved much. I can't have been asleep long. Whew. But I've gotta try and stay awake.

I tug my t-shirt down over my middle as far as it will go and rub my bare arms. Tempting to get out and lie in the sun for a while. No. Dad and Uncle Z will be here soon. It's not worth the risk. I just gotta stay put and keep awake.

I peer out at the distant bank, searching for the tell-tale glint that will probably be my first hint of the 'Vi's approach. A stealthy movement at the edge of the marsh draws my eye. What's that?

Huh, it's my friend from yesterday. At least, I think the allosaur over there has blue crest feathers, so it's probably the same one. He's got his sights set on that duckosaur grazing nearby. Some bushes grow at the border between marsh and normal ground, and the allosaur is making good use of them for cover. He's almost close enough to launch an attack.

What's he doing out hunting now, though? I glance at the sun. I s'pose the heat of the day really is nearly over, now. Everything will be coming out to hunt soon. I wish Dad would get here.

The allo's making his move...his powerful legs splash through the marshy ground. He's three quarters of the way there before the duckosaur realizes it's in danger. It springs forward and begins to flee. Too late. The allosaur powers into it, huge jaws sinking into its neck as he carries it to the ground. Heck, I can hear it screaming even from here. The wind's my way.

Faintly, I hear a sickening crunch as the allosaur bites down harder. The agonized cries cut off. I think it's dead. Lucky duckosaur. An unusually clean kill. Regardless of city-folk's "fond fantasies" about nature, as Dad puts it, few predators care about more than disabling their prey before they begin to feed.

Which the allosaur is now doing. Biting off hunks of meat and gulping them down. He's making my mouth water. The rest of the herd of duckosaurs have stopped at the far side of the marsh, gabbling nervously to one another. But soon, they dip their heads and begin to feed again. The allosaur's no threat to them now.

I've seen animals hunted my whole life. Hunted them myself. But right now, I can't get the duckosaur's screams out of my head. I keep hearing that crunch. The way its cries cut off...

That coulda been me. So easy. A shudder interrupts my shivering. My stomach feels all cold and churny. I wrap my arms around my chest and draw my knees up tight, fighting the feeling, but it's no good. I start to sob.

Heck, why am I crying over a duckosaur I never even met?

I can't stop, though. Not for a while. When I finally manage to get a hold of myself, I remember some'at Dad told me in my survival training. *"If you're out there, Josh, then it's gonna be hard. It's gonna be real tough. And sometimes it's gonna seem like too much, and mebbe you're even gonna get all upset for a while."*

"No, I ain't!" I told him fiercely. "Hunters never cry during a crisis!"

"If you're out there, you might, Josh. And that's okay, under the circumstances." I scoffed slightly, but he just went on firmly, "Survival ain't just physical, Josh. So as soon as you manage to get yourself together, you stop and you think why you're getting like that. And you think whether you can do anything about it. And how dangerous that might be. And then you weigh up whether it's worth the risk. 'Cause you gotta stay positive and focused, understand?"

Why *did* I lose it like that? Not over the duckosaur. I'm scared. And I'm cold. And tired. And so *hungry*.

Well, there's only one of those things I can do anything about right now. If I can find a straight stick and sharpen it up for a fishing spear, I can shinny down that cliff and catch a couple of fish, and be back up here within a quarter-hour. Mebbe I should do it. The afternoon's half gone, and they ain't here yet. What if they're delayed? What if I'm even further downriver than I think? What if they won't get here until tomorrow?

Yeah, I gotta eat. I'm gonna do it.

After inspecting my various injuries as best I can, to make sure the sap and mud still cover them well, I make a quick check for danger. Then I slide out of my hideout and search the woods until I find a good enough stick. Long, straight, with a little branch sticking out at just the right place. I saw through it and carefully cut off the branch about an inch from the stick. After sharpening the end, I sharpen the base of the branch as well, for a barb. One fishing spear. Perfect.

My stomach churns with excitement as I lie at the edge of the cliff for a few minutes, staring down as I recheck the other half of the island—or rather, the second island—for danger. No, I can't see any dung around that cave. On bare rock like that, it's the only thing likely to give away occupation by a large carni'saur. But there ain't none. And what large creature would be living in an awkward place like that? Below, the silver fish glint.

I slip my legs over the cliff and climb down. My hands ache and sting as I grip the rough rock, but I'm too hungry to care. Soon I'm leaping and splashing my way to a likely-looking boulder in the middle of the shallow stream. A slightly deeper channel runs between me and the far bank, though I could wade across if I didn't mind getting in up to my waist. No need. This rock is perfect.

Readying my makeshift spear, I take a breath, trying to focus. My stomach aches and my hands shake. I can do this.

It takes me four tries to catch one—terrible by my standards—but the spear ain't totally straight and feels odd in my hands, and I'm definitely not at my best. I wanna eat it at once, but I force myself to drop it on the rock at my feet once it stops flapping and try for another. I'm so hungry I reckon I can eat two straight off. So I'll catch three, then I'll have one for supper if...if the 'Vi's not here before then.

It only takes me three tries to catch a second one. I'm getting used to the spear. And I get the third, first time! Knowing food is coming is steadying my hands.

Right, I'm gonna have to put them all on the spear, I guess, to carry them up. Or should I eat them right here to avoid taking scent to my hideout? Yeah, but no. I'll carry them up the cliff and eat them at the top. Feels safer up there, somehow. I'm so much closer to the mainland here.

Yeah, mebbe I should get one more, while I'm down here... I could probably eat another two tonight, right? Hang 'em on a tree away from me until I want 'em or wrap 'em in the strongest scentCam I can find. Or both.

I've just raised the spear, my eyes tracking a plump fish, when there's movement at the corner of my eye. I glance around.

There on the bank, barely ten feet away, stands a fully-grown Dakotaraptor. Looking straight at me.

My gut clenches. I've got seconds to live.

Oh Dad, I'm so sorry!

ISAIAH

From my earpiece, I hear Zech mutter a swearword.

"What's wrong?" But I know what he's gonna say.

"Rock just crumbled again. This outcrop's no good neither. I'm gonna try the next one."

He moves upslope, lugging the heavy drill. He's already drilled four holes in the best located outcrop, but all of them failed, the rock cracking and falling away before he even tried to insert any rings. This is the third hole in the second site. The rock he's headed toward is even more off-center, an even worse angle for getting the 'Vi out. But if the bolt won't hold, there ain't nothing doing.

I don't reply, 'cause there ain't nothing useful to say, but I shoot a frustrated look at the sun before going back to scouring the landscape for signs of danger. It's after the heat of the day now. For a second time, big predators will be stirring and roaming around out there. With my little Josh...

Saint Des, please look after him...

Lord, protect him...

JOSHUA

My heart's pounding, *thud, thud, thud, thud*, each beat so hard it hurts, and a strange ringing fills my ears as I stare at my death. I wanna run for the cliff, but she'll be on me in one bound. My body's shaking and I can't stop it. The raptor raises her muzzle with a little jerk, sniffing...about to spring? For a moment I'm afraid I'm gonna wet myself. Or just run away, wildly, screaming like an idiot.

But I can hear what Dad said to me once. *Someday, Josh, there might come a time when it's all up. When it's over and there ain't nothing that will save you. Then there's only one choice left—whether to take it like a man.*

When Dad imagines this moment, that's what I want him to picture. Me taking it like a man.

And I want it to be true.

I'm not gonna run. I'm not gonna scrabble at the cliff like a panicked puppy while the raptor drags me down from behind.

I stand straight and look her in the eye—and wait.

ISAIAH

Zech has barely started running the drill when he shuts it off and swears again.

"Hey, easy on the language," I tell him. "You want Saint Des mad at us right now?"

"Saint Des ain't gonna take it out on an eleven-year-old boy 'cause I flapped my tongue!" snaps Zech, kicking the rock and making a piece fall off. "Argh! This stuff is useless. I'll try lower down."

"Lower down this slope is the last place we wanna shift this 'Vi. It's still sodden."

"You got a better idea?"

I don't, so I keep quiet again. This is like being trapped in a nightmare. The better part of the day is gone, and we're not even close to getting moving. At this rate, it'll be dark before we've even got enough bolts in.

Heck, no. Don't even think that, Isaiah.

JOSHUA

The raptor stares back, nostrils flaring as though she's trying to get my scent. Her head turns a fraction this way, then that, as though she's aiming her ear cavities my way too.

Weird. I mean, she's looking right at me. But...I focus more closely on her great head, trying to ignore the razor-sharp teeth peeping from her slightly parted lips. She's looking my way, no question, but her amber eyes ain't really focused on me. In fact, they ain't very focused on *nothing*. And it's hard to see from here, but they almost look a little cloudy. Can she actually see me? It ain't possible for a blind raptor to survive in the wild, right?

But this island...so protected from danger. But there's no dung, nothing to suggest... My eyes go to those broken-open logs. Argh, of course there's no dung! If she's so hungry she's breaking open rotten wood to get bugs to eat—her, a big proud Dakotaraptor!—then she'll definitely be eating up her own dung, too, to get any nutrients missed the first time around.

Staying very, very still, I look her over carefully. Her legs are sticks, her body real thin under her feathers. The once-fine ruff of blue feathers around her leathery face is tired and faded. This raptor is *very* old. And—still she just stands there, sniffing—at least half-blind, I'm more certain of it by the moment.

But even her tired old nose and what's left of her sight and hearing are probably five times better than mine. If I move, she'll be onto me. And—my eyes go to her feet—there ain't nothing wrong with her nine-inch killing claws. Or her teeth. Carni'saurs can grow as many new teeth as they need, she ain't gonna run out of *those* if she lives to a hundred.

So what do I do? Does her blindness change anything? Do I have a chance?

My heart sinks. Probably not. She knows I'm here. She must've caught a movement or heard me fishing. She's either not sure enough what I am or not sure exactly where I am, that's why she's waiting. But if I try to creep away... Well, it's worth a try, but it probably ain't gonna change nothing. If only this stream were making more noise, but it's rippling very quietly over the shallows.

Her nostrils flare again, and she steps forward, one great, bony foot splashing into the cold stream, her head lowering and moving from side to side. Searching.

Heck, the fish! *Idiot, Josh!* I've got three bloodied fish at my feet, stinking away...

Very, very slowly I tilt my spear down and stab it into one of the fish, then raise it until I can give it the smallest flick necessary and send the fish flying onto the shore. Her head jerks at my sudden movement—no, she ain't totally blind—and she moves forward, but as the fish hits the rocky shore beside her, she spins around and lowers her muzzle, sniffing, grabbing the fish almost at once. *Gulp*, she swallows it whole.

I've already got the next fish on the spear and manage to chuck it before she can turn and pay attention to me moving. While she's distracted I chuck the last one, too. But they won't keep her occupied for long. Mebbe...mebbe before I try to creep away, I should do my best to fill her up with fish. It's risky, 'cause I'll have to keep moving, but I don't fancy the odds of giving her the slip while she's hungry and alert. Taking the edge off her hunger first might be my only chance.

Quickly, I turn my eyes to the water, looking for

another fish. The side of my body prickles and tingles as I wait for her fangs to sink into me, my belly clenching as I wait for a killing claw to slit me open. But I force myself to keep watching the river. My arm is shaking. No. I've gotta catch another fish, fast! I force my muscles still. And...strike!

The raptor surges forward at my movement, her head rising, teeth parting, killing claws drawing back—but I toss the fish onto the same spot I threw the others, and she turns back to eat it. Heart pounding wildly, I stare into the river. Another. Another, quick!

Plop! My spear drives into one—the raptor starts to move—I throw the fish...and again she goes for it instead of me.

Quick, another!

Plop! This time, she tenses when I strike—but don't move towards me. Instead, her head turns slightly to the left... Heck, she's waiting for the fish, ain't she? Smart old lady. I toss the fish quickly, she grabs it—*gulp, swallow*—and she's standing there again, staring toward me hungrily. Why wade into a cold river to try and catch who knows what, when tasty fish keep dropping down in front of your nose, huh? I'd better keep them coming.

Quickly, I turn my attention to the next fish.

Plop! She waits again. *Splat. Gulp.*

Plop! Yep, she's totally got the idea. *Splat. Gulp.*

Plop! This time the noise makes her drop her muzzle to that spot of shore, ready to eat. *Splat. Gulp.*

How many fish does it take to fill the belly of a starving Dakotaraptor? Eighteen foot long and as tall as Dad. Heck, this could take a while.

But.

Amazingly.

I'm not dead.

Yet.

Oh yeah, I'll fish for you all afternoon, old lady, if that's what it takes to stop you eating me!

ISAIAH

"This rock might be slightly better," says Zech, making my heart leap—until he adds, "but we're gonna have to drill a lot deeper than usual if there's any chance of getting the bolt in well enough to be of any use."

I think a few words that Saint Des wouldn't like, 'cause whatever Zech says I'm not saying them out loud.

"Well, at least you've found somewhere," I manage to say—'cause it's good news really, right? Even if it will take longer.

"I ain't promising." Zech sounds wary and discouraged. "But it's our best chance."

Best chance ain't good enough, I wanna yell at him.

Josh is alone out there!

But I manage not to. He really is doing his best.

JOSHUA

It's seriously weird having a Dakotaraptor for a fishing companion. There she lounges—the weary old thing settled down on her tummy a while ago—eagerly gobbling up each fish as it arrives in front of her, like a very large, feathery version of Dad chilling on the river bank, while I stand and fish.

But she still ain't et me. And surely she must be getting full soon?

I still can't believe she's survived like this. Half-blind? It don't seem possible.

Plop! Splat... Gulp.

Hold on, I found *two* Dakotaraptor prints up by the log bridge. Last spring there were a male on this island too. I pause my fishing for a moment, glancing around uneasily. No sign of him now. Please God only *were*.

Yeah, but *were* makes sense. I bet she's a former matriarch who left the pack with her mate after losing a leadership challenge. They came over to this island and made their home here, safe from attack, no doubt slipping over to the mainland now and then for a bit of sneaky hunting. And the pair-bond with raptors is super-strong, so as she got older and began to lose her sight, I bet her mate hunted for her. But some'at happened to him—pretty recently, from the fact that she's starving but still alive—and now she's completely alone.

Well, not *right* now. Right now she has a personal chef, but since I'm also a possible dessert, I doubt I count in the companionship department.

Plop! Splat... Gulp.

Eventually I'm gonna have to make a move. The sun is dropping in the sky. But I need to think this through. Which way do I go? The cliff? If I could get high enough, she'd have trouble following me, but I'd be a sitting duck while I got up the first bit. First, I need to try creeping away, but the moment she sees me I'll have to go for speed. She's shown no sign of springing on me—a Dakotaraptor in its prime can leap twenty feet with lightning speed—probably because she just can't pinpoint my location precisely enough. So mebbe I have a tiny chance.

Still, can I *really* outrun her? Depends. From the stiff way she settled down on the bank, and from her reluctance to enter even this shallow water, she's probably got aching joints. But how much will they actually slow her down when there's a meal at stake? My life will probably depend on the answer to that question.

But I can't go for the cliff, anyways. She can see movement too well for me to succeed in creeping over there, and if I bolt that way, the moment I stop running to climb, she'll have me. No, I need to go across the clearing outside the cave, around the far end of the curving crag where it's low and I won't have to slow down to climb, and then...over the channel to the mainland? Where the allosaur and the deinons and the velociraptors are waiting? Or double back to the log bridge and return to my hideout with the perfect view of the 'Vi's approach?

That island sure ain't as safe as I thought it were, with a Dakotaraptor in residence next door. But I didn't find any fresh tracks. There's no evidence she goes over there anymore. With bad eyes and arthritis, having to cross the log is probably enough to keep her away. But if she thinks there's food over there? But there's food over there already, rabbits and small mammals in abundance, and she's not been venturing in search of it...

Whoops! Stiffly, the raptor is rising to her feet, staring my way. I've spent too long thinking and not enough time fishing. Aargh! Quickly, I fix my eyes on the water, trying to concentrate despite that deadly interest. But when I toss the next fish onto the bank, she's still just staring my way, waiting. She gulps the fish down but stays on her feet. No more slacking, Josh! This old matriarch ain't having it.

There's still far more hunger in her stare than I'd

like. Ain't I managed to fill her up at all? I guess the fish are mere morsels for her. A pack of Dakotaraptors can pull down a juvenile triceratops and strip the carcass to the bone before lying down somewhere to sleep it off. Like many predators, they can consume a vast amount in one meal.

I try to picture how many fish it would take to equal a Dakotaraptor's share of a kill. My heart sinks. There's no way I'm actually gonna fill her up. Not before dark. The light's fading already.

Yeah, if I crossed the channel to the marsh and the shore beyond, I'd be walking straight into the twilight hunting spree again. I'm gonna have to just go back to my island. *If* I can get away. And I dunno how I will if she's gonna eat me the moment I stop fishing...

Quickly, I stab and toss another fish onto the bank. What am I gonna do? Have I fished for hours just to be dessert after all? Mebbe, but what else could I try? What else *can* I try? Fishing's keeping me alive. *Plop, splat.* Mebbe she'll get tired and take a nap or some'at. I've just gotta keep going, buying each minute or two of life with a fish.

So much for her taking a nap. She stays on her feet as though afraid lying down will make the flow of fish slow again. Demanding old lady.

The fishing don't require enough movement to keep me warm, I still ain't et nothing, and I'm getting colder and colder. My wet feet are turning into blocks of ice. How fast am I gonna be able to run on them? A stumble may kill me.

Every time she's busy gulping a fish I bend my legs and flex my feet, trying to warm them and loosen the muscles. The sun is dropping and so is the temperature. We're not late enough in the season for a deadly killer-chiller storm, but a more mundane fall storm is definitely on the way and will be dangerous enough in a t-shirt and shorts. I should be gathering extra bedding in case Dad don't get here tonight.

Yeah, at this moment, bedding really is the least of my worries.

But it just confirms that I can't wait much longer. I'm gonna have to make a move. Josh vs. a Dakota-raptor. Heck, it sounds like a bad joke.

But it ain't.

ISAIAH

"Okay, we're set." Zech gives one more cautious tug on the sling he's somehow managed to get around a bit of the central outcrop, shakes his head—he don't reckon it's gonna stay on—and heads for the 'Vi.

We've got one winch cable hitched to the tree again, one to the extra sling, and one to the bolt Zech finally managed to set deep into the lower outcrop. Hopefully with the 'Vi's weight spread between all three, we'll be able to get out onto the traction boards Zech's laid in front of us and rammed under the wheels for grip.

Zech swings straight into the cab and I get ready on the winch controls.

Once he's started the engine, I ask, "Okay?"

"Yep. Take it gently."

He's stating the obvious, and I clamp my teeth on a sharp retort. Setting the winch controller to maintain equal tension in all three cables, I very slowly apply the power. Pained whining from the winches and no movement from the 'Vi. I maintain the power, low and steady. The ground's still wet enough that there could be some serious suction to overcome.

But eventually I say, "It ain't moving, Zech. I'm gonna have to give it some more."

"Yeah." Zech speaks reluctantly. "Slow as you can and be ready to stop."

I bite my tongue some more and very gently increase the power. The 'Vi shifts slightly. My heart pounds in my throat. I hold the power lever, waiting, giving the 'Vi time to ease free as Zech tries applying a little gas, but he's got no traction. No movement, nothing. I run the winches a little harder and get another movement. I wait again. No good. I inch it up further, my eyes flying from the screen to the winch points. Heck, we'll be up to full power soon and the 'Vi ain't even coming out y—

"Watch it!"

Even though we've both been alert for it, it happens too fast to stop. The sling slips off the rock, throwing the force onto the other two points, and a split second later the rock shatters and the bolt flies out. The tree is already rising out of the ground by the time I can slam the winches into reverse. It settles back, mebbe not damaged too bad to survive, but it ain't no more use to us, and that's all I care about right now.

Heck! I pound on the console and mouth swear-words under my breath. We're running out of options. Normally if we were stuck this bad, we'd kick back and relax and wait for the ground to dry out properly. And if that didn't work, try to get a message to the nearest 'Vi-park, if we got a signal, that we needed some help.

With Josh out there, I'd even call Highway Patrol, but there ain't been a blip of a signal yet and I have a bad feeling we may be in a blind alley—no satellites orbiting close enough to get a line of sight with us. The technology that allows such rapid transfer to cities also requires very directional beams—or whatever the technical term is. You've gotta be pretty much dead underneath to get a lock-on. No problem for cities, the orbits are routed to go right over them. But it limits our Net access in the wilderness, even at the best of times. We've never cared before.

Now we couldn't care more.

The sun is dropping lower. We need a new plan, fast.

JOSHUA

Tossing another fish onto the bank, I eye the shore, planning my route, scanning the ground for pebbles or loose bits that might slow me down. I'm gonna need every millisecond. Can I really outrun her? *No,* says a cold voice inside me. *Of course you can't.*

Mebbe I should just creep to the cliff and inch up it until I'm out of her reach. But she's staring intently at me again, everything about her showing disapproval. Yeah, I'm not making the tiny movements I make while fishing, and she already connects them with another fish being on the way. No, she may not be able to see well enough to gauge the distance and spring right on me, but she'll notice if I start trying to sneak off.

Quickly, I bend over the stream and I sense her relax slightly, satisfied. Heck, what do I do?

I'm breathing too fast as I eye the fish in the water. If I go for the cliff, she'll get me. If I run, she's gonna get me. She's still too hungry to nod off, not while either the fish or the heron are available to eat.

Plop. Splat. I chuck another fish onto the bank. *Gulp.* It's gone in an instant. I am so done for.

The temperature is still dropping. I've gotta make a move or I'm gonna have hypothermia by morning, even if I do get away from her. I eye the route again. I'm just gonna have to go for it. I'll be too cold to run at all if I wait much longer.

Mebbe I should try and hold back a few fish, so I can chuck her a bunch at once just before I make my move. I'm gonna have to fish really fast, though, 'cause she ain't patient, and she can smell them.

I try to keep back every other one, but have to reduce it to one in three as she stares and sniffs with far too much interest as the pauses between fish get longer. It seems to take forever to collect even four fish at my feet. But from the way she's sniffing, she ain't gonna put up with this stockpiling much longer. Fortunately, right now she looks away, checking for a new fish on the bank, then lifts her tail slightly and drops dung.

Dung! The sudden stab of hope is like an electric shock through my body. If I can keep her from eating it... If I can *get* to it... Despite my scentCam, she's probably keeping tabs on me partly by smell. She'll have connected the blurry movements of the heron with the scent of sap and mud by now. But if I can smear myself with her own dung, change my scent, and *then* run...! She'll be hunting the wrong scent, then.

But she's already turning around to eat it, still too

hungry not to. I bend and grab the four fish, chucking the first one into the usual spot, then swiftly lobbing each of the other three further along the bank. Getting her even slightly further away will help.

She's already turning to eat the first fish. As she steps towards the second I lower myself from my rock into the icy channel. Ooh! It's more like chest deep and the cold has my teeth chattering in moments. I clamp them together, trying to stay silent. I'm afraid to risk drawing her eye with speed, and terrified I won't get to the dung in time if I don't hurry.

Aw, heck! By the time I'm dragging myself up the bank, my chilled body heavy and numb, she's gulping the third fish. I stumble the few feet to the dung, grab a fistful in each hand and clap it to my armpits, then my groin. I distinctly hear the swallowing sound that'll be fish number four. Frantically, I rub it in my hair and over my arms...argh, no time, she's turning, she's looking my way, her head and tail are raised eagerly, she knows the heron has finally left its rock and her intentions are all too plain...she's coming, she's *hunting*...

I tense to run, but she's already so close, and despite her stiffness there's still a bounce to her stride that tells me flight is useless.

To a raptor, everything is pack, predator, or prey. I can't run, and I sure can't intimidate her...

Saint Des, help me!

I chirp like a Dakotaraptor hatchling welcoming its mother back to the nest, bending over to adopt the most raptor-ish position I can without actually having a tail, my arms tucked up as though they're wing-arms.

Her steps slow. Her head cocks slightly, listening.

Come on, Josh, sound like you mean it. Pretend she's Dad, coming for you...

I pour emotion into my cries, as though a pack of piranha'saurs had come lurking around the nest while she were gone and I've never been so glad to see her back.

Her tail lowers, her head tilts forward in an anxious maternal way. Oh yeah, she's an old matriarch, alright. Probably raised dozens of chicks over the years. I've gotta keep triggering those maternal instincts.

She hurries forward again, but there's no hunting signals coming off her, now, just maternal curiosity. Heck, all or nothing...

I hop to meet her, making my movements as raptor-ish as I can, crying out continually in welcome. Careful not to hesitate, I go right up to her and rub my cheek against her thigh the way a chick would do, keeping up my pitiful peeping.

I paw slightly at her side and keep rubbing against her as I sense her head turning to inspect me. My dung-clumped hair ruffles a little as she sniffs at it. She could take my head off in one bite... *No, stupid, don't smell scared. She's your mom. She's Dad, come to save you...*

I peep and fawn against her happily, as though the idea that she could hurt me is unimaginable. She carries on sniffing, nudging me here and there with her nose. Puzzled, I guess. Knows on some level that she don't have no chicks right now, but her maternal instincts are well triggered, and I do smell like her, so she ain't sure what to make of me.

Keep it up, Josh. Keep it up...

I ramp things up a notch, flopping down beside her great clawed feet and screeching like I've just hurt myself.

And she replies. Finally, she replies. A soothing, rumbling muttering sound as she lowers her head to nudge me less in investigation and more in comfort. *Are you all right, chick? Get up, chick...*

Bingo. I stay down for a little longer, then get up with the sort of whiney sounds a chick makes when it's not really hurt that bad.

The relieved raptor-mom inspects me, nostrils flaring, trying to check I'm okay even though she can hardly see me, then nudges me forward. Obediently I move in the direction indicated, pausing only to crouch in the most raptorish way I can manage to grab the last few balls of dung. I shove them into my pockets for safe keeping.

She's shepherding me to a spot nearer the cave,

tucked behind an outcrop, where the rock gives way to a small area of sandy soil, patchily covered with long grass. Ah-hah, here she has a little 'day bed'—a scrape she can sun herself in. With a warning chirrup to me— *don't wander off, chick*—she settles into it. Oh yeah, no wonder I didn't spot her earlier. Only one corner of the bed could possibly be visible from where I were, and her drab old plumage blends into the grasses beautifully.

I guess it's nap time. Becoming a mother again at her age must be tiring—to say nothing of standing around watching someone fish for hours. Obediently, I settle close enough to satisfy her, which is way too close for comfort, but she still ain't eating me, so... As soon as she's asleep, I can sneak off. *Please, Saint Des?*

Sprawled on my tummy, my chin on the ground, raptor-style, I keep my breathing deep and slow, as though I'm napping obediently, fighting not to actually fall asleep. Hard to believe I could be this close to nodding off with a deadly carni'saur's jaws two feet from my nose, but I'm too far gone to stay alert.

She seems to have settled off quickly, though. I give it a little while, to be sure she's deeply asleep, then, as quietly as I can with legs that feel like numb jelly, I ease up to my feet and tiptoe away. I take the nice flat route I planned, stumbling faster and faster as I get up above the cave. There's the log bridge! I'm shaking so hard with cold and hunger and relief that I crawl over it on hands and knees—and finally...safe! Well, as safe as I'm likely to get.

I need...what do I need to do now? My mind feels as sluggish as my body. Bedding. That's what I need. As much extra bedding as I can, and get myself under that rock again. Try to get warm.

Yeah, right. I'm shivering even harder in the growing twilight. Soaking wet, no food, pathetic shelter. Get warm, huh?

There's nothing I can do about it, though. I locate a suitable bush and fumble my knife out, dropping it several times as I hack at the greenery. Hauling it over to my sloping rock exhausts me. I need more. This ain't enough. But when I step that way my legs buckle, and I end up on my knees. I can't get more. I'm done.

I crawl under my rock instead and weakly arrange the extra greenery. A small amount at the back, to insulate me from the stone and keep me out of the rainwater that will probably pool there. A glance up at the cloudy sky tells me that the storm is well and truly gathering. Then I pull the rest in as close as I can, not leaving a gap to look through now. It's so close to dusk that Dad and Uncle Z will have stopped driving, in case they'd miss me in the twilight. What if they drove past while I were down there at the stream for hours? I shudder. Nothing I can do now. They'll be back, even if they did. I'll just have to...have to...

Thinking about it is too hard. Shaking with cold, I try to tug the bedding closer still, then I let my head rest on the dirt. My eyes close...

ISAIAH

We spent the rest of the daylight digging again. We've exhausted the obvious belay points, so it seemed the next best option. Since Zech had done so much heavy work, I took a turn. It's a lot drier now, so we hope we can dig a ramp for each wheel and line them with traction boards. But, honestly? It's still wet enough that normally we'd just accept we weren't going nowhere yet and wait.

But that ain't an option. Not with Josh out there.

Hopefully he's found a safe place to den up. If he hasn't by now, he's probably dead. But 'safe' den or not, this is taking way too long.

JOSHUA

I shudder as cold air strikes my wet body, and the shudder drags me fully awake. What? My bedding's moving away from me. Some'at's pulling it...

Maternal muttering reaches my ears. *Don't worry, chick. Don't worry. I'll get you out of there.*

Oh... I mouth some'at Saint Des wouldn't like. The raptor's woken up and come looking for me. *Misfire.*

Guess I convinced her a little too well that I'm her chick. Raptors are super-good parents. Best out of any 'saurs. I guess I shouldn't be so surprised she were prepared to wobble her way over that log in search of a missing baby.

She's making short work of dragging my bedding out of the way, half-blind or not. And this rock is no way low enough to stop her getting her head in. Quickly, I grab a bit more dung from my pocket and rub it over myself as thoroughly as I can. By the time I've finished, her muzzle is there, looming large and blocking out the feeble remains of the daylight. She sniffs and lips at me, then grabs my t-shirt as though it's tough raptor skin and simply drags me out. Her *strength*—even this tired old creature... For a moment fear chokes off my breathing.

But she just puts me down at her feet and sniffs at me, doing her 'trying to check my chick's okay though I can't really see him' thing again.

I launch into a barrage of relieved and grateful sounds. *Momma, you found me, you saved me!* If I can keep her relieved that she rescued me from where I'd got myself 'trapped,' mebbe she won't get angry that I wandered off. If she decides to punish me with a nip she'll probably draw blood from thin-skinned me, and

I'm not sure how she'll react to the taste. Out here in the wilderness, she might never have even encountered a human before—but I still won't taste like a raptor.

In between adoring peeps, I eye the nearby woods. Could I make a run for it? But she can fit between all those trees and it'll take me too long to climb one—even assuming I could, the way I feel right now. I mustn't blow my cover unless I'm sure I can get away.

Like any good parent, I guess she senses that I'm thinking of misbehaving. At any rate, although I'm large enough to be a young nestling, she grabs the back of my t-shirt again, picks me up as though I'm a newborn hatchling, turns her head and deposits me on her back.

What the—!

Automatically, I clutch two handfuls of feathers to stop myself sliding off. Heck! I've seen raptors carry their little ones like this often enough if they have to leave their nest site, babies clinging all over them, but...what the heck? I'm really riding on a wild Dakotaraptor's back? Mebbe I'm hallucinating.

I resist the temptation to sit up, and instead cling, flat and close, just like a chastened chick being carried home in disgrace 'cause it can't be trusted not to wander off.

She plods off along the cliff, back toward the log.

I'm too tired and off-balance to do nothing but lie there shivering. And her warm feathery back feels amazing against my cold skin.

Crossing the log is kinda hair-raising, the way she teeters from side to side, but soon we're on the other side, and she's carrying me down into that clearing outside her cave. When she stops, she gives a little whistling call that I interpret as permission to get off, so I slither down her side, land on my feet and promptly tumble in the dirt as my legs give way again. I am so beat.

And, after hours of effort, here I am back where I started — at the feet of a hungry Dakotaraptor.

ISAIAH

I dig the spade in yet again, ignoring the gathering darkness around us. In my ear, Zech is muttering to himself as he weighs the risks of leaving the floodlights off and mebbe not spotting some'at coming, versus putting them on and attracting every nosy raptor in the area.

I leave him to it, digging frantically. If we can't get all four ramps dug tonight and make an attempt to get out, there's no telling how much of our work will be left in the morning. The ground's still that sodden. But I'm working on the last one. If some'at can just not eat me for another twenty minutes—half hour tops—we'll be ready.

"You should come in, Isaiah. Finish in the morning." Zech speaks half-heartedly. He don't want me eaten, but he's as worried about Josh as I am.

I don't bother replying. We're nearly done. *Saint Des, please keep those critters away from me for another few minutes. Unless there's anything bothering Josh, that is. Send those to me. Even if they eat me. Seriously, Saint Des, if my life will save him, anyway, anyhow, just take it...*

"I might as well go put some dinner on; I can't see a short-circuiting thing," grumbles Zech. But I don't even need to look to know he ain't moving from that turret. He's still got the heat sensors.

I drive the spade in yet again. Almost time to start laying the traction boards.

JOSHUA

I've managed to drag my weary body up onto a little ledge over the cave entrance, where the motherly raptor can't follow me. I'm safe from her, finally, but it's horribly exposed. The wind is rising and between that and the cold stone under me, the last shreds of warmth are being sucked from my body super-fast.

Below, the Dakotaraptor peers up in my direction and calls anxiously. *Come here, chick. Come here. Storm's coming.*

I can't go down. She only needs to change her mind about me, and I'm dinner. But, heck, it's cold up here.

The last of the light seeps from the evening sky. I can't see the raptor no more, but I can hear her, still calling to her naughty chick. She's a good mother, all right.

Eventually scrabbling sounds tell me that she's trying to climb up to me. I don't think she can, but it's still a relief when the first flash of lightning gives me a glimpse of her—still safely near the bottom.

Come down, chick, she calls. *It's cold and late. Time for bed. Come down.*

Sorry, Momma Matriarch, I think to her. *What big teeth you have.*

More thunder rumbles in the distance, but rain begins to splash down in big drops—or rather, fly sideways in the wind. I hadn't really dried much, but it still feels icy on my skin. I ain't feeling quite so bad no more, though. Mebbe I can just curl up and sleep and tough it out 'til morning... Yeah, I'm not even shivering so much, now. I'll just let my eyes close...

Screech! More scrabbling sounds jerk me from my doze. *Screech.* The raptor's getting herself in a state, trying to reach me. Why's she so worried? I'm okay now. I'm just gonna get some sleep...

Screech! "Give up," I murmur, "you can't get up

here."

My noises throw her into even more fevered cries. *Come here, chick! Chick! I'm worried!*

"*Don't* worry," I tell her, "I ain't cold no more..."

I close my eyes again. No, I ain't cold no more. The icy rain lashes down on me. The wind whips over my skin. The stone sucks at me. Why *ain't* I cold no more?

I try to jerk my eyes open and only manage to drag my lids up slowly. No shivering—heck, I'm hypothermic! *Misfire, misfire, misfire...*how did I let this creep up on me? How did I...

My eyes are closing again, my mind wandering. *No! NO! Move, Josh. Move!*

But where?

The cave. The cave will be sheltered. It's my only chance.

I can barely move. My limbs feel heavy and numb. I turn clumsily, lowering my legs over the edge, trying to feel for footholds, but I can't find any and my body slides. My hands don't remember how to grip and the next movement I'm sliding, falling, sliding, falling...

Thud!

Am I on the ground? Am I...? Where am I? What am I doing? Some'at...some'at about a cave? I can't remember. I thought it were important, but it don't seem important, now. I'll just rest a moment and then...mebbe I'll remember. I'll just...

Zech eases off the gas pedal and slams a fist into the steering wheel.

"No, keep trying!" I snap.

"It ain't working!"

"Let me try!" I half-drag him from the driver's seat and throw myself into it instead, ramming the 'Vi into the lowest possible gear before clutching the steering wheel in my blistered hands.

Of course, no matter how gently or how hard I play with that gas pedal, the wheels just spin and fishtail around in the bottom of their slippery little indents, just the way they did for Zech, unable to get enough purchase on the traction boards we've tried so hard to force underneath.

"Heck!" My turn to pound on the steering wheel. "This. Is. Not. Happening! We've *gotta get outta here!*" I grab the gear stick again, but Zech grabs me.

"Stop it! You're gonna dig us deeper! We've gotta wait for morning!"

"Wait for morning!" But I leave the gear lever and pound on the wheel some more. "*Again?* Josh. Is. Out. There!"

And then somehow I'm not hitting the wheel anymore, I'm slumped over it sobbing and Zech's got his arms around me.

But I'm not too sure he ain't sobbing too.

Eventually Zech fries a couple of edmo steaks and forces me to eat one while he stares glumly at the other. We turn in almost immediately afterward, knowing we ought to rest after all the heavy work. But I can't get to sleep.

I lie listening to the rain lashing against the 'Vi as thunder rumbles. Josh is out there for a second night, and the weather could hardly be worse for the time of year. The temperature's less'n half what it were last night. I picture Josh, barefoot in his shorts and t-shirt, and shudder. Lord willing, he's found a darn good shelter, and he stocked up really well on bedding. He'd have read the coming storm in the sky all day, it's not like he'll have been taken by surprise.

But he's still hugely undersupplied for this weather. And there ain't. Nothing. I. Can. Do. 'Til. Dawn.

Sleep finally sucks me down, but I jerk awake in the small hours after a nightmare in which Josh is trapped in a giant hailstone and I'm hammering and hammering on it, trying to get him out, but I can't.

I don't sleep again, just lie awake waiting for the sun.

Josh, I'm coming. I swear.

DAY 3

JOSHUA

Mmmm, I'm toasty and warm. I lie for a while, enjoying it, before waking up enough to wonder why I'm enjoying it so much.

Some'at's tickling my nose. My entire face. Raptor scent fills my nostrils. Dakotaraptor.

My eyes fly open.

Feathers. My face is pressed into a feathery side. That weight over my hips is Momma Matriarch's neck. I'm inside the cave. Her wing-arms encircle me, tucking me close under her breast. Yep, I'm lying in a raptor's nest and she's swaddling me. That's what hunters call the way raptors tuck their young up at night, not just keeping them warm but also stopping them wandering off. More young raptors die because of curiosity than anything else.

Once the chicks get too big to all fit under the wing-arms of the parents, they start parceling them out to the unmated pack members to swaddle at night, until they get big enough to escape from it.

I'll never be big enough to escape a Dakotaraptor that wants to swaddle me, even if I grow to Dad's size.

Well, I don't need to. Dad's gonna come get me soon enough.

Just so long as Momma Matriarch remembers I'm her chick when she wakes up, or there won't be nothing much for him to find. As soon as she shows signs of waking, I'll risk moving and put some more dung on.

Right now, I'm just gonna enjoy being warm. My clothes have even dried. I guess she picked me up and brought me inside. I have a vague memory of some'at lipping at my t-shirt, lifting me... Yeah, I'd be dead by now if she hadn't warmed me up.

Hypothermia and you didn't even notice. That were stupid, Josh!

Yeah? What did I do that were so stupid? I were dangerously hungry, so I tried to get food. Then I were trying and trying to get to shelter without being eaten, with enough time to gather bedding, 'cause I knew I were in danger of hypothermia. Whole point about hypothermia is that you're very lucky to notice it in time, even with training. What could I have done different?

Not much, I guess.

Thanks, Saint Des.

Thanks, Momma Matriarch.

Now, if you could just carry on being nice to me...

Yeah, carry on being nice to me, Momma, and I'll catch us

both a fish breakfast, how about that? My stomach's empty and aching—I ain't never been this hungry in my life. Mebbe she'll wake up soon. Seriously? I want the raptor to wake up? *Let sleeping raptors lie* is a saying for a reason.

Yeah, but whenever she does stir, she'll either eat me or she won't, and I won't get no food 'til she's up. I don't want her getting out of the wrong side of the nest, though, so I won't disturb her. I'll just lie quiet until she wakes up by herself, and then we'll see what it's gonna be for breakfast: fish or boy.

ISAIAH

I rise before the sun and open the side door an inch to check the ground. Barely any drier than yesterday. *Outage.* That's that, then.

I dig a backpack from a cupboard and start laying out supplies on the table. Flares. Ammo. Scent-sealed packs of emergency food. Josh's clothes and spare boots. What about his rifle? But the stuff's piling up already. I need to travel light and fast. Above all, fast.

I'm weighing the decision in my mind when little noises and slight movements in the vehicle tell me Zech's getting up. I fight to keep my mind on what I'm doing, but I'm soon rehearsing what to say—yet again. It would help if there weren't such a compelling case for staying to help Zech get the 'Vi out as soon as possible. Even I can argue it either way. But enough is enough. I gotta get to Josh.

Before long, the cab door opens and Zech steps through. He stops as his gaze falls on all the gear. No, he won't like this. Frantically, I ready my arguments...

His hands go to his hips as he scans the table. "Have you got enough flares and ammo?" He steps forward and starts flipping through Josh's clothes, checking the complete set of thermals and other layers.

I stare at him as he continues inspecting things. "You ain't gonna try and stop me?"

Still bent over the gear, he glances up at me, anguish in his eyes. "We ain't moved one foot yet, and there's no telling when we will. If someone don't get to him soon, he won't be alive to save. This is as good or bad a plan as any. You go get him, and I'll come meet you in the 'Vi, if Saint Des ain't totally turned his back on us. And if it won't come free, well, so long as you get him back here, we'll be fairly safe while we wait for things to dry out. Most important thing right now is to find him 'fore it's too late. That storm won't have been easy on him."

"Mebbe we should both go."

Zech twists his lip, clearly desperately tempted, but speaks reluctantly. "Two guns ain't enough to put up much more defense than one. You need at least four men before a pack of raptors will take you seriously, you know that. And every mile you and Josh don't end up having to cover increases your chances considerably. So I need to stay here and get the 'Vi out. Somehow."

That were my conclusion as well, and I know he'd rather stick with me if at all possible. "I can't decide whether to take Josh's rifle along. It's so darn heavy."

"Let's pack this gear up, and I guess the question will answer itself."

Zech kinda elbows me out and packs the rucksack himself, but he does it with painstaking care and puts everything just where I'd put it, so I stand back and let him. He's just worried about me.

When it's done, he hefts it and shakes his head. "You gotta leave that extra rifle. Your first responsibility is to survive long enough to find Josh. You can't do that if you can't move fast. He'll be safer with just you and your rifle than with nothing at all. I guess he could use the flare gun, in a pinch. If it comes down to shooting at anything, you're gonna be giving your position away to every raptor in earshot, and you'll be in such doo-doo that it ain't hardly gonna matter."

"Well, thanks for that pep talk, Zech."

"Just telling it how it is, little bro."

Yep. Surviving out there has more to do with remaining undetected than with brute force.

Lucky for little Josh.

Please, Saint Des?

JOSHUA

The raptor is waking up. At any rate, I can feel her heart beating faster, where her chest presses down on my stomach. I slide my left hand, which ain't wedged under a third of a ton of Dakotaraptor, into my pocket and pull off a good chunk of dung. I don't wanna use it all up, but if she's forgotten about me when she comes fully awake it's gonna be an all or nothing moment. I apply dung liberally to my hair and anywhere I can easily reach, then wriggle a hand in to do my other armpit and my groin again, the two places where my not-raptor scent will be strongest.

She responds to my movements by raising her head and shaking it, blinking in the dim dawn light. I roll over like a sleepy chick, making just-waking-up peeping sounds, and quickly dung my other side too. Not a moment too soon. Arching her neck, she dips her head down to me, sniffing. I hope it's just my imagination, but she seems puzzled to find me there.

I break into a far more enthusiastic morning greeting, rubbing my cheek against her feathers. Her teeth sink into the back of my t-shirt and she drags me out from half-under her, depositing me between her wingclaws. My heart pounds like mad. What's she doing? Is she gonna eat me?

Her head drops to mine and she lips at me. Then her teeth are running through my hair, removing clumped dung, old and new. Heck, she's preening me. Morning bath.

Good. I'm still her chick.

It don't take her long to do my little head of hair, and then she's lipping over the rest of me, hunting for more 'feathers' to preen and coming up short. Sneakily, I gather any scattered scraps of dung large enough to pick up, squeeze them into a ball and stuff them back in my pocket. Clearly puzzled by my featherlessness, she spends some time inspecting me thoroughly, before accepting defeat and giving me a little push with her nose that clearly means my bath is done and I can go play — so long as I don't go far away.

I get to my feet, adopting my raptor pose, and hop toward the river, chirping excitedly. *Come on, Momma Matriarch. Come on. Let's have breakfast!*

She rumbles disapproval that I'm straying from her side again *already* as she gets stiffly to her feet. Ignoring her objections, I grab my spear from where I dropped it yesterday and move to the riverbank, eyeing the shallow area where the fish are easily accessible. Now that I'm her chick, I don't want her to connect me more than I can help with the heron she spent several hours yesterday hoping to eat. There's only so much I can do about that, but I can at least choose a different spot to fish from.

Heck, I'm hungry.

I splash out to the rock furthest from where I stood yesterday and take up a fishing position. *Plop*. Missed. I may be warm at last, but my hands are shaking with hunger.

Plop. Got'ya.

I draw my knife and in a few quick movements I've gutted the fish, tossing the innards onto the bank for Momma Matriarch to eat once she gets over here. I scrape the worst of the scales from the outside, then raise the fish to my mouth and bite into it. Ignoring the mess and the rawness, I gorge myself just like that bald creature in that classic movie we watched one Christmas. Even if I could risk a fire, I'm too hungry to wait.

The cold wet fish flesh tastes like the nicest birthday meal Dad ever prepared for me. *Food. Yummmmm. Thanks, Lord. Thanks, Saint Des.* I chew my way through five delicious bites before Momma Matriarch finally arrives at the bank and lowers her head to gobble the guts, before looking over at me hungrily.

Okay, I'm your nestling now, not a heron, but I'll catch you some fish.

Cheeping like an excited chick, I put my half-eaten

fish by my feet and pick up my spear again. But I only catch three fish for her before picking mine up again— just enough to prove myself as a source of food, not a food item myself.

"Sorry, Momma." I kinda cheep the words, so it'll sound like raptor-talk to her. "I'm real hungry. You had all the fish yesterday."

As I start munching again, she cocks her head, listening to the sounds of me chewing, but then she just settles down on the bank to wait. I guess she don't mind her chick feeding, even if she's hungry herself. Good mother.

But, after I've finished the first fish, I catch some more for her before gutting and descaling another for myself. She saved my life last night, after all. And it's no different here, further downstream; there are plenty of fish.

ISAIAH

Zech insists on sitting me down and making me a bowl of oatmeal, a meat sandwich and a big mug of coffee.

"It's still dawn," he tells me firmly. "Worst possible time to be moving, with everything converging on the water to drink and hunt. Get that food down you. Last hot meal you'll have for a while."

Mebbe ever. But even for Zech, saying that would

be keeping it too real. I eat obediently, though I'm desperate to set off. He *is* right. Getting eaten in the first mile won't help Josh.

Zech triple-checks my backpack while I eat, and when he's done he even picks up my rifle and inspects that, which is super-rude, but he's my big brother so what do you expect? When I drink my last swig of coffee and stand up, he inspects me too, even pulling back my collar to check for under-layers, which really is too much.

I pull away. "Leave off, Zech. You really think I don't know how to dress for a jaunt like this?"

His tense face makes me almost wish I'd just put up with it. He must be crazy-stressed. Josh already lost out there, and now I'm going off too. He'll have to work outside without cover, but at least he can get in the 'Vi the rest of the time. He's gonna be the 'safe' one by comparison, but we'll all be chancing it, big time.

I feel bad leaving him here like this, but if even he thinks it's best... I slip into my outer jacket and heave the backpack on.

"Isaiah..."

I turn to Zech, and he grips my shoulders, tight. "Isaiah, promise me some'at."

"What?"

"That...that whatever happens, whatever you... find...you'll stay safe and come back."

Heck, he's afraid that if I find Josh's gnawed bones I'll just lie down and wait for some'at to eat me. Mebbe I will.

"Isaiah." Zech sounds so insistent—I reluctantly meet his eyes. "Isaiah, you promise me that, or I'll take that backpack and go find Josh and you can stay here and get the 'Vi out."

What? No way! I'd go crazy left here by myself, not knowing if either of them were okay! 'Course, that's exactly what I'm asking of Zech. And if Josh *is* dead, making Zech lose us both won't help him.

"Okay, okay. Whatever I find, I promise I'll do my best to stay safe and get back here. Promise. Now, I gotta go."

"Yeah." He pulls me in for a long, hard hug, then climbs up into the turret to check for danger without another word.

I almost say *don't bother*, since I'll be uncovered in less'n three hundred feet, but I bite my tongue. Getting eaten right outside the 'Vi door would win me a place in the hunter hall of shame, for sure, and wouldn't help Josh.

"All clear," says Zech's voice in my ear, since I've put my earpiece in automatically, though that will also be out of range in a quarter-mile. We had some of those retro handheld radio units for some years, but they broke eventually, and we'd never used them, so we ain't gotten around to replacing them. Stupid us.

"Okay, I'm off." I touch the door 'open' button and leap down. "I'll be back with Josh, hopefully in no more than a few days. Depends how far downriver he ended up." Stating the obvious, but what else can I say?

Settling my rifle into a comfortable position from which I can raise it swiftly, I let the door hiss closed and head down to the riverbank. The water level is still much higher than when we arrived. In fact, the night's rain has raised it again. What if Zech can't get the 'Vi out? What if this ground's gonna stay too wet now right through until spring?

I turn and begin to follow the river, almost immediately passing out of sight of the 'Vi and pausing to make a terrain inspection, checking for danger.

If I can just get Josh back here, it won't matter even if the 'Vi is stuck until summer. We'll lose a lotta money on missed contracts, but we have water, and plenty of fish and meat available nearby. We've got a good supply of weapons and ammo. We can find wood and dried dung to burn. Hunters frequently survive for months after getting stranded. Won't be a lotta plants to eat throughout winter, but we keep plenty of vitamins in stock for just such a situation. And that's all assuming our friends from Technicolor 'Vi don't come looking for us, which they almost certainly will.

Nah, all we've really gotta worry about is finding Josh and getting him back here. Mebbe Zech *should* come with me.

For a moment, I waver, on the point of speaking, urging him to come along after all. No.

No sign of danger ahead, so I walk on in silence.

We've both run all the calculations, probably over and over. Getting the 'Vi out will be more help to Josh and me than his presence. He needs to stay.

"Everything's still clear back here." His voice comes in my ear, crackling, 'cause the crags are already blocking the signal.

"Great." I speak very softly, to avoid drawing attention. "I'll be back before you know it."

"Sure you will. You and Josh will be heroes at the 'Vi-park."

"So will you."

But I'm not sure if he heard me. At any rate, he don't reply. Signal's gone.

I'm on my own.

JOSHUA

After several hours of fishing, Momma Matriarch and I are both finally full. At any rate, she's calling me back to her in a way that brooks no argument.

The temperature's about half what it were yesterday and my belly may be full, but I'm thoroughly chilled. I splash back to shore and hop obediently over to her, eager to convince her that I am a well-behaved chick, really. Idiotic, mebbe, for wandering off yesterday, but not really a disobedient chick that needs nipping. Not good little me.

Really, I need to think about what to do next. But I'm tired and so cold. When Momma lies down in her day bed and calls sharply to me, I simply hop right up to her. She grabs me by the collar of my t-shirt and tucks me under her breast, scooping me close with her wing arms. Yep, she don't trust me not to wander.

Never mind. I can warm up again and decide what to do while she sleeps. She's just laid her head down, neck pressing over me, and—yep, if I crane I can see— closed her eyes.

Mebbe...a yawn stretches my jaws and I nestle into her warm feathers...mebbe I'll have a nap, first, too...

ISAIAH

It's always hard to believe how slow it is making safe progress when you don't have anyone to provide cover. I'm horribly torn between speed and safety, but since each time I'm kinda choosing between getting to Josh fast, and getting to Josh at all, I mostly manage to rein in my impatience.

Completing my painstaking inspection of the terrain ahead, I move forward, avoiding sudden movements but making steady progress over the ground I've just checked. Scanning the riverbank beside me for evidence that Josh has been there, and watching the landscape for danger, my eyes are never still.

I've already paused beside a patch of smelly mud to smear some over myself, hoping to conceal the not completely odorless scentBlocker cream I applied before leaving the 'Vi. It's very unlikely, right out here in the wilderness, that raptors would associate the smell with humans the way they do in less isolated areas, but they might come to check out the strange scent, with the same result.

It's nearly noon, and the day remains cloudy and gray. But I've been making steady progress all morning. I ain't seen the slightest sign of Josh, yet. I've gotta keep my eyes open. He'll be looking and listening for the 'Vi, for flares and engine, but I can't let off flares. They're only for attracting the 'Vi's attention when Zech—*please, Lord*—comes to get us.

I keep pausing to inspect the other bank, either by eye or through the telescopic sight of my rifle when it's a bit further away. But there's nothing to suggest a boy climbed out there two days ago.

There were that long stretch of ravine, not long

after I left the 'Vi, where he *couldn't* have got out. Hopefully he didn't try; he'd have been dashed against the walls. But could he tread water in the heaving flood long enough to get through it?

I shudder and keep moving. I have to assume he's alive. If he ain't, there ain't nothing I can do.

Josh, where are you? Are you safe?

JOSHUA

When I wake, I'm dry again. The sun—a lighter patch behind the damp clouds—is well past noon. I musta been tired. Momma Matriarch is still sleeping.

Decision time. What am I gonna do? I've got a choice between the mainland, which is crawling with predators, an island Momma Matriarch will just fetch me back from—and, what? Staying right here? As her chick? They always say if some'at ain't broke, don't fix it, but this is crazy. A Dakotaraptor's lair for my safe den? Living with a Dakotaraptor?

To a raptor, everything is pack, predator, or prey. She ain't imprinted on me, so it ain't safe. That's how it works. That is true, but...those army trainers, who raise velociraptors for guard animals and military use, they get their raptor to imprint on them at birth—but they *also* then try to get them to pair-bond with them, once the raptor's grown. Like folks used to do way back, with birds of prey. The double bond makes for a safer relationship and easier training. And a pair-bond *is* a bond that's formed once a raptor is grown-up.

So if it's the right bond, it *can* be done—if not relied upon. And right now, she thinks I'm her chick. Or a chick that she's ready to take for her own, anyway. Senior raptor females are commonly known to try to steal chicks from other mothers, if they can't have any themselves.

I ain't in no position to hold out for one hundred percent perfect, am I? I'm out here with hardly any clothes, no safe place to den up, and the weather's turned full into fall. If she's gonna keep me warm and give me some protection and *probably* not eat me, then that's safer than going back to the mainland where every fanged and clawed critter I meet will *definitely* eat me. Looking at it like that, I guess it's leaving that would be crazy.

Right, so I'm staying. This is home for…how long? It's been *two nights* already and no sign of Dad and Uncle Z. Have they been held up? How badly? Am I looking at extra hours or whole days? Not weeks; they'd up and walk to me if there were some'at that wrong with the 'Vi.

A cold prickle runs up my spine at the thought, and I frown. *Please, Saint Des, don't let them have to walk. I don't care how long it takes, as long as they arrive safe* and alive.

A breath of actual cold air against my exposed shoulder just makes me frown harder. Okay, they kinda do need to get to me before too long. The weather's only gonna get worse from now on. But…

Two nights. Two nights already. I'm either really far downstream, they've missed me, or there's some'at very wrong. Whichever, my hopes of a super-quick rescue are getting shakier. I'll prioritize keeping a low profile until tomorrow morning, but if they're not here by then, I'm gonna have to start thinking slightly longer term.

Just in case.

DAY 4

ISAIAH

Seething with impatience, I managed to make myself wait out the first few hours around dawn, when all sorts of critters would be visiting the water's edge—*Zech, I hope you're proud of me*—but it were torture.

Avoiding the morning and evening bursts of activity eats into the daylight hours so badly.

I got lucky last night, though, finding a crack in a cliff face tucked behind a good bush of scentCam. It weren't safe foliage to sleep with, so I had to go further afield to find some bedding, but it makes my hideout safer. I have a lightweight thermal blanket, so I only needed the bedding for scentCam. I didn't have to cut much. It all took about as little time as I coulda hoped.

Saint Des knows what I'll find tonight, though. Sometimes you drive through an area and you can see perfect hidey-holes right, left, and center, and some-times you drive all day and there ain't nothing. I hope Josh came ashore in an area like this one.

Only when I judge enough time has gone by do I take a sealed bar of emergency food from my pack, rip it open, and chomp it down. I put the biodegradable wrapper on the ground and kick some dirt over it, double-check all is clear, and head on my way, immediately distancing myself from any lingering food smells.

Back to the riverbank, and onward.

JOSHUA

I crouch on my fishing rock, shivering as I gnaw the last of the flesh from the skeleton of my second fish. The last pink streaks of dawn still show in the clear sky, but here on Matriarch Island, we've been up for hours. Momma Matriarch has preened me, and I've had more of a real bath wading over here to fish—a cold one. Momma's had enough fish to take the edge off her hunger, and I've had two, enough to fill me up.

No sign of Dad and Uncle Z by dark, yesterday. What am I gonna do? Eventually, they'll get here, and they'll see that big X and come find me. But until then…

I wriggle my toes frantically, trying to warm the blocks of ice that are my feet. I've got goosebumps all over, and I can't stop shivering. The clear sky means drier air, which is welcome after yesterday's dampness, but it also means colder air temperatures, which cancel out any benefit. Even with Momma to cuddle up to now and then, I can't go much longer without better protection from the elements. I need to try and make some sorta clothes. And shoes. Heck, would I love some shoes.

And if there were a way to get more food, that would be good. For Momma. She's a heck of a lot better off than she were before I got here, but I'm not able to catch enough to feed her properly. I mean, if I just stood here and fished for hours every day I could, but I'd die of exposure. I ain't been out here that long this morning, and I'm more than ready to tuck myself under Momma's warm breast again. But the better fed she is, the less likely she'll forget I'm her chick and have me for dinner instead.

First things first, I gotta get warm again. I splash back to the shore and hop hopefully towards Momma's day bed. When it's clear that there are no more fish coming her way, she soon joins me, settling down and swaddling me firmly. Once I'm warm and dry, I'll have to try to coax her into letting me out to play nearby. And then I can see what I can do.

+

I wear Momma down eventually, just the same way I woulda worn Dad down when I were little. When I won't stop wriggling, she finally lifts her head and opens her wing-arms, hissing sternly as I scramble to my feet. I make sure to mess around very close by, like a good little nestling, interspersing my raptorish play with little stints of unpicking the thin paracord that binds the edge of my belt. It comes out easily, like it's designed to. I coil what I've unwound around my wrist, since my pockets are full of dung. Some I split down further, pulling out the snare-wire that forms one of the strands. That, I coil carefully around my other wrist. The fishing line, firestarter cord, and thinner strands I leave in place for now.

Momma's calmed down, now, reassured that I'm always there when she opens an eye to check. In fact, she's sound asleep again. Creeping away, I dash up to the log bridge, dart across, and hurry into the wooded area. Working as quickly as I can without wrecking my chances of catching some'at, I set three snares and dash back to the den site.

Once Momma's checked on me and dozed off again—guess there are some advantages to her being so old other than the eyesight!—I'm back onto the other island to set three more. Back to the den, and I wait for Momma to notice I'm there again—then set another three. Nine. Good. That will do for now.

After her next check, I head along the shore in the direction away from the cliffs. I can see some taller vegetation, and hopefully…yeah, here's some long grass. I cut some big armfuls and hurry back to the den area with it. By the time Momma opens her eye yet again, I'm sitting near her once more, braiding the ends of tufts of grass into strands of paracord to make some of the simplest garments known to man—a grass cape and skirt. Okay, so they're prickly, but they'll keep me warm. Warmer, anyway. And I don't have to call it a skirt, I can call it a kilt.

Mebbe, just mebbe, I'll have some rabbit skins by tomorrow. My feet would love that. But I can only use them if I can find…

It takes me several hours scanning the ground around the den site, dashing back regularly to avoid worrying or angering Momma, but eventually I spot the distinctive leaves of a stink root plant. Digging up several of the fat roots, I return to Momma again. I don't need to go far from her for my next activity.

Using a big leaf, I carry water from the river to a couple of depressions in the stone of the cliff that look watertight. When they're full, I crush the stink root with some rocks to keep it off my hands and push it into my basins of water. It don't actually smell that *bad* to me, but it's so strong it acts on predators' sensitive noses like total scentBlock. Perfect.

Momma wakes up before long, seeming much more rested and alert, so I try to engage her in play. It's a risk, little thin-skinned me playing with some'at her size, but it's an important part of chick-parent bonding.

Choosing the safest game I can think of, I creep toward her tail, wriggling my bottom in the air like an impatient nestling that thinks it's being stealthy—even waving my leg occasionally to imitate a tail—until I see the slight shift of her head that tells me she's noticed me. Now that I know I won't take her by surprise, I inch closer and closer—then pounce!

Her tail whisks away from my grasp at the last moment. Oh yeah, she knows this game. I pounce again like an over-excited chick—pounce, pounce, pounce—until finally she lets me catch it. I press my nails in just enough to be felt, as the best way to imitate tiny teeth, making triumphant noises.

She allows me to "chomp" on her tail for a while before pulling it free and rising to her feet. Heading over to the rotten logs, she breaks them into even smaller pieces, sniffing for grubs. Not yet used to simply waiting for me to feed her. Which is for the best, since Dad and Uncle Z will come get me soon enough.

How will she survive the winter? I shake my head and try to think about some'at else. 'Cause I know the answer.

She won't.

ISAIAH

The constant awareness that I've absolutely no way to know how Zech is gnaws at me all the time. *Saint Des, guard him, please?*

But what can I do? Other than keep going.

As for Josh, I ain't sure whether to be happy or sad that I ain't found nothing yet. Not one single trace of him having been here. I mean, no news may be good news, right?

Mebbe he were swept quite a long way before he got out.

But how long could he have kept his head up, kept swimming, in that raging flood?

A long time, if he found some'at to hold onto. Firmly, I push the fearful, negative thoughts away and try to concentrate on the terrain ahead.

What's that? A dust cloud on the horizon sends me motionless. Avoiding sudden movements, I slowly raise my rifle and take a look through the sights.

A bachelor pack of allosaurs. Seven of the brutes, approaching full male size—the pack won't hold together for much longer. Over twenty-five-feet from nose to tail tip, with a mouthful of four-inch teeth.

And coming my way fast.

But my caution has paid off. I've spotted them long before they would've spotted me. I ease sideways into a thick bush and stay motionless until they've run on by.

Yeah, I gotta keep going slow and careful.

Getting et won't help Josh.

DAY 5

JOSHUA

I've caught a total of four rabbits when I check my snares in the morning, which ain't bad considering how much I were rushing when I set them.

I leave them well away from Momma's den area at first, skinning two at a time in between trips back to Momma's day bed to reassure her I'm there. Only once the skin and bones are safely separated out from the meat and offal do I carry my haul back with me. The skins, bones, and guts I immediately shove into my little rock pools of stink-root water, weighting them down with rocks. The meat and the remaining offal I give to Momma.

Heck, would I love to sink my teeth into a nice spit-roasted rabbit! Memories of cook-outs with West, Thiago, and Ed—my almost-uncles from Technicolor 'Vi—and other 'Vis fill my mind.

Or, even better, one of Dad's rabbit pies!

I try to shake the thoughts away. Lighting a fire would be real stupid—attract any predators intelligent enough to be curious—and I'm far more likely to get parasites from raw rabbit than from raw fish.

The rabbits make a slightly bigger mouthful for Momma than fish, leastways. From the speed at which she gulps them down, she appreciates the change of menu just as much as I woulda.

I'll hafta let those skins soak for a bare minimum of a few hours before I can use them for anything. Right now, Momma's awake and showing interest in me.

I guess it's playtime.

ISAIAH

Four nights. *Four* nights!

Yet again I force the thought away and try to focus.

The sun shines from a blue sky today, but the temperature is low. Frost stiffened my fancy thermal blanket when I woke up and, honestly? I were a little cold.

Josh has no blanket.

I push that thought away as well. Josh knows how to gather natural bedding. He'll be sleeping under a huge mound of the stuff, in some well-sheltered cave or crack. He's probably warmer than I am. The best I could manage last night were to sleep on top of a large boulder. It put me above the easy reach even of Utahraptors—but I woulda been at perfect snacking height for an allo.

Who cares. I made it. I'm alive. And I'm on my way

to Josh.

Please, please Saint Des, let me find him soon?

I peer around another outcrop, pausing for my next terrain inspection. A faint, ominous buzzing sound reaches my ears.

There's a carcass nearby.

O God, please, please don't let it be... Don't let it be!

Nausea tightens my throat. I force myself to stay where I am, to complete my careful survey of the landscape. And only then move forward, slow and careful.

Where there's a carcass, there may be scavengers. Or the predators that made the kill.

Everything's quiet, though. I move cautiously around a largish rock by the riverbank and finally spot the source of the noise, out on a flat area beside shallow water.

A piranaha'saur squeaks and bolts away from a scattering of blood and splintered, clean-picked bones that could belong to anything, at first glance—but the quantity of feathers still billowing around the area in the breeze provide swift identification.

A golden ornithomimus.

The wave of relief that sweeps over me weakens my legs and catches at my breathing, but I stiffen my muscles and continue toward the remains.

The golden ornithomimus, the one Josh were

chatting to? They're rare, so...probably.

It ain't Josh, and heck, am I happy about that. But if it were swept away the same time as Josh—and here it is dead—that ain't encouraging.

I move closer still and crouch to inspect the bones, just to make absolutely certain.

Yeah, it's an orni.

Thank you, Saint Des. Thank You, Lord.

JOSHUA

I only took the skins out of the water a coupla hours ago and they're not really quite dry yet. But the temperature is plummeting as night approaches once again.

Still no sign of Dad and Uncle Z.

My feet are so cold. I can't wait for these things to be bone dry. Momma will dry them off with her heat quick enough once we go to bed, anyways.

I take the first skin and wrap it around my foot. It's just large enough. I use the strips of leg skin to tie it roughly in place, then make some holes with my knife and thread the guts through to make it fit better. It'll all tighten as it dries.

The skins ain't been properly cured, so they're gonna reek as they dry. But the stink-root will hide the smell well enough—I hope. Most large carni'saurs are scavengers as well as predators. At least walking in my new footwear will keep them flexible, so eventually I'll have near-enough tanned moccasins.

Well, hopefully, Dad will be tossing them in the incinerator by tomorrow.

But if Dad and Uncle Z don't come quite that soon, at least I've got shoes now. Even slightly damp, they feel amazing, swaddling my sore feet in soft, warm protection.

I ain't never gonna take my boots for granted again.

DAY 6

JOSHUA

I wriggle out from under Momma's breast, peeping reassuringly. She opens one eye, then closes it again. I'm allowed to play.

Heck, it's cold this morning. I were so glad to cuddle up to Momma again after catching our breakfast. Quickly, I tie my grass kilt and cape back onto myself. That's better.

Momma can't get the hang of straw clothes. If I'm wearing my grass-things when she wants to preen me, she starts to dismantle them ever so diligently, thinking she's getting bits out of my feathers. Cute but annoying. I've gotten in the habit of taking them off whenever I'm gonna get swaddled, to protect them.

I need them now, though.

Dad, when are you gonna get here? It's gone to full fall, now.

The fact they ain't here yet is bothering me more and more.

I push the worry aside again. Better to get on with some'at useful, like checking my snares.

ISAIAH

The landscape is peaceful. Several undulating hollows lie ahead, all empty of movement, empty of life. At least every part of them that I can see.

It's safe to proceed.

Then why am I still standing here?

Forcing myself to be patient, I scan the terrain all over again. But it looks safe. So what's triggering my alarm bells?

Very slowly, very smoothly, I begin to make my way down into the first hollow. Nothing stirs. But some'at still has me on edge.

I'm halfway across the open area when I register a faint whistly sound. And...am I feeling...vibrations?

I stop. I stand absolutely still.

Finally, moving only my head, and that as little as possible, I inch my gaze around the sides of the hollow.

There.

Hidden behind one of the boulders that were blocking my view is a full-grown male T. rex. Smaller than a female, but quite large enough to make an appetizer out of me.

Fortunately, Mr. Rex is sprawled flat on his belly, asleep, thick eyelids closed over his great eyes.

I let out a huge, too-long-held-in breath absolutely as quietly as I can.

Thanks, Saint Des.

Very, very slowly, as soundlessly as I can manage, I creep on my way.

The soft snoring gradually fades until...finally, I'm out of the darn thing's sight, should it wake.

I'm coming, Josh.

JOSHUA

Six whole rabbits today! I return briefly to Momma, then start preparing the first two up on top of the crags above the cave.

I'm gonna save the skins in my stink-root pools until I've got enough to make a cape. I dunno what Momma will make of stink-rooty drying skins, but it's worth a try. Mebbe if I put the fur outwards, it'll feel a bit like feathers.

Or will it just feel like fur? I frown. She ain't shown no sign of acting like I ain't her chick—but is that some'at I really wanna risk?

Guess it depends on how cold it gets. I mean, it shouldn't *smell* much like fur. My moccasins are fur side inwards, and she hasn't really reacted to them, other than avoiding sniffing them too hard. Mebbe I should carry on taking a furry cape off, though, just like the grass kilt. To be on the safe side.

That's two done. I'd better get back to Momma.

By the time I've skinned the last two, I'm cold

again. Carrying my haul, I hurry down the slope which follows the curve of the crags down to the cave — then jerk to a halt as a tan and cream form that's taller than I am appears ahead of me.

A deinonychus!

Chucking the bloody rabbits as far away from me as I can, I screech at the top of my lungs, like a panic-stricken chick.

The deinon — a thin, scruffy juvenile, sodden and muddy from crossing the marsh — barely glances at the rabbits, darn it, eyes fixed eagerly on me.

Yeah, mebbe a chick's not the best thing to imitate — except I ain't got a stick, I ain't got nothing to fight this thing off with except my belt knife — and it ain't gonna be enough.

I screech again, backing up toward the closest rocks in the hope I might get behind them and slow it up for a second — but it's already bounding forward. I wait, then dodge at the last second, sprinting down the slope as fast as I can.

Not fast enough. I can hear it catching up at lightning speed.

I ain't gonna reach the closest rocks, let alone the cave.

It's almost here!

I spin around, drawing my knife. Mebbe if I let it

run right onto the blade, it'll hurt it bad enough to scare it off...

ISAIAH

As I begin to descend into the next hollow, I'm just glancing back to make absolutely sure I'm out of the rex's sight when an apparently secure boulder turns suddenly under my foot, tumbling me down the slope.

At the bottom, the ground drops off about ten feet above the hollow. But I don't fall as far as that, landing on a knobbly boulder the size of a small city-car and collecting bruises from both that and my rifle.

Oof.

Uh-oh...

The knobbly boulder spins around violently with an angry squeal, shedding me from its back at once.

An armadillion!

Ankylosaur, their proper name is, but who calls them anything but—

I get my feet under me—sorta—and scramble away. It's a male—the larger sex in most herbi'saurs—and it's really peeved, never mind the fact that landing on it did far more harm to me.

Misfire!

I hurl myself flat as it swings its huge tail

club. The air thrums as it passes over me. It swings again...I roll frantically, another near-miss, I make it to my feet at last, and back rapidly toward a crack in the rocks that's smaller than the armadillion is.

I almost make it. But the tail lashes out, a short, fast swing that takes me by surprise. The world slows down as the club smashes into me, shocking impact, catapulting me backward.

Josh, Zech, I'm so sorry...

Everything goes black.

JOSHUA

The deinon's almost to me...I grip my knife tight...

This ain't gonna work—

A large brown feathery form hurtles past me with an ear-splitting screech, one shoulder clipping me and sending me spinning like a top.

As I fall, I see Momma Matriarch's teeth sink into the deinon's shoulder, hard.

The deinon screeches in pain, struggling, as I sit up and turn to look. Half-blind Momma's failed to get a good neck hold, and the deinon's teeth rake her face as it snaps at her. But what Momma lacks in aim, she makes up for in size. She bites down harder, crushing the deinon's entire shoulder with a sickening crunch. It's a catastrophic injury, and almost at once the deinon's struggles grow weaker.

Momma releases it at last, dropping it at her feet and opening up its underside from chest to guts with a casual swipe of one huge killing claw.

The deinon jerks feebly, unable to fight back as she lowers her head and begins to gobble the soft innards.

I stay where I've fallen.

I lie very, very still.

I don't want Momma to notice me, not while the hunting frenzy is on her.

She finishes off the guts and tears through the rib cage, going for the lungs.

Then pauses and turns her head toward me.

And chirps encouragingly.

My insides relax. She's calling her chick to come feed. It's okay.

She arches her neck proudly and calls again. Yeah, today, she's feeding me, and she's real happy about it.

Giving myself a quick rub with some dung from my pocket, just to be on the safe side, I hop forward, chirruping like a hungry, grateful chick.

Momma wants me to feed. And I am so sick of fish.

There's far less risk of parasites from 'saur meat than from mammal. And a bit of the liver would be a good idea. For the vitamins. Getting sick won't help me.

Momma's feeding in that area, though. I need to be

careful. But when she raises her head to gulp down another chunk of flesh—the heart, I think—I glimpse the dark, smooth, slimy organ that I'm after.

Quickly, I dart my hand in and grab it. A quick slash with my knife, and I rip it out. Retreating to the other end of the carcass to give Momma's hungrily gobbling teeth some space, I inspect my prize carefully.

Despite the disheveled appearance of the deinon, the liver is healthy enough. Guess it were just a bad hunter, not sick.

I bite off a mouthful and chew. It's so hot in my mouth. I ain't had hot food since breakfast the day before my birthday. It's soft, too. Kinda melts in the mouth. Well, not quite. I have to chew.

But it sure does make a change from fish.

I mustn't eat it all, though. I could easily overdose myself on Vitamin A and have the opposite problem.

After three good bites, I toss the rest to Momma, who could probably do with it too. No point trying to keep it. Sure, if I could dry it out, it would be a good source of vitamins. But all my darn rabbit skinning musta drawn the deinon over here in the first place. Last thing I need is to keep a hunk of raw meat lying around.

Besides, Dad will be here before I need more vitamins.

Right?

While I tuck into a big hunk of prime deinon rump, Momma eats almost the entire rest of the carcass by herself. Well, she's a big lady, the deinon were skinny, and she's overdue for a good feed.

Her feeding finally slows about when she's reduced to crunching up the smaller bones. In a few days, she'd probably crush and eat even the larger ones, but for now, she's full.

Yeah, sorry, Momma, but the skeleton ain't gonna be here in a few days. I'm chucking it in the river next time you take a nap.

It feels cruel to deprive her of food—but it's for her own good, as well as mine. What if that had been even a pack of deinonychus, not just a loner? That coulda been more than Momma could fight off, and they'd be just as happy to eat her as she were to eat one of them. Let alone some'at larger.

Yeah, I've gotta get rid of it as soon as I can.

Right now, I just wanna wash all this blood off.

When I hop down to the river, Momma follows, dipping her head to drink. I clean my hands, then suck a bit of water through my filtration straw, before moving to Momma's head, trying to get a look at her wounds.

While she starts preening herself, I scamper off to where I've noticed the most soothing plant available, and some yarrow to clot blood, and return before she can do more than lift her head and chirrup slightly.

Now, how do I get her to let me help her?

She's lowered her head to drink some more, so I gently scoop water over her gashed cheek, washing the blood away. She draws back slightly, shaking her head to dry it.

Blood still oozes from the wounds. I crush up some of the yarrow and try to press it as gently as I can to the largest wound. Momma jerks away.

"Come on, Momma," I chirp, in my raptor-ish way. "Let me help you." But mebbe I'm doing this the wrong way. Soother first. Or both together? I crush some soother in with the yarrow, and try again.

She pulls back, but when I reach out yet again, she don't withdraw so violently. The soother is working. I risk taking hold of a handful of her faded feathers to encourage her to stay still.

"You musta had a glorious blue ruff when you were younger," I chirp, trying to distract her from what I'm doing. "I bet you had gorgeous coloring. The very best raptor-blue is a right rich color, and I reckon you had it."

I press the plant paste into the second larger cut and she flinches away with a slight hiss that sends my heart to my mouth.

"It's okay, Momma. It's okay. It's making it better.

Stopping the bleeding. No blood, no unwelcome visitors, right?"

I try again. She tolerates what I'm doing for a few more moments—just long enough for me to cram paste in almost the whole length of the cut—then pulls away. This time she rises to her feet, muttering disapprovingly, and moves toward the cave. She calls commandingly over her shoulder. Pausing only to rinse the crushed leaves from my hands, I hurry after her, shedding my grass clothes.

She goes right into the cave to her night nest, clearly settling down for a long digestion sleep. She gives me a quick preening, then scoops me close under her breast, so I wriggle until I'm comfortable. The best position is with my feet tucked under her armpit and my head tucked almost in the other one. Her feathers cover me cozily and her wing-arms keep her full weight from crushing me, just as though I were a real chick.

Hunt, eat, preen, nap.

Hunt, eat, preen, nap.

At this rate, I'll turn into a raptor for real.

+

Momma's still sleeping, but I've slept off my modest human belly-full, and I could eat a fish. And I really need to pee. I wiggle my way free—Momma's sleeping too deeply to react—and head for the cave entrance, tying on my grass clothes.

But I make a careful survey of the area before heading outside. This island had seemed so safe I'd gotten complacent, but the deinon turning up has shaken me out of that. Clearly a hungry critter will cross that marsh more willingly than I imagined, even outside of winter. I'd better make me a proper spear, for defense.

Nothing stirs, except a pair of kingfishers by the water's edge. Evening light has turned the sky red. I'd better be quick. Even here on the island, I don't want to be out at dusk, which it almost is.

I head a short distance from the den to relieve myself. On the way back, I locate a solid branch I'll be able to sharpen into a spear. Then I hurry to the river, picking up my thin fishing spear from where it leans against a small tree. Time for dinner.

But before I can enter the water to get to my rock, I pause. What's that in the shallows?

I move upstream and pick up the big, plasti-starch wrapped packet.

It's meat. Freeze-dried meat. And...it feels like one of the cold fish has jumped live into my belly as I check the stamp...it's from our 'Vi, the Wilson 'Vi.

What's it doing in the river?

Calm down, Josh. One pack of meat don't mean nothing.

I glance around, scanning the shallows. My gut

clenches as red evening light glints off another wrapper. I rush over and lift it out as well. Both packs are completely sealed. The contents should be edible.

So why would Dad and Uncle Z throw them away?

ISAIAH

My chest hurts.

The pain overwhelms every other thought as I swim slowly toward wakefulness.

Throbbing, aching pain. Deepening to intense stabbing pain every time I breathe in or out. I find myself delaying each breath for as long as I can, even though it makes me feel faintly light-headed.

Eventually it occurs to me to open my eyes.

A red evening sky hangs above me. No 'Vi ceiling. No concerned Zech peering down at me.

Darn it. Where am I?

I turn my head slightly, but even that sends fresh pain stabbing through my chest.

I'm lying in some kinda rock gully.

Finally, memory rushes back. The rex—and the armadillion!

Coldness washes over me. I took an armadillion club to the chest? How am I still alive?

How *long* will I be alive?

I tilt my head and try to see my chest, ignoring the

pain.

Huh? No bloody, gory, smashed crater meets my eyes. Not really much to see at all. I unzip my waterproof jacket—it's ripped on the chest and both sleeves—and unbutton my shirt, my head swimming as every movement intensifies the agony.

Working my underlayer up high enough to get a look is almost too much. But I ain't quite passed out when I finally manage it. No crater. Instead, wicked bruising runs across my chest in a straight line. Across my arms too, from the feel of them as I move them.

What the—?

I gotta get up and figure this out. But if I try to sit up, I ain't too sure I won't pass out. I've got cracked ribs, best case scenario. Broken, mebbe. Worst case scenario—internal injuries. Ain't no way to tell that, nor nothing I can do about it.

I'm lying on my pack. Painkillers in the pack. I gotta get them. But that means getting the pack off…

Move, Isaiah. Move or lie here and die.

I try to roll onto my side and red hot knives slide through my chest, drawing a smothered groan from my lips, however hard I try to hold it back. My head goes white and rings and spins.

When I come to myself again, my cheek is pressed to the dirt, and I'm still on my side. Thank God I didn't roll back!

Now I just gotta get my pack off, and round in front of me.

I ain't sure I can...

Move, Isaiah. Move, or lie here and let Josh *die.*

Teeth clamped together to keep me silent, I flex one shoulder back—*aaaaaaaah*—and manage to slip the backpack strap off. Drawing my arm out is like self-mutilation. Then I have to reach, and pull the pack around, dragging the other strap under my other arm.

And it's off. I lie, breathing in ragged breaths that are almost sobs.

Now I've just gotta get it open...

+

I swallow two mild pain pills, the kind that don't put me to sleep too bad, then pull out the strip of morphine syringes, each pre-loaded with a single dose. I really don't wanna take none. Strong painkillers put me out like a light. Not quite as bad as little Josh, who can barely stay awake after even the milder kind, but worse than I wanna risk while I'm out here. How can I reach Josh if I'm lying down to nap all the time or ambling along with my head above the clouds?

On the other hand, how can I reach Josh when I'm lying here in agony or walking along too distracted by pain to be careful?

No, if I take that stuff I'll probably lie here and sleep until morning, and this ain't a good place to spend the night. Not narrow enough to provide protection even from a determined Dakotaraptor, let alone velociraptors. And I saw velociraptor dung and tracks earlier.

I gotta just get up and move. I close the pack, every moment sending fresh pain through my ribs, then attempt to swing it onto my back.

Red hot machetes slice through me.

My guts heave unstoppably as I vomit, and the machetes hack me apart. My head spins in screaming circles of pure white...then everything goes black again.

JOSHUA

I catch and eat my fish without even thinking about it, then carry the two packs of meat into the cave and stash them right at the back, where the ceiling drops down too low for Momma. Since I can't safely cook it, it'll be better food for her than for me, but this stuff will keep. No point letting her gobble it all at once.

But...why were it in the river?

As I quickly sharpen my new spear, I can't get the question outta my mind.

Did they throw it in, in the hopes I might fish it out? That would be crazy. The size of this river, they could empty the whole meat locker into it and not expect any of it to wash up near me.

But why else would perfect, sealed packs be in the water?

Once my spear is nice and pointy, I stand it by the cave entrance, then, I wriggle back under Momma's breast, shivering. The evening's cold, but my thoughts are making me colder still. My imagination insists on showing me a large, hungry she-rex ripping the 'Vi open like a tin can, freeze-dryer and cupboards and meat locker bursting apart by the riverside. Or an angry bull triceratops bellowing as it shoves the vehicle over a cliff edge, tumbling down into the ravine, into the water, splitting open, everything spilling out...

Stop it, Josh! There's probably a harmless explanation.

But what is it?

ISAIAH

A foul stench fills my nostrils as I slowly come awake. Vomit and...bad breath?

Carni'saur breath?

I snap alert, trying not to move a muscle, and listen. Slight scuffing sounds from only feet away. Some'at large?

Very, very slowly, I ease my eyelids open.

I'm looking straight up into a mouthful of very fine

rex teeth. Not the largest rex teeth ever—it's my friend Mr. Rex. But if I had a cull permit and took him down, they'd sell very well in zoo gift shops and the like. Normally, I'd rather look at them in the rex's living jaw. But this is a bit too close.

Nostrils the size of my hands flare, sending another wave of rex breath into my face.

He can smell my vomit, can't he?

Careful not to move my head, I glance from side to side with just my eyes. I don't think he can get his head quite low enough to reach me. His cheeks are right up against the rock sides of the crack. Thank God it narrows so much at the base.

My legs, on the other hand... The crack widens, so I reckon he could reach those. If he realized they were edible. Fortunately, the reeking puddle that's drawn his interest is right beside my head, from the smell. Did I get any cuts on my legs falling down that hillside and dodging—failing-to-dodge—the armadillion?

I sure hope not. 'Cause there ain't much I can do other than lie absolutely still and hope he don't sample my lower limbs. Despite their hunting lock being triggered by movement, rex will scavenge from carcasses. But they rely on the movements of other scavengers or a smell of decomposition to find them.

I ain't decomposing. But what does he class vomit-smell as?

His muzzle moves along my body slightly, sniffing, then returns to my head, thrusting down in a vain attempt to reach the source of the fascinating smell.

An angry squeal rings out nearby—the rex spins around and with only a slight roar over its shoulder, bolts out of the hollow just ahead of a swing of the armadillion's tail club.

Great. That territorial beast is back. Luckily for me, the rex ain't dumb enough to mess with it. And the car-sized critter can't reach me in here. It's far too wide.

All the same, I lie still until it wanders off again. Then I drag the fallen backpack to me, avoiding the puddle of sick, work it open again—all the activity leaves me gasping in pain—fish out a morphine syringe and jab it into my leg, injecting half the contents.

So it's gonna leave me groggy. I ain't got no choice.

I lie for a few minutes, waiting for the stuff to kick in.

Ahhhhh. That's better. Grinning, I manage to get myself into a sitting position, leaning against the rock walls. Oh yeah, I could just loll here and take a nice little nap...

Uh-oh. I dip into the first aid kit again for some caffeine tablets and a pair of heavy duty stimulant pills, which I gulp down with some water. Taking all this stuff together is unhealthy as heck, but what else can I do? The sun is setting, and I ain't safe here.

Only when I've repacked my backpack do I finally realize that I ain't got my rifle.

Misfire! Where is it?

What were I gonna do before, wander off without it?

Heck, am I out of it!

Getting shakily to my feet—sheeesh, that still don't feel good!—I stagger along the crack a few steps and peer out at the hollow. But the armadillion and the rex really are gone.

That's weird...my fingers trace a pair of deep gouges in the rock at the very end of the crack. Like some'at metal were driven into it?

Never mind, where's my...*there!* Lowering myself to one knee with a huff of agony, I ease the rifle up into my lap. *What the*—? Did the rex step on it? It looks very much worse for the wear.

Nasty scratches on the barrel and stock draw my gaze back to the gouged rock as it all snaps together with the memory of that mysterious bruised line across my chest and arms.

Heck. The armadillion's club didn't hit my chest directly, it hit my *rifle*. And my rifle were too wide for the crack, so as I were flung backwards, it caught against the rock, taking enough of the force of the blow that I were just left with these bruises—and cracked-broken ribs, mebbe—but saving me from having my chest caved in and obliterated.

"Saint Des, you sure out-did yourself, here," I whisper. "Thank you. *Thank you-thank you-thank you!*"

But—my sudden euphoria at my near-miraculous escape sinks suddenly into stomach-clenching panic—what's it done to my rifle?

I retreat into the crack, since it's the best shelter in sight, lower myself back into a sitting position, then carefully inspect my battered gun. My heart sinks. It's damaged, all right. But how bad? Only one way to find out.

Chafing at the delay—the evening shadows are long and the light level in the crack's dropping inconveniently fast—I methodically strip down the weapon, examining each piece as I do so. Last of all—gripped by hopeless certainty but knowing I gotta check anyway—I sight down the barrel at the darkening sky.

What the—? I turn the barrel slightly this way and that, but... My heart finally lifts again, just a little. The barrel—astonishingly—does seem to be straight. Which means the rifle *will* still fire. But the telescopic sights are smashed and the auto-loading mechanism is trashed. Once I have it back together—which I'm making happen as fast as I can—I'm gonna have some'at like an ancient carbine. One shot at a time, manual reload.

Sheesh. Better than nothing at all, I guess. But I sure wish I'd brought Josh's rifle now, despite the weight.

No use thinking about that. I empty the rounds from a mag into my jacket pocket, so I'll be able to grab them as quickly as possible, and finally get to my feet again, heave—*ouch*—my backpack back on, and totter forwards.

But only a few steps. Then the feel of the half-night closing around me, and the memory of the smooth undulating landscape of hollows and boulders that lies ahead sends me back into the crack.

Sure, velociraptors and piranha'saurs can get in here. But nothing else, not easily. It's far too late to be moving around. And I ain't in a great state to be doing it, neither.

I settle myself in the narrowest part of the fissure with my blanket.

I gotta wait here till morning.

DAY 7

JOSHUA

As soon as I can persuade Momma to let me up, I head out into the crisp dawn air—checking carefully first, of course—and hurry to the river, still tying on my outer layers. I ain't thinking about the cold, though. I'm thinking about—

Oh no.

Fumbling with the paracord, I unfasten my grass kilt again and throw it aside, then wade into the shallows.

Plasti-starch packs of freeze-dried meat litter the rocks like a school of grounded fish.

I collect them several at a time, piling them carefully on the bank to avoid damaging them.

Most of the contents of our meat locker musta gone in the river, for this many to wash up here. Sure, it's a natural spot where stuff comes ashore, but there are so many of 'em.

I put off thinking about it while I hunt around the area a bit more widely, making sure I ain't missed none. I even check a little way around the back of 'my' island, but there ain't nothing there.

Momma's on the beach when I return, sniffing eagerly at the pile. Guess at least one must be breached.

I go through the pile carefully, checking each pack.

I know which one it is before I even find the tear, because Momma gets so excited, almost getting her teeth into the packet before I can rip it open and toss the meat a little way along the bank for her. I chuck the wrapper straight back into the river. It'll biodegrade, and I don't want her figuring out that meat comes inside that stuff or, if she does manage to reach the stash, she could eat the entire heap in one meal.

Yeah? And why am I so worried about that?

I move the packs to the rear of the cave, ripping open two more damaged ones for Momma to eat at once. It takes quite a few trips, but finally a satisfying stack of meat takes up part of the low-roofed area.

I catch a fish, then, and eat it for breakfast. And after that...there's nothing that needs doing that's urgent enough to stop me thinking about things.

Why would Dad and Uncle Z empty our entire meat supply into the river, voluntarily?

Sure, they might unload the 'Vi if it were stuck somewhere, to lighten the weight. But they'd just stack it nearby, and put it back in as soon as the vehicle were free.

Why would they get rid of it *all*? It's freeze-dried, it ain't like it could spoil.

Try as I might, the only scenarios in which the meat would end up in the river are...catastrophic.

What if the flood were worse than I realized, and washed them and the 'Vi away too? Smashed it all to pieces?

It don't mean they got drowned, I remind myself. *The 'Vi might be gone, but they might not be. They're still coming for you.*

They *might* still be coming for me. Only might. I can't hide from the doubt no more. They're days late, and now this?

They only might be coming.

And mebbe not very fast, if they're on foot.

They might even be...gone.

And if they are? What am I gonna—

Apparently, I'm gonna cry. It ain't useful, but I can't help myself. I wrap my arms around my knees and cry until my eyes are all puffy and my nose is all snotty and my cheeks are burning hot and my whole head pounds and aches.

Dad and Uncle Z may be dead. I ain't never gonna see them again 'til I die too, and I'm all alone out here.

Huh.

Guess I might see them quite soon.

Rather than panicking me further, the thought steadies me slightly. I sure don't wanna die, and I know my chances have just gotten worse. But at least if I do, I'll be with Dad and Uncle Z again, right?

Mebbe they ain't dead. I don't know that. Mebbe they're still coming for me...

I sniff and sob and try to believe it, but all I can think about is the meat.

Stinky breath and tough raptor-lips lipping at my salty cheeks finally dry up my tears.

"I know, Momma. I'm being silly. I'm sorry. I'm sorry."

She lips her way over my face up to my hair, clearly sensing there's some'at wrong but confused what it is. Guess most chicks don't go in for...what's the word? Ex...ist...ent...ial angst, that's it. Worrying about dying and stuff, s'what Dad said it means.

But the misery sits too heavily in my guts to shake off, and the thought of Dad brings more tears. I wrap my arms around Momma's warm, feathery neck as she makes concerned noises.

"I know. It's okay, Momma," I sniff. "It's gonna be okay. We're gonna look after each other. We're gonna be fine. We'll take care of each other."

She lets me cling to her for a while, then does what any parent does with a child that won't stop crying—she picks me up by the scruff of my t-shirt, carries me to her day bed and puts me down for a nap, swaddling me firmly.

I cuddle close. I gotta think what to do. But the

crying's left me cold and shaky inside, and exhaustion sucks at me.

Looks like I'm gonna be a good chick and take that nap.

ISAIAH

When I drag my sleep-clogged eyes open, a blue sky hangs overhead again. Clear, but cold. Yet again, my mind shows me Josh, barefoot in his shorts and t-shirt, and I shiver.

I'm coming, Josh.

Thanks to the morphine and my injuries, I've slept well past dawn. But nothing's et me. As soon as I've drugged myself up again and eaten some'at, I can get moving.

It takes another half dose of morphine and full dose of caffeine and stimulants to get me upright. So much for a good night's sleep helping. I'm more tired, and the pain is worse now that everything's stiffened up and bruises have developed.

Well, it's normal to feel much worse before you feel better with broken ribs. It don't mean nothing. Don't mean I have internal injuries. I can still make it to Josh.

I can.

JOSHUA

When I wake, my cheeks and eyes crackle with teardust, but I'm calm again. Momma's still asleep, busy digesting three packs of meat on top of the deinon. I'd better get up and get going.

But I lie snugly for a while under her warm feathers, thinking.

What am I gonna do? I mean, if Dad and Uncle Z come, then no problem. But everything I do from now on, I have to do assuming that they probably ain't—that they *might* not be—coming.

I guess I need to work out roughly where I think I am, and which way I need to go to reach a road or a settlement. And then work out how long it'll take to get there. And then think when the first snow might be. And that'll give me the latest date I can possibly wait for Dad and Uncle Z to show up.

And what I've most gotta do is make sure I'm fit and healthy for the hike.

The closest thing to make for would be the main road to the south. Ain't no farms or hunter camps out here. There's one camp to the west that's probably slightly closer than the road, but I don't really know exactly where, so my chances of finding it... The highway, well, that I can't miss.

And when—if—I reach the road? Flag down a vehicle and get a lift to Exception City 'Vi-park, I guess.

There'll be guys there who know me, who can contact Technicolor so they can come get me.

But...unease twists in my belly...what if whoever picks me up don't wanna take me to the 'Vi-park? What if they take me to the...to the *social workers? They* won't give me to Uncle West, Uncle Thiago, and Uncle Ed, will they? They'll hand me to some city-folk, keep me locked up in-city till I'm eighteen or I manage to run away or Technicolor track me down and steal me back. Whichever's first.

I guess...I guess I could hide and wait for a HabVi to pass? But what if I didn't have a choice? That road down there, it's awful exposed on either side. Not much cover. I could get et waiting for a 'Vi to come. I might have to flag down any old car—and then I'll be locked up in-city. What if I can't escape? How would Technicolor even find me in all those apartments and condos?

Shivering, I cuddle closer to Momma. Mebbe hiking outta here ain't the right thing to do. I mean, Technicolor will miss us soon enough, come looking for us. Even if the 'Vi's destroyed, Dad and Uncle Z will have logged the flood on our WhatHap box. If Uncle West and the others find that intact, they'll come look for me downriver, sure as sure. Then I don't need to go nowhere near the city-folk.

Technicolor might not show up for a month or

more, though. Could be getting real cold by the time they come. And if they never find me...I guess I need to focus on winter preparations.

Seriously? How can I winter out here? With Momma to feed as well as me? Momma will keep me warm, though, if I can keep her fed. That will save me having to light a fire. I can make more stink-rooty clothes out of rabbit skins. Teach Momma to leave 'em alone. Improve the cave, to make it warmer. I've got that stash of meat already. Collect firewood in case of a killer-chiller...

I'd have a real bad chance on my own, sure. Like Momma's got a real bad chance on her own. But we ain't alone. Together, Momma and I can do it. Anyway, if the alternative's getting stuck in-city...

Yeah, I'm gonna wait right here for Technicolor.

Even if they don't make it till spring.

ISAIAH

I inspect the landscape, my head ringing with painful hyper-alertness from the stimulants, even while I fight an urge to giggle at the sight of a sleepy rodentosaur bolting up a distant tree to escape from the cranky armadillion.

Darn morphine. This is serious. Josh is waiting for me.

I can't stop myself grinning, but I manage to give the pea-brained mini-tank a wide berth. Walking soon sobers me up. Any way that I hold my single-shot rifle bangs it against some part of me that hurts like heck. And every step, every movement, sends stabs of pain through my chest, morphine or no morphine.

I gotta reach Josh. I gotta.

But I hope to heck Zech ain't far behind me, 'cause the thought of walking all the way back again...

Well, that don't make me wanna giggle at all.

JOSHUA

With Momma so sound asleep, this is a good time to work on the cave. The most important thing is a windbreak, to narrow the entrance and trap heat inside. If it snows, I can pile snow against it, too, to insulate it even better.

I'll have to leave an open gap, for now. When Momma's used to the screen, mebbe I can make a curtain out of reeds or skins and teach her to push past it to go in and out. That would really keep us warmer.

There ain't much to attach nothing to around the cave entrance, though—it's mostly bare rock on the ground and above, too. In the end, I tie branches together to make a large rectangular trellis, then fasten it to the cliff at the top by tying it to sticking out bits.

Inside and outside, I weight it with heavy rocks. Then I thatch it with reeds, and when it's as windproof as I can manage, I add plenty of foliage for extra insulation. I am able to peg down the sides and bottom in just a couple of places where there's bare dirt. I hope that will be enough. I'm kinda worried that if Momma takes a dislike to it, she might manage to push it right over.

And if she could push it over, so could the wind. Once it snows, it'll be thoroughly weighted down, of course. I'd better add some more rocks another day, before we get a storm. Right now, I should start collecting firewood. It's far too early for a killer-chiller, but if one did come, a fire in the cave is the only thing that would save me—and probably Momma, too.

A very big fire.

ISAIAH

Mebbe my watch got damaged when the armadillion attacked me, 'cause time's gone into first crawler gear, like I'm the 'Vi we were trying to get unstuck, and however hard I try to go fast, the mud sucks at me, barely allowing me to move.

Of course, I am moving, unlike the 'Vi, it just feels so slow. Every step is agony. Every breath is excruciating. Every stumble is like dismemberment. The weight of my backpack is slow torture; the bump-bump-bump of my rifle like knife blows.

Is it just the ribs, or am I hurt inside?

I push the question aside. Ain't nothing I can do. I gotta get to Josh.

You could take a full dose of morphine...

Yet again, the temptation whispers at me. I force the idea away, blinking gluey eyes as I fight to concentrate on the terrain ahead. A bunny sits a few feet from its burrow, washing its long ears with elaborate care. Mebbe it's got a date! Is it a buck or a doe? Very long ears, so silky. Josh would love to stroke them. So would I, come to that.

Only when a herd of ornithomimus—normal ones—spooks the rabbit back into its burrow do I realize that I've been standing here watching it for...how long?

This won't do. I gotta get to Josh. I cannot take more morphine. I can't keep my mind on the job as it is.

It looks clear ahead. I can skirt around the ornis. The thought of getting kicked right now...

I start walking again, each step one more pain.

But every halting stride takes me closer to Josh.

DAY 8

JOSHUA

Dawn again. Another new day. I'm gonna lose track how long I've been out here, if I ain't careful.

I wriggle free of Momma, who's still sleeping even more than normal as she digests the food, and head outside. I pause after checking the area for danger, scanning the sky as well.

Well, that don't look too good. There's another storm on the way. Not a killer-chiller, just a regular storm. Almost certainly too early for snow. But high wind and heavy rain are gonna make me very glad of our cave tonight.

In case the stormy weather don't clear quickly, I'm gonna work extra hard today on my winter preparations. The fact Momma's still happy napping and don't wanna be fed will give me extra time.

By noon, I've weighted down my windbreak much better, and Momma finally stirs. When I hear her yawn, I bounce toward the cave with my raptor-ish stride. Sure enough, she's sniffing suspiciously at the mysterious new screen.

"It's good, Momma," I cheep to her. "Keep us nice

and warm, that will. You're gonna love it when you see it in action, I promise."

When she pushes at it with her head, I pounce on her tail to distract her, 'cause I know she won't wanna play when she's just got up. I trust her not to be rough with me now. If she ever went the slightest bit too far I made sure to whimper and cry out like a hurt chick — no Mr. Tough Guy—so she's figured out she needs to be extra gentle.

Yep. Pulling her tail free with a scolding mutter, she heads past the windbreak and to the water's edge to drink, then settles in her day bed and firmly calls me for my morning preening.

Whew. The windbreak is safe for now. It is much stronger after my morning's work. But Momma weighs a third of a ton and if she really hated the thing...

By mid-afternoon, I've made a reed curtain for the doorway, though for now I roll it up and put it safely at the back of the cave. Let Momma get used to having the entrance partially closed off first.

I make a couple more grass kilts and capes as well, so I'll have dry ones when it rains.

Even more excitingly, I've used guts and paracord to fasten my collection of rabbit skins together to make a little cape. It's messy and smelly, but I'm sure looking forward to trying it on as soon as it's dry. I lay it out at the back of the cave for now. Mebbe I can put it in the nest tonight, let Momma dry it off quicker.

The wind is rising when I rush off to check my snares in the late afternoon, rain starting to fall. But when I return with five rabbits—and more importantly since Momma ain't very hungry, five more rabbit skins for my stink-root pools, half a rabbit fur kilt—Momma is scraping out a new nest in the cave.

Huh, she's already realized that the spot behind the windbreak is far warmer than our current nest.

I can't help her dig without risking getting in the way of her claws, but once she's satisfied with the depression, I'm able to gather armfuls of dry grass and feathers from the old nest and carry them over much faster than she can. We'll be even warmer and cozier tonight.

Well, I've been plenty warm and cozy already, but Momma will be. And the less energy she has to use to stay warm, the less food I'll have to catch for her.

My hard work is already paying off.

ISAIAH

Shelter or distance? All afternoon I've agonized over which to choose as I plod on my painstaking way.

Make sure I've found the best possible shelter from the brewing storm—or get as much closer to Josh as I can while daylight lasts? How much longer can he survive by himself? What if he hasn't found good shelter? It's hard to believe that Josh would struggle to feed himself from the wild, at this time of year—but what if he were injured or sick? If he's in bad condition, can he even survive another storm?

I found a perfect cave mid-afternoon, but I couldn't bring myself to stop, despite the forbidding sky. How can I nestle myself into a cozy cave while Josh might be lying injured on a bank somewhere?

Ignoring the bleak voice that says that if Josh were at all badly injured he's probably dead by now, I plow onward.

The sun is dropping.

The wind is rising.

Little spurts of rain begin to patter onto me. I peer down at my ripped waterproof jacket. It ain't gonna be much use in a downpour.

I go back to scanning the landscape as I walk. I gotta hole up now. I can't keep walking into the dusk, into the gathering storm. I'm in bad enough condition already.

Of course, now that I wanna stop, there ain't no good hidey-holes. The rain's beginning to fall more persistently, and I'd take anywhere with some kinda roof.

But there ain't no caves. Few outcrops, even. I'm

crossing an area of open ground. My head splits and my eyes ache from trying all at once to check the riverbank for signs of Josh, look out for danger, and hunt for a sheltered place to den up for the night.

I can already feel water soaking through my shirt, wetting my aching chest. The temperature's dropping fast as black clouds bring an early dusk. I shouldn't be moving around.

I gotta stop. But where?

JOSHUA

I lie on my belly inside the cave, watching the rain hammering down on the rocky ground outside. *Misfiring rifles*, what a deluge. I sure hope Dad and Uncle Z are still tucked up safe in the 'Vi—or at least in a nice cave like this one—or they're gonna be soaked to the skin.

I got a real good day's work done, so it's nice to relax now. Momma's preening herself carefully like the proud old lady she is, and I'm glad to see it. Yeah, she's a bit old and stiff, but it's her eyes that are her main problem, ain't it? I can be her eyes and her hunter, if she can be my heater and bodyguard. We make good partners.

A little voice in the back of my mind whispers that I can't be sure her eyes are the only part of her that's really worn out. Her mind might be too. Mebbe that's why I convinced her so easily to take me as her chick.

And mebbe one day she might forget it just as easy.

I push the thought away. She ain't shown no signs of serious forgetfulness. If anything—I think how she fetched me back from my island that first day—the opposite.

Besides, chicks are the ultimate status symbols for she-raptors. Only the matriarch—and if there's a large enough pack and enough prey, the next few senior females—get to mate and raise chicks. All the other pack members can expect to spend their lives as professional aunties and uncles, helping to raise their alpha females' chicks but never have any of their own. Having a chick—even a slightly weird one like me—makes her feel young again, I can tell. It makes her feel important, like she has some'at of her old position back.

Yeah, I reckon she'd have to be really, really forgetful to change her mind about me, especially when I'm feeding her so reliably.

Momma finishes her preening and chirrups to me. Bedtime.

I'm getting a little chilly lying here, anyway. I shed my grass clothes and slide into the new nest. Momma gathers me close and settles down, her neck resting across me as usual. I wriggle a little until my feet are snug in her armpit and her feathers cover me.

Ah, that's nice. I'll be toasty warm in no time.

ISAIAH

My teeth are chattering, sending rapid-fire jolts of extra pain through my chest. The wind and rain snatch the warmth from me, even if they can't pierce the foil emergency blanket that I broke out when I finally accepted that I couldn't find any better shelter than another crack in a small crag.

Unfortunately, by the time I wrapped it around me, I were already soaked through. The gaping rips in my jacket had let the torrents of water straight in. My regular thermal blanket's wet from my clothing too, now, 'cause I couldn't face trying to take it all off while hiding under a blanket with my ribs like this, though I know I shoulda.

It's the middle of the night and it's still pelting down. I am so cold. I can't stop fantasizing about fishing Josh's change of clothes from my backpack and wrapping them around me under the survival blanket as well.

But I can't do that. I have to keep those dry. If I find Josh, and he's in bad condition—especially after this storm—those dry clothes could be the difference between life or death.

I press closer to the cold shelter of the rock. Eventually it'll be day again, and it'll get a little warmer. I can walk, and warm up that way. Whether it will stop raining...

Not looking likely.

I'm starting to warm up a little. Finally. I rest my cheek against the hard stone. Mebbe I can get to sleep at last.

A great splatter of icy rain down my neck drags me fully awake again. *Aaah*, the moment I began to doze my arms slumped and dislodged the emergency blanket...

Clumsily, I try to rearrange it. I just wanna sleep. The wind slaps my hair against my forehead, yanking on my blanket, blowing harder than ever.

Yeah? How have I managed to warm up, then?

A faint wash of panic sends an equally feeble jolt of adrenaline through me.

Don't go to sleep, Isaiah. DO NOT *go to sleep.*

Dragging my belt knife out with fumbling fingers, I cut a hole in the foil blanket. Knotting my regular blanket around me like an ancient Roman's toga—*misfire*, my fingers feel like numb sausages—I heave on my backpack and pull the foil blanket over the top as a poncho. Rifle strap over my head. Flashlight on my head, 'cause there ain't no moon nor stars.

I stumble forwards, out into the wet, dark,

dangerous night.

Walking is my only chance of getting warm.

Walking is my only chance of not falling asleep.

Walking is my only chance of making it to dawn.

Saint Des, please don't let nothing eat me.

DAY 9

JOSHUA

The sound of the rain still pattering on the rocky ground outside fills my ears before I even open my eyes, only faintly muffled by Momma's feathers. Dawn, but the storm ain't let up yet.

I ain't hungry enough to go out and get drenched, though eventually I'm gonna have to run out to pee. Mebbe there'll be a lull.

Momma shows no sign of getting up neither, so I stay quietly in the nest, enjoying a rain morning. I guess eventually I'd better see if there's some'at useful I can do inside the cave.

I'd better get good at napping, though. When the days get shorter, there'll be hours and hours and hours of darkness to fill.

I think you can make a lamp just by putting oil in a dish with a little wick in it. If I saved rabbit fat and mixed it with stink-root, would it still burn?

Yeah, but the fat has to be rendered first, right? Over a fire. To make it more like oil. And I don't wanna attract attention to the island.

If the fire were in the cave, it wouldn't be so obvious. Bit of a smoky smell, mebbe, but no strange light to be investigated.

I guess I'd better think about it some more. A lamp sure would be nice—but I dunno if it's worth the risk. Ain't like I've got nothing to read.

I sure hope Dad and Uncle Z or Technicolor come get me before spring. If I don't get to read nothing all winter, I really am gonna turn into a raptor!

ISAIAH

I ain't needed the flashlight for some time, but I ain't going much faster. I walked all night, but I ain't warm. Am I somewhat in shock from my injuries, or is it just the wind and me being so wet?

I ain't warm, but I ain't lain down and succumbed to hypothermia, nor been et, neither, so I'll take that as a win.

Heck, I wish I could get somewhere out of the rain, take these wet things off. But I ain't got nothing dry to put on.

Anyway, I can't stop. The longer the storm goes on, the more vital it is that I get to Josh.

JOSHUA

The rain hammers steadily down as my bladder swells and aches more and more. No way I'm stinking up the cave by going in here, and Momma would probably nip me if I tried.

Finally, with an irate mutter, Momma rises and heads outside to do her own business. No, she ain't fouling her own nest. I scurry along under her on all fours, taking advantage of her size. When she stops to relieve herself, I quickly do the same, and we head straight back inside. I pause to snatch the new skins and guts from the stink-root pools, though, and settle a little way from Momma's sensitive nose to start work on my fur kilt.

Okay, so it's a fur mini-skirt, so far, but another day or two of rabbits and it'll be the bunny's knees. *He he.*

"Get it, Momma?" I chirp in my raptor-ish way. "Bee's knees, bunny's knees?"

She cocks her head and peers poor-sightedly at me that way she does sometimes when I speak to her, like she's trying to figure out what I'm saying.

She can't, of course, so I speak full-raptor to her instead, telling her with a far simpler vocabulary that she's a great mom, and I'm glad to be her chick. That makes her arch her neck in response and make happy broody noises, so I put aside the half-kilt to go play with her.

ISAIAH

The clouds are lightening. I peer upward, worried it's wishful thinking. No, the rain is easing a fraction. 'Bout time, it's mid-afternoon! I ain't sure if the storm is actually over, or if we'll just get a lull for a few hours, but who's complaining?

I gotta find proper shelter tonight. Even if the storm don't come back, I'm too wet and cold and tired and hurt to spend another night exposed. I gotta find a cave, or deep hollow, collect a LOAD of bedding, get my wet clothes off, and get good and warm through — or I ain't gonna make it to Josh at all.

I scan the landscape ahead, my mind so numb and foggy I almost wonder why I'm bothering.

No signs of movement. I try to make myself examine every knoll and rock, but I can barely do it.

I need a cave. I need to stop. I know it's only mid-afternoon, but I can't go on no longer. I'm about this close to collapsing on the ground and sobbing and not moving again.

I head onward, but more terrain opens up almost at once. I stop, breathing raggedly as frustration and pain tug at me.

And...it gets worse. It's marsh ahead, by the look of it. I'm gonna have to make a big loop inland to get around it, risking missing signs of Josh if he washed ashore there, or wade through it, getting wetter than ever, which I don't reckon I can handle right now.

Can I find somewhere to stop near here, and tackle the marsh tomorrow?

No, that don't make no sense, wading into the marsh just when I've spent all night getting—*please Lord!*—dry. I gotta cross it now, then den up after.

I eye the reeds wearily, but I don't see nothing but a few duckosaurs in the far distance. I'm about to attempt a more thorough inspection when my gaze catches on some'at in the river. An X, carved into a cliff on a...is that an *island*?

My heart rate kicks upward, hope exploding in my beat-up chest.

An island! If Josh found an island, he'd definitely den up there! How fresh is that X? Looks clean and clear. And what are the odds someone else woulda been marking the cliff right around here?

If Josh carved it, then he's *alive*. Was alive... He's there, he's gotta be!

So close...

I almost stumble forward when I remember my terrain inspection. Seething with impatience, I scan the marsh, adrenalin finally sharpening my attention again.

Seems safe. Adjusting my rifle so it presses against a different patch of bruises, I head forward, fighting to stay alert, to look all around me, when all I wanna do is feast my eyes on that X.

Hang on, Josh! I'm nearly there!

JOSHUA

The rain has finally eased. I slip out of the cave ahead of Momma, spear in hand, and make a real quick trip to check my snares. But they're all empty. The bunnies have been hiding in their burrows too.

I hurry back down before Momma can worry, and swap to my fishing spear before splashing out to a rock. My stomach's been rumbling for hours. Momma comes to the water to drink, then raises her head in a hopeful way that suggests she's done enough digesting to be getting peckish.

Guess I'll catch her a few fish first.

I wish I could figure out how to preserve meat without it smelling. Fishing is far easier now than it will be once it snows. I can bore a hole in the ice with a stick or my knife and drop a line in, but it's gonna be slow by comparison. Mebbe I could bore several holes, have more than one line down at once. And I'll be able to keep at it for longer, if I'm snug in my furs and not having to get wet no more. But if I could stockpile some food now, that would be even better. I guess I can store some of the roots and tubers and edible plants I've been having for veggies, that'll help feed me. Momma might even eat some, if she were real hungry. I don't want her to get as hungry as that, though—for more reasons than one.

I stab a fish and toss it to Momma, who gulps it straight down.

Stink root ain't poisonous, it just don't taste great. If I soaked some fish in the pools for a while, then hung them up to dry, would they still smell fishy? But the stink root won't get right into the fish the way it can get into hide or straw. And fish is a real strong smell. Rabbit meat, mebbe? I guess I could try. Then leave it lying around and see if Momma found it. As good a test as any.

Yeah, next rabbit I catch, I'll stick a leg into the stink root and see what happens.

"Here, Momma." I toss her a real fat fish. "Here's another."

ISAIAH

The marsh gives way to more of an actual river channel, which I'm real glad to see 'cause it makes Josh safer. But soon I'm wading in water up to my chest. It's freezing, probably coming from some glacier up in the mountains somewhere, but the flow is only sluggish this close to the marsh.

It could be ten times colder and ten times faster and

I wouldn't care. Josh is just over there.

Please, Saint Des?

Finally, I'm scrambling up onto the bank of the island. Despite the adrenaline that's been pouring through my veins ever since I saw that X, I'm shaking violently. My legs wobble under me when I push to my feet.

I am so tired.

On the other hand, if I'm shaking, then the cold water ain't pushed me back to hypothermia. Quite.

Unless the shaking is pure muscular exhaustion.

I move forward, my gaze flying here, there, and everywhere as I hunt for any signs of Josh.

There! My heart constricts in my aching chest. A small footprint in a patch of mud, blurred by more than the heavy rain—Josh must have some'at wrapped around his feet for warmth—but quite clearly human. Quite clearly the right size.

I hurry on, fighting to stay alert, to check for danger as well as for Josh, but I almost can't control myself.

No. Get it together, Isaiah. Ain't that hard to get to this island. You ain't got no idea what's over here. Go steady.

Josh has been on his own for days. A few minutes more won't hurt him.

I hope.

I peer over the top of a rise—and there he is! He's perched on a rock, in the river, a little home-made fishing spear in his hand, intent on the water. Alive.

Joy hits me like another tail club to the sternum.

Hang on! My eyes focus on the bank, where a full-grown female Dakotaraptor crouches, intent on *Josh*. The out-of-control-emotion-armadillion strikes me again—this time with heart-stopping terror.

I swing my rifle to take aim, fighting for calm as I line up the manual sights on the predator. I'm Josh's only hope, but I've only got one shot. I can't afford to miss. I do practice now and then with just the manual sights, like any sensible hunter, but I ain't as used to them, and that's a fact.

Don't spring on him yet, don't, don't...

My arms are still shaking, curse it. Head shot's no use. I readjust my aim to the carni'saur's body instead.

Quickly, quickly...but she ain't sprung yet.

Josh stabs sharply downward with his spear, then swings around toward the bank, his gaze going to the danger, though he screeches in a way that sounds more triumphant raptor than frightened boy.

But he don't try to run, or show any sign of fear at all. Instead, he just flicks the spear, sending the fish flying to land at the raptor's feet.

Clever boy. Probably the only way he can distract her. But he *still* don't run. *Aah, don't be all brave and dignified, cub!* Sure, if I weren't here, running wouldn't help, but right now it would buy me a few extra moments to take my shot.

The she-raptor dips her head and gulps the fish down, then looks at Josh again.

Oh no, you don't!

I check my aim, my finger tightening on the trigger.

JOSHUA

"Have you had enough, Momma?" I cheep. "Hope so, 'cause I'm starving. Next one's for me. Ah, there it is..." I stab, hauling out a good big fish, and splash quickly back to the shore.

I shake and wipe the water off as best I can and pull my shorts back on, and the grass skirt and cape too. It ain't warm today. Then I scrape the fish quickly with the descaler on my knife, toss the guts to Momma — *gulp* — and tuck in.

Momma yawns, giving me a good view of her excellent teeth, then tilts her head up as though inspecting the slight brightness that is now making it through the clouds. There's barely any heat in it, but she settles into her day bed anyway.

Yeah, might as well enjoy some fresh air before the rain comes back, and we have to go inside again.

It's really not warm, though. I shoulda put on my new fur cape. I gobble my fish as quickly as I can, rinse my face and hands in the water, then shed my grass things and wriggle under Momma. She obligingly lifts her head a little and opens her wing-arms to let me in.

I settle my feet in the warm spot and get cozy. But, if it's this chilly already, what's winter gonna be like? I'm only in shorts and t-shirt, though. When I've got enough skins I'd better make myself some pants and a long-sleeved top, rather than just capes and kilts. Then I'll be okay.

Then I'll be able to *do* more, rather than spending so much time cuddling up to Momma just to get warm again.

Yeah, proper winter gear is a must.

ISAIAH

I still ain't fired the shot. I can't believe what I'm seeing. Josh is totally calm and comfortable around that huge predator. In fact, crazy though it seems, she acts like she thinks he's her chick. He acts like *he* thinks he's her chick.

He just walked straight up to her—hopped up to her, very raptorishly—and wriggled right underneath her, like he had every right to.

And she let him.

Am I hallucinating? From the...the morphine, and the exhaustion?

But my last morphine is wearing off—in fact, I'm

desperate to take some more—and I ain't had no hallucinations before. Nor would I expect to on so small a dose.

So what the heck has my son been doing out here?

Finally daring to ease my eye away from the sights, I glance around the area, taking stock. There's a cave behind that very solid, very man-made (or boy-made) windbreak. A much fatter spear leans against a boulder nearby. Josh's grass clothes lie where he left them. Raptor tracks and boy tracks wind all over the area.

Unless I'm mistaken, Josh has been here for most of the time he's been missing.

Only my son could interpret 'find a safe place to wait' as 'den up with a Dakotaraptor.'

How in Saint Des's name did he pull this off?

JOSHUA

I'm warm again. Once Momma's good and asleep, I'll do some more winter prep. I should gather some extra veggies for my winter stores. I saw some real promising plants a little way down the bank.

Momma's breathing has deepened, her heart thudding more slowly against my hip. Not long now.

Finally! Josh is moving, wriggling out from under all those feathers that were hiding him from me. I were starting to hope he hadn't suffocated down there. But then, chicks don't usually suffocate.

The raptor raises her head, yawns—a cold shudder runs through me at the size of her mouth—then grabs the tattered scruff of Josh's t-shirt and pulls him back toward her.

I snap my rifle up and take aim—but Josh is laughing and wriggling much the way he used to when he were little and didn't want his shower.

But I should shoot, right? This is crazy-dangerous. That raptor ain't imprinted on him—*misfire*, she's older than he is—so it ain't safe.

But in my head a distraught young voice screams: *I hate you! I'll hate you forever!*

But if he's in danger... Zech weren't *wrong*, even if he coulda handled it more gently.

Yeah, but that's just it, ain't it? Zech only thought about Josh's physical safety. Josh's heart took a real hit that day. *And* his relationship with his Uncle Z, and that weren't good for him neither.

The mouthful of razor-teeth brushes Josh's head as...as she preens him? Yeah, she's keeping him clean and tidy.

Finally, after what feels like six million years, she

gives him a little push with her nose and puts her head on the ground again. Bath done, he can play. She's gonna nap. Sun's virtually out.

Lowering my rifle at last, I consider getting my flashlight, but it will take too long, and the thought of getting the backpack off...

I fish my mirror from my knife sheath instead, while Josh fools around raptorishly down below. The she-raptor opens an eye now and then to check on him, then settles off more deeply. Josh musta been waiting for that, because he snatches up the heavier-weight, defensive spear and scurries off along the bank with a more boyish stride. Boy in a hurry, too. Guess she don't like her chick out of her sight for long.

Now he's further from the danger, I tilt my mirror to reflect some light onto his face. Carefully. Very carefully. I sure don't wanna get the sun in the raptor's eyes and wake it up instead.

Although my hand is still alarmingly shaky, it ain't long before a beam crosses Josh's eyes, once, twice...

He goes motionless. His head turns, and for a moment he looks for the source. I get a third glint onto his face. He'll see where the light comes from, though I'm well hidden behind my bush. He can come straight to me.

Nope. He spins around and dashes right back to the area outside the cave, putting himself between me and the sleeping she-raptor. Then he leaps up and down wildly, waving his arms in exaggerated 'no, don't shoot' gestures.

Yeah, yeah. I figured that out.

I glint my mirror at him again, but he stands there, staring anxiously, clearly afraid to remove his shielding presence from his foster-mom.

Guess he ain't got no way to know if it's me or his Uncle Z up here.

Smothering a sigh, I tighten my shaking hand muscles, marshal my fuzzy brain, and painstakingly send some Morse instead, slow tilts to produce long flashes, and fast tilts for short ones.

DAD WONT SHOOT COME

His lips move as he sounds out the message, though they keep quirking into a gratifyingly happy smile. He glances at the raptor, probably to see if all his dancing around has woken her, then he bounds up the slope toward me with appalling energy.

So much for my nightmares about him injured and starving away out here!

JOSHUA

It's Dad! He's alive! He's *here*!

I'm so happy I could screech like a juvenile that's just helped take down a large kill for the first time. But I mustn't wake Momma.

Here he is!

I beckon to him and bound on, only stopping when I reach the marsh-side river channel. Far enough away that we can talk without Momma hearing. 'Cause she's used to me talking funny, but if she hears Dad... Well, she may just try to feed him to me.

And we don't none of us want that.

Dad's taking his time, though. I watch him walking to join me, painfully slowly. His shoulders are real stiff. He's wearing a survival blanket like a poncho, so it's a good thing he's going slow, or the rustling might wake Momma. He must've been desperate if he put that on and walked around in it, risking making noise. Is some'at wrong with his waterproof jacket?

His legs certainly look real wet. Didn't he undress to cross the river, and put his clothes in his waterproof pack? Guess not. I peer up at his face as he finally reaches me. Cheeks an unhealthy grayish color, and his eyes are black-circled like a badger, his pupils dilated like he's taking some'at real strong.

No, he ain't okay.

ISAIAH

Every cell in my body screams for me to scoop Josh into my arms and hold him tight, never let him go again, but if he latches onto my chest like a baby bat I reckon I might pass out on the spot.

"Don't grab me," I blurt, just as Josh says,

"Don't hug me!"

Josh stares up at me. "Why not? You okay?"

"Sure." I try to stand less stiffly, but it's impossible. I really need more morphine. "I just banged up my ribs a bit, that's all. Hurts like heck, but not dangerous; y'know how ribs are."

Josh eyes me suspiciously, gaze narrowing on my battered rifle. "What happened to *that*?"

"It took a nasty blow. Just in case you need to use it, you'd better know—the sights and auto-loading mechanism are broken. It will fire one shot at a time— I think—but you have to reload manually."

He frowns. "How on earth did that—"

I cut him off quickly, "Why can't I hug *you*?"

"'Cause you'll get your scent on me, and I don't know what Momma would think of that."

"The raptor, huh? Don't matter, though, right? We're leaving."

"Is Uncle Z okay?" Josh waits for my reply, practically quivering with tension, his eyes intent on my face.

"Yeah, sure. Well, he were when I left. The 'Vi were stuck real deep in the mud. So eventually I came to get you, and he stayed to finish getting it out. That's the only reason I'm alone." Though I *am* surprised he ain't caught up to me, yet.

I keep that last thought to myself, but Josh don't relax as much as I expect. "Why did you put the meat into the river?"

"What meat?"

"From the 'Vi. I fished a whole loada it out the other morning. Whole locker musta gone in there. Perfect sealed packs."

An icy chill runs down my spine. All our meat? Why would Zech dump it *all*? I can't think of a reason that ain't bad, but then, I'm struggling to think, period.

I fight to keep my face calm. "Some'at to do with getting the 'Vi free, I guess. I'm sure he ain't far behind me, by this time. Come on, we'd better start heading back that way."

Josh eyes me from head to toe with a right skeptical look on his face, then glances around at the sky. "You got a place picked out for tonight?" he asks.

What? "Uh...no, I...I saw the X and came straight here."

"The storm's coming back. You look like death warmed over. You'd better spend the night in the cave, and we'll go tomorrow."

I stare at him. "In the cave? I thought you don't want me to shoot the raptor."

His eyes fly wide with alarm. "I don't!"

"Then I can't sleep in her cave, now can I? Whatever the heck it is you've got going with her, it don't include me."

Josh just nods in an annoyingly patient way. "Sure, but the cave gets real low at the back. She can't get in there."

"She'll see me. If I even make it in there alive, I'll never get out again without culling her."

"She's half-blind, Dad. Listen, I'll cut a whole loada scentCam and bedding and drag it in there now. Then you sneak in. I'll keep her outside as long as I can to give you time to get your wet things off and get settled. Then you lie very still and quiet all night, and don't make noise. You look half-frozen, you gotta get warmed through. Don't see how else you can do it."

This is insane. Okay, I guess the "half-blind" thing makes it fractionally more understandable how Josh stopped her eating him long enough to convince her she were his mother, but *me*?

Josh is right, though. I gotta get warm. My vision's swimming and graying slightly, from standing here so long. As casually as I can, I rest my haunch on a boulder. I can't think. I can't...I can barely stay upright.

"Fine. Yeah. We'll...we'll do that. Sure." I wanna lie

down.

"Okay, Dad." I don't miss the worry in Josh's voice. Darn it. "You go back to where you were," he tells me, "and I'll beckon you to come down when the cave's ready. 'Kay? Oh, take that silver blanket off and leave it there. Too noisy."

He's off again, bounding back up the slope to get my accommodation fixed up. I let him get out of sight before hauling my rump off the boulder, just in case I end up crawling back up there after him on hands and knees.

I want more morphine. But I'll never get my back-pack on again if I take it off. I gotta wait 'til I'm in the nice, safe Dakotaraptor's lair.

Saint Des, watch over all three of us tonight!

JOSHUA

Dad ain't fooling me. He's in bad shape, and he needs to get warm. But as soon as the sun goes back behind the clouds and the rain starts again, Momma's gonna go inside, and then he won't be able to sneak past her, half-blind or not.

I dash back and forth frantically—but as quietly as I can—carrying great armfuls of foliage into the cave. I stuff a load of feathers and dry grass from the old nest right into the back, on the other side from the meat store, then pile plenty of bedding next to it, leaving a gap for Dad to get in, and finally I arrange a good big wall of scentCam in front of that, dipping some of it in the stinkroot pools just for maximum protection.

I toss anything else I think he needs in there too, and hurry out again. The sun has gone into hiding as the clouds thicken. *Uh-oh.* Temperature's dropping. Momma will be stirring soon. Positioning myself in front of Momma so I can obscure any sound Dad makes with some noisy play, I beckon urgently toward Dad's bush.

For a long time, nothing happens. Is he okay? Passed out up there? Gone hypothermic while I were getting it all ready?

Ah, no. Just picking his way down that bank real slow, like he's considering falling down in a heap and sleeping right there. He has taken the rustly blanket off, though.

I keep beckoning to him, silent encouragement, and finally he trudges past me. I hear his smothered "oof" as he ducks to enter the cave, and I mess around a bit to make some noise. Is he gonna be able to stay quiet all night? I sure hope so.

He's in, anyways. Now I just gotta give him some time to get settled. However long I think he needs, then at least double it, 'cause of his ribs.

Momma's stirring, though. Quickly, I try to engage

her in play. She won't oblige by moving her tail, though. In fact, she looks like she's gonna rise to her feet.

No, no, no!

ISAIAH

Teeth clamped together in a not-wholly-successful attempt to keep silent, I flex my shoulders—*aaah*—to get my sodden shirt off. I can just about sit upright here at the very back of the cave, where the ceiling rises again.

Quickly, Isaiah! You're taking too long!

Along the length of the cave and through the gap beside the windbreak, I can see Josh... *Misfire!* Clambering up the raptor's side right onto her back, peeping like a chick that really wants some attention. What if he makes her mad?

Hurry up, Isaiah!

The shirt's off. Now the underlayer. That don't unbutton, so it's even worse. Pants next. I've already taken some more morphine as my first priority, 'cause I don't reckon I can stay quiet all night without it, but it ain't fully kicked in yet.

Finally, my clothes are in a damp heap. I'm shivering in my bare skin, but no longer covered in wetness. And...what are these?

Josh has left dry "clothes" for me. Three grass skirts and three grass capes, and...ah, bliss! A rabbit fur cape, too. Nasty, stink-rooty, and not-tanned—and boy-sized—but I sure ain't complaining! I wrap it around on top of the grass things, feeling like I've died and gone to heaven. Mebbe the raptor caught me on my way in here.

There's another small rabbit fur garment...but I can't figure out what it is. Mebbe it's half a skirt or some'at. But I wrap it around my icy feet real gratefully.

Since Josh clearly don't need them tonight and they won't get wet in here, I spread Josh's spare clothes over me as well, to use for a patchwork blanket. Now I just gotta pull all the bedding into position and— *Uh-oh,* the raptor's on her feet, heading purposefully toward the cave.

I can't keep moving, or she'll hear me. But if I can't get that bedding close around me, I ain't gonna warm up...

A screech like a chick in real trouble makes me start—I hafta smother a groan as it jolts my ribs. I ain't even a raptor and it makes me wanna rush out and help the poor hurt little thing. The raptor's spinning around, hurrying to where Josh is lying in the mud on the far side of the clearing, lowering her great muzzle to him. She makes anxious crooning noises while he flops about and whimpers.

Good boy, Josh. He's saved my bacon.

I ease the foliage into position a branch at a time, as quietly as I can. There are only a couple left when I hear Josh's voice, talking human, but in a very raptor-ish way.

"Can't stall her no longer, Dad. We're coming in, ready or not."

I switch off my flashlight at once, adjust the loose clothes over me, and make sure I'm comfortable, my back firmly to the wall—insulated with some bedding—so I can't easily turn onto my back and snore. I've arranged myself so I can see down the cave, and a moment later I understand why even Josh's inventiveness is at an end. The raptor's got him by the scruff of his t-shirt and she's carrying him, hanging from her jaws like a helpless kitten. She's making slight disapproving hissing sounds around her naughty mouthful. It's pouring again outside, which is probably why. His theatrics have gotten them wet.

She deposits him in the new-looking nest beside the windbreak, shakes herself, and settles firmly on top of him, gathering him close. Then she turns her head toward the rear of the cave—I hold my breath, keeping absolutely still. She sniffs a couple of times—scenting the foliage?—before putting her head down to sleep without any sign of interest. I guess Josh has been doing all kinds of projects involving wood and vegetation around her for days. What's one more?

Josh is right that she can't get to me. If she lay flat she could slide her head into the gap, no problem—but it goes back too far for her to reach me. I guess I really am as safe as I can hope to be.

Which means I can sleep.

Whether I should be sleeping when my son is cheek to breast with a deadly predator...

Zech woulda shot her already.

Yeah? And then Josh would be shivering beside me, instead of being toasty...toasty...

A huge yawn wipes the rest of the thought from my mind.

I ain't warm yet, but I'm warmer than I've been for...for... Huh?

Meat... Some'at about meat... *Please be okay, Zzzzzzzzzzzzzzz....*

JOSHUA

I sure hope Dad ain't gonna snore.

I sure hope he warms up, as well. He ain't got Momma to cuddle up to, though she will be heating the whole cave to some extent. Hmm. Mebbe I should try to hang that door curtain, trap as much heat in here as possible.

But when I try to wriggle out, Momma ain't having none of it. *Make your mind up,* she scolds me. *Are you unwell or not?*

She's faaaaar stronger than me, so I give up. Mebbe in an hour or so, once she's asleep and has forgotten my little drama, I can get out. It won't quite be dark. I might still manage to hang the thing.

DAY 10

ISAIAH

Rain is pattering somewhere a little ways away. My chest is killing me—morphine's worn off again. I'm lying down, though, dry, and relatively warm. Which feels strange.

Memory rushes back, snapping my eyes open.

Dimness fills the cave. From the chinks of light from the entrance, it's day, but some'at now covers the doorway. Some kinda reed curtain. Were that there last night?

Mebbe. I were so out of it.

The raptor's still asleep in her nest, and judging by the muddy moccasin peeping out under one wing-arm, Josh is in there too.

He musta been up, though, 'cause my wet clothes and thermal blanket are gone.

What's that? At the other side of this rear section of cave some'at reflects the light in an un-rock-like way. Almost...plasticky? Now that I'm not looking at the entrance, my eyes slowly adjust. Oh. It's the meat I vaguely remember Josh telling me about. He fished it out of the river? A lot of it? Well, that ain't good. I sure hope Zech's okay. It's weird he ain't caught up to me yet.

What time is it? I am *so* stiff. I don't think I've moved a muscle all night. I really need to change position, but not while "Momma" is in here.

If it don't stop raining, how long before she goes outside?

But the cave steadily lightens as the sky clears. The rain peters out. Soon I can make out a large stack of firewood beside the plasti-wrapped meat. Why did Josh gather all that? If Zech and I never turned up, he shoulda hiked to safety long before killer-chiller season.

Everything aches all along my side and back, screaming to be moved, but I lie stubbornly still.

I do *not* wanna have to shoot Josh's raptor.

JOSHUA

When I wake after yet another nap, the rain has stopped. Finally! I wriggle out from under Momma and tie the curtain slightly to one side, so the way past it is obvious but we're not losing all our heat. I'll leave it up—it will help her even after we've left.

I head to the back of the cave first, and crawl under the low section to check on Dad. He's asleep again— I'm pretty sure I saw his head moving earlier—but as far as I can tell in the dim light, his color's better.

I put a hand to his forehead, to double-check. Yeah, he don't feel too cold now.

I crawl out again without waking him, and head outside. I wanna catch Momma one last fish breakfast before we leave. I should drag those meat packs out of the back, too. The plasti-starch wrappers will gradually biodegrade, allowing her access to them throughout the winter. Might make all the difference.

It sure is nice to think so, anyways.

I fish for longer than usual, keeping going well after the cold would normally have driven me back to the bank. As soon as I set off with Dad, I can put some nice warm socks and boots on, and full-length pants too. But Momma needs all the help I can give her.

Finally, Momma's gobbling the fish in a downright lazy way, and I'm so chilled I know I have to stop. I splash to shore, dry off, and pull my shorts back on. Dad's got all my extra layers, so I put my arms around Momma's neck, cuddling close, my feet tucked under her warm breastfeathers.

"I'm gonna miss you, Momma," I whisper. I hate that I have to just leave her here, all alone again.

Calm, full, and content—suspecting nothing—she lips at my head for a moment, then flicks the tip of her tail nearby, inviting me to stalk it. Just like it's a normal day on Matriarch Island. Choking back a real big lump in my throat, I get on hands and knees.

Dad's probably still sleeping. I'm gonna play with Momma one last time.

ISAIAH

"Dad?" Someone pokes my shoulder. *Ouch.* "Don't make any noise."

Josh? I open my eyes. The raptor's cave. It's bright outside now, and the cave's inhabitant is asleep on the riverbank. It must be at least late morning. *Huh.* Has the meat stack moved or am I really losing it?

"How are you feeling?" asks Josh, distracting me from the puzzle. "Ready to travel, or do you wanna rest today and set off tomorrow?"

"We should go," I say, very softly. "I'm fine."

He shoots me a suspicious look, but don't argue.

"Okay, well, I fed Momma, and she's taking a nap," he tells me. "You should be able to sneak out once you're dressed."

Ugh, my clothes will still be damp. They're back beside me—folded, now. But when I reach for the stack, they're completely dry. Dry, and smelling of stinkroot. Dull brown feathers cling to the fabric here and there. Josh musta rinsed them in stink-root water to hide my scent and lined the nest with them to get them dry quickly.

I guess that's one way to do laundry.

JOSHUA

All too soon, Dad's safely out of the cave, waiting for me at the top of the slope. I eye Momma, who's still sleeping. Just the way we want, I remind myself. I wanna hug her goodbye or some'at, I wanna so much. But I'll wake her, and then we won't be able to sneak off.

"Bye, Momma," I whisper. "I'm always gonna pretend you were my real mom."

Quickly, before I can do some'at stupid like stroke her or hug her anyway, I turn and hurry up the slope to Dad.

ISAIAH

I do take my clothes off and put them inside my nice waterproof backpack before crossing the river this time, pain or no pain. But the icy water chills me to the bone again.

Having dry clothes to put back on helps, but heck, I'm tired. Josh stripped off for the crossing too, but strides along beside me afterward with his energy apparently unaffected by the cold dip. I don't say much as we travel, 'cause despite me telling Josh I'm fine, and despite my determination to get back to Zech as quick as we can, it takes all my energy to stay alert and just keep walking.

Mebbe we shoulda stayed another day. Nah. If I have got internal injuries, I have a very short window of time in which to get Josh safely back to Zech before I collapse. Assuming Zech ain't in trouble too.

Josh don't say much, neither, so I reckon he's feeling sad about leaving his raptor-momma. Half-blind, huh? And alone. She ain't gonna make it to spring. Poor Josh. I can tell he's gotten too attached.

I pause and slip my arms around him at last, giving him a very gentle hug. His arms go around my waist, hurting less than my chest, though the movement still shifts my ribs.

I don't let go. Holding him is worth the pain.

JOSHUA

Dad's going real slow. I wonder if we *shoulda* stayed another day, let him rest up. Then again, ribs are real slow to heal, ain't they? Uncle Z were cursing and groaning for weeks, that one time. Like sharing the 'Vi with an unhappy bear.

Thankfully, Dad calls a fairly early halt when we find a nice-sized crack in a stony hollow near the river.

The rock formations make it unlikely large critters will come to the water's edge here, and even velociraptors would have to enter the crack one by one. It's a good spot.

Since it ain't twilight yet, I strip off my ragged t-shirt and shorts and wash the dung and mud from my body, then pull on the clean clothes Dad brought for me. I've got my boots on already. My old ones, a little tight, 'cause my normal ones washed away, I guess. But they're real boots, swaddling my feet.

The clothes smell so wonderfully fresh. They smell like soapnuts, which is what we use for laundry. They smell like the 'Vi, like home.

Home...

I sure hope Uncle Z is okay. Where the heck is he?

ISAIAH

Josh insists that I stay still in a patch of late afternoon sun and stand—well, sit—guard while he scurries from bush to hideout, bush to hideout, loading it with bedding and building a nice wall of scentCam. With clothes and blanket dry, and Josh's extra straw and fur layers, and all this bedding, we should be okay tonight. Especially since we can cuddle up together. I'm gonna be a poor substitute for a Dakotaraptor, though, heat-wise.

I sure am looking forward to getting horizontal and shutting my eyes. Though, now that there are two of us, we really ought to take it in turns to keep watch. But I ain't actually sure if I can stay awake, the way I'm feeling.

Josh has collected a whole mountain of foliage, and the sun is nearly gone. I'm about to tell him that it'll do when a movement catches my eye.

JOSHUA

"Josh!"

Dad's voice is sharp. I look around and he points down the riverbank, raising his rifle. I peer that way. Some'at's moving...

Brown plumage. Faded blue ruff feathers...

"It's Momma! Don't shoot her, Dad!"

Misfire, she's followed me! *Momma, you're too good a momma!*

"D'you wanna get in the crack and hope she goes away?" Dad asks.

"She tracked me all this way; she ain't just gonna give up and go." I hesitate, watching her coming slowly closer. "But I washed her dung off..."

Dad snorts. "If you've been sleeping with her for a week, she knows your scent, no matter how much dung you smeared over yourself."

Dad's right. No way she won't recognize me, strange-smelling clothes or not.

I hope.

"Okay, I'll...I'll see if I can get her to go home." Heck, how? "How do I do that, Dad?"

"Convince a third of a ton Dakotaraptor to go somewhere and do some'at it don't wanna? You know you can't. We've either gotta let her tag along behind until she gets too tired to keep up, or I cull her. Which, y'know, would be a mercy, really."

"No! I left her all that meat. If she'd just go back... We don't need to do that."

"If she tries to drag you away, I won't have no choice."

"No! Soon as she puts me down, I'll just come back to you. Don't hurt her."

Dad hesitates. "She may know your scent, but you're wearing weird clothes, and smell like me too, now, and you've been a very naughty chick wandering this far. If she makes the slightest dangerous move I gotta take her down, Josh. Okay? So it's up to you whether you engage with her, or we just hide in the crack and sneak off in the morning when she's sleeping."

I swallow. I know what Dad's saying. Mebbe I should get in the crack, play it safe—for me and for Momma. But...

A thought creeps into my mind. A wonderful, awesome, perfect idea. What if...

Momma's almost here. Her head rises, nostrils flaring as she catches my scent. Dad eases backward into the crack, his rifle aimed. If Momma puts a claw wrong, he's gonna kill her.

Momma sniffs again, then chirrups in joyful relief. Her tired plod breaks into eager springy steps as she rushes toward me, stumbling over a too-large boulder she can't see. My heart melts. I gotta try.

Cheeping eagerly, I hop to meet her, rubbing my cheek against her feathery side.

Don't get angry, Momma, don't nip me, don't...

It's so good to see you, Momma, I tell her. *So good to see you.* Her muzzle hovers over me, her breath tickling my skin as she sniffs me, taking in the strange scents. I cheep more sweetly than ever. *It's just me, Momma. Just your dear little chick. Just me.*

She grips the back of my nice warm—until now unripped—thermal top and scoops me off the ground. For a moment, I'm afraid she's gonna march off back toward the island, but she only walks as far as the looming rock wall not far from the crack, where she deposits me, settling herself and gathering me close. She chirrups a stern warning to me not to roam, and puts her head down to sleep.

Poor thing. After trekking all afternoon, she's too

tired to even be real mad at me. She just wants to rest in a sheltered spot. Lucky for me—and her too, since I don't reckon Dad were gonna just stand there and let her nip me.

"Uh, Dad?" I chirp, hoping he can hear me through all the feathers. "Guess you're sleeping on your own."

DAY 11

ISAIAH

Soft animal voices draw me up from a deep sleep. A Dakotaraptor mother and chick are talking, not far away. I associate the sounds they're making with mealtime, though there's some'at a little odd about the exchange.

A meal? With the sudden awareness that I'm out-'Vi, a spurt of adrenalin snaps me more awake, and I open my eyes. Me?

But I'm nestled in the base of a deep, Dakotaraptor-proof crack, packed around with good scentCam bedding. Peering through the branches, I make out an old she-raptor with a faded blue ruff sitting by the river.

Josh's unlikely momma. Memory returns in a rush. Heck, I slept deeply. Musta needed it.

Josh is standing on a rock, fishing, wearing nothing on his lower half but his underpants. It makes me cold just looking at him, but he's right to keep his pants dry.

Ah. Of course. The dialogue they're having is backward. *He's* feeding *her*. From the way she's lying there by the river, merely tilting her head to grab each fish, she's still exhausted after blundering after us for so many miles yesterday, following her nose.

Guess Josh is getting his own breakfast, anyways. I'd better sort myself out, and once that inconveniently devoted old raptor settles off for a nap, we can get on our way.

Wrapped in a mix of grass skirts and untanned rabbit skins and my thermal blanket, I'm pleasantly warm—almost too hot—but my rib-pain is up to full force again. I shift as little as possible until I've got my medicine from my pack and taken everything I need. I fish out a food packet too, and force the contents down, though I ain't that hungry.

Aw, heck. I were *asleep*. Really asleep. So much for keeping guard over Josh. Still, the raptor were at least as likely to hear or smell danger as I were to see it in the dark, and with my one-shot rifle, she's almost as likely to be able to fend it off too. Though, Mr. Rex would make short work of either of us. I've been particularly keeping my eyes open for *him*.

Hmm. If this raptor's gonna keep turning up, I'd better take what precautions I can. I apply a fresh layer of scentBlock cream with particular care, then break off lots of small sprigs of the best scentCam and tuck them all over me. If I finish up looking slightly like a walking bush—and smelling like one—so much the better.

Raptors don't feed on bushes.

JOSHUA

I eat my cold fish breakfast, trying not to think about the trail rations in Dad's backpack. I am so sick of raw flesh.

By the time I finish, Momma's napping again, but she's restless. Now that she's slept off her deepest exhaustion, she raises her head regularly, peering around with her useless eyes and cocking her head nervously to catch the unfamiliar morning sounds.

Heck, she's vulnerable out here. And part of her knows it. She needs to get back to her island.

Or...

Dad has emerged from the crack, looking more bush than man this morning—anti-Momma-precautions, clearly—and is creeping along the back of the hollow. I wait until he's well upstream and standing waiting for me, then paw at Momma's side with my not-wing-arm.

"Come on, Momma," I chirp. "Come on, it's time to go."

She raises her head to check on things again, then rests her chin back on the ground. "Come on, Momma." I paw at her again. She lifts her head and makes a little lunge, trying to catch me to swaddle me now that breakfast is done, but I hop away upstream, interspersing my speech with appropriate raptor calls. "Come on, Momma. We can't stay here all day."

She makes a grumpy sound, clearly still too tired to wanna move.

"Come on. We can't stay here. We gotta go."

Steeling myself, I head on along the bank to join Dad, ignoring her anxious calls.

Get up, Momma. Come on. You hafta follow us.

"What are you doing, Josh?" Dad quietly asks when I reach him. "I thought the whole idea were to give her the slip so she'd go home?"

Uh-oh. Busted.

ISAIAH

Josh eyes me shiftily. "Yeah, but..."

"But what?" He's up to something.

"But it's a long way to the cave. And now that my trail's gone cold, she might not even find her way back. Raptors ain't bloodhounds. Good noses, sure, but they're sight hunters."

"Obviously I know that," I tell him, "but what other option does she have? She can follow the river." Does my chest have to hurt this much before we've even set off?

"How will she know where to cross the marsh?" he objects. "Besides," he sidles from side to side slightly like a juvenile raptor that's afraid it's in trouble with its parents—or about to be, "I were thinking...if she followed us all the way back to the 'Vi...why couldn't we put her in the rear pen and take her to a zoo?"

I draw a breath to tell him that she's hardly in prime condition, but he rushes on, "Zoos love a good story, don't they? Just think, the only known blind raptor to survive in the wild! Rescued in the nick of time, just before winter! Real heart-warming stuff, right? They'd have people lining up during those slow cold months to see her. And she could have a heat lamp, and unlimited food, and a comfy den..."

I pause, rethinking my first response. He ain't wrong. It *is* a good story, even leaving out the whole adopting-a-human-boy angle, which no one would believe anyways. "She couldn't be housed with the other Dakotas, though. Far too old to join a new pack."

"Sure, but she don't exactly need a large paddock, at her age. Just a little space to putter around in. I reckon you could get several zoos interested, no problem; let them bid against each other."

This pitch ain't really aimed at me, is it? He's rehearsing for his Uncle Z. Josh knows that *she's old and tired and she helped me so why not take her to a nice heat lamp instead of shooting her?* would work just as well on me. Probably better.

Except...however cozy they may be together, she ain't imprinted on him. Strictly speaking, every moment they're together Josh is at risk.

Admittedly, at this precise moment, having an extra pair of claws and teeth to add to my crippled rifle to defend Josh is more desirable than worrisome. If she's gonna protect him through the long, dangerous nights, I ain't gonna drive her off or cull her unless she starts trying to eat me.

As for the whole *putting her in the 'Vi and taking her with us* idea... Half-blind or not, she is still a very large, powerful, dangerous predator.

"I'll have to think about it, Josh." His face falls, making me feel like a heel.

"She saved my life, Dad!" he cries. "Twice! The second night, I had hypothermia, and I woulda died, sure as anything, but she tucked me in her nest and warmed me through. And then another day, this deinon were gonna eat me, but she took it down, and we ate it instead. She's such a good mother that she left her safe place to follow me. If we cut her loose so far from home, she's done for. After the way she's looked after me, how can you do that to her?"

My insides clench uncomfortably. This pitch is aimed squarely at me.

"The rear pen ain't designed for a wide-awake Dakotaraptor," I say, trying to buy thinking time. Thinking still ain't my favorite thing, right now. "She'd have to be tranquilized."

"Sure. Won't do her no harm." Josh is beaming like

I've just agreed to the crazy scheme.

"I ain't said yes," I add quickly. His face falls again. "And you know it ain't up to me. Your Uncle Z is the 'Vi-boss.'" And by quite a considerable amount, too. I only own a twenty percent share of our happy home, thanks to Josh's charming biological mother.

We start walking.

Y'know, I'm liking his *new* mom much better.

JOSHUA

I walk in silence for a little ways, to give Dad time to think. But I start to suspect that drugged up and in pain, his mind's wandered elsewhere. The terrain, mebbe. Which I guess I ought to be concentrating on too.

"You could help me persuade Uncle Z, though," I say firmly, when we stop for our next proper terrain inspection.

He blinks, then grimaces as he remembers what I'm talking about. "I wouldn't bet on it."

"Yeah, but won't you at least try?"

"Just gimme a chance to think about it, Josh, okay?" His voice is slightly sharp. Guess he's still feeling crummy. I'd better drop it for now.

I glance behind us again, looking for Momma. *Come on, where are you? Don't give up now...*

I tilt my head back and give a good chick screech, but Dad claps his hand over my mouth, a slight huff of pain escaping him at the sudden movement.

"No." His voice is stern. "Too loud, Josh. No noise, okay? You know better than that."

My cheeks get real hot. I feel like a little kid. Yeah, of course I wouldn't normally make noise, but I just wanna help Momma. I guess I don't want some'at to eat Dad, though. Or me.

"Sorry," I mutter.

Sorry, Momma. You're gonna have to follow your nose.

"It ain't raining, Josh." Dad reads my mind. "She'll find you no problem, same as yesterday."

"Yeah. I just hope nothing eats her."

"Sure, but I'm more worried about some'at eating us."

ISAIAH

I'm real glad of that deep night's sleep as the afternoon wears on. I were tired enough yesterday, and the full day of walking is almost more than I can manage. Josh surges along like a ball of youthful energy, but for the first time in my life I'm getting an insight into what it'll be like to be old.

Tired all the time. Everything hurting. My mind working real slow.

Mebbe a few of Josh's kids or grandkids to bounce on my knee, heh? So I guess it may not be too bad.

Josh don't bug me no more about Momma and the zoo, and thank Saint Des for that. I can't concentrate on nothing extra right now.

JOSHUA

Dad's face is gray again by the time we find a deep niche in an outcrop, which he reckons is the best shelter we're gonna find in this area. It's barely large enough for both of us along with enough bedding, but then, I won't be sleeping in it, right? I hope not, and I guess Dad merely expects I won't be.

I work hard gathering bedding, 'cause Dad don't look like he can do it, and it takes my mind off wondering where Momma is.

Even worse, where Uncle Z is. Dad's been scanning the far distance, every single terrain inspection he's made, and so have I, but there still ain't no sign of the 'Vi. I can tell Dad's getting more and more worried. How can it have taken Uncle Z eight *days* to get the vehicle free?

I guess HabVis do get so badly stuck sometimes that they're stranded until spring—or even forever. But it ain't likely.

Nor is it likely that some'ats happened to him, I

remind myself. What's that fancy thing Dad said once? "Hunters always have cover when they go out-'Vi 'cause of statistics, not real-time risk." In other words, any one time you go out-'Vi, the chances of some'at bad happening are real small. It's only over a lifetime that they get not-so-small.

I eye Dad's stiff shoulders and strained face. Well, or if you go a long way, I guess. He still won't tell me exactly what happened. He either did some'at pretty darn stupid, or it's so bad he's afraid it'll totally freak me out. Unfortunately, I'm getting more and more sure it's the second.

That's enough bedding, anyways. I sit beside Dad.

"Dad, did you think about—?" But his pain-glazed gaze has sharpened on some'at in the downstream direction.

"Josh." He tilts his head that way, gently, to avoid jerking his ribs, no doubt.

It's Momma!

ISAIAH

The raptor's real tired, that's clear enough. Her legs are scraped and sore from tripping over things she can't see properly.

She greets Josh with relief, but at less length than last night, then tries to sit down and swaddle him right there on the riverbank. He lures her to a more sheltered spot nearer my niche, managing to swipe a handful of crushed yarrow and some'at soothing over her legs just before she settles on the ground.

Then she has him securely swaddled, and I'm guessing she ain't letting him out until morning. I sure wouldn't, if he kept running off on me like this!

"Night, Dad," a muffled chirp reaches me. Yeah, if raptors used words, they'd sound just like that!

DAY 12

JOSHUA

One more day to the 'Vi, Dad said yesterday, mebbe two, since he ain't going so fast. Can Momma manage another whole day's traveling, let alone two? With her bad sight, it's seriously hard work for her.

I spend as long as I can fishing for her, trying to make sure she's had plenty to eat, letting Dad sleep in. I mean, he needs the sleep, and she needs the food. Ain't much else I can do for either of 'em. I snatch some bites of fish for myself, and only come to shore and get dressed when I see bush-Dad crawl out and stagger to his feet in a disturbingly wobbly way.

Mebbe he's just stiff.

I make a good fuss over Momma while he gets clear of the area, stroking her blue ruff and rubbing my cheek against her and giving her a pep talk.

"Ain't you brave and clever to have followed me so far? Just a little further, Momma. Just a little further, and we'll take you to a nice new home, okay? A really nice home. It's warm, and safe, and there's more food than you can eat. It's worth walking a little further, I promise. Come on. Come on, Momma. You can do it."

I dodge an attempt at swaddling and hop away from her at last, and she screeches. Not just anxiety, this morning, but outright distress. She knows I'm gonna vanish again. The sound knots my insides into a tangle.

"Come on, Momma. It's worth it, I promise. Just one more day. Please? You need a new home. The island's no good for you now." As I head toward Dad, she lurches up to her feet and begins to follow at once, calling pleadingly. Not wasting time waiting for me to come back, like she has every other morning.

She seems so confused and uneasy, I hate to see it.

Yeah, she don't even know what to do, now, does she? She ain't stupid, she knows she's come too far to go back, she can't feed herself, she can't see... She followed me out here because she wanted to take care of her chick, but that ain't the only reason she's following me now.

She needs me every bit as much as I've needed her.

ISAIAH

Josh let me sleep later than he shoulda, but it ain't done no good. My chest screams, my head aches, and I got a nasty feeling I'm running a temperature.

Am I coming down with a cold? No surprise if I were, after getting near-hypothermic and wet through.

Or do I have internal injuries? Not the kind of big dramatic ones that drop you almost at once, but subtler ones that more slowly cause problems. Damaged tissue seeping blood rather than gushing. Wounds inside can fester and get infected too, and ain't much one can do about it without intravenous antibiotics and operating rooms.

How much longer am I gonna be able to stay on my feet? I took extra caffeine tablets and a little more morphine this morning, I were so desperate.

Zech, where are you? We need you here.

JOSHUA

I eye Dad anxiously as he stands, leaning against a boulder and staring at…nothing?…on the ground in front of him.

"Dad? You okay?"

He starts slightly, winces, and focuses on me. "Uh, yeah, I think I'm just coming down with a heavy cold or some'at. I'm, uh…I think I'm gonna have to concentrate on walking today. Let you take more responsibility for the terrain inspections. Can you do that?"

"Sure." I try to sound calm. Heavy cold? He ain't sniffing or sneezing. Is it some'at to do with his ribs? He *still* ain't told me what happened to him. He brushed the question away again, and we've been keeping quiet most of the time while walking for safety. How sick is he?

I glance over my shoulder, looking for Momma. I wanna stall, make it easier for her to keep up, but Dad needs to get to the 'Vi as soon as possible. There are more medical supplies there—and it's the only way to get him to a hospital.

Momma ain't in sight right now, but the terrain ahead is clear and we can't wait.

"Come on, Dad. Let's move."

ISAIAH

My head pounds harder and harder, hotter and hotter. I'm starting to feel sick. No, no, no, I do not wanna puke, not with my ribs like this.

I'm so tired. I just wanna stop…

JOSHUA

By noon, Dad's stumbling along behind me like a zombie. Sometimes I even hold onto his hand and lead him for a while. His skin burns with fever. It ain't a cold. It's either full-blown flu—or some'at worse.

Saint Des, please let it be the flu!

I nag him to keep drinking water from his bottle.

Eventually I take the half-broken rifle from around his neck and transfer some rounds to my pocket. But I can't carry the backpack, fully loaded. If he gets much worse, I'm gonna have to abandon a ton of stuff and just keep the essentials.

I can lug the rifle, though. It's far too big for me, but Dad ain't up to using it right now. I wedge a bit of wood on the point of my spear for a safety cap and give it to him to use as a walking stick. He leans on it hard.

At lunchtime, I stop us at the top of a gentle slope, with a good view ahead, and try to bully Dad into eating some'at.

He sits, hugging himself and shivering, so I fish out his blanket and tie that around him.

We really ain't going fast, today. How far to the 'Vi?

Guess that depends on where the 'Vi is.

ISAIAH

I feel like death warmed over. I'm furious with myself for dumping the terrain inspections on Josh, but I ain't got no choice. I can't *do* it. I can't *think*, I can't… Barely keep going…

I'm scaring Josh to death, I can tell. He's even taken my rifle, now. I feel naked without it, but it's horribly easy to resist the urge to ask for it back. The backpack crushes me. *So tired…*

What do I do if...? What does Josh do if...? Thinking is *so* hard.

What if I can't carry on?

It ain't some'at I wanna consider, but I gotta.

Painfully slowly, I unfasten my backpack and fish around until I find a thin trail pad. I failed to mark much detail on it as I were walking here. I were far too impatient to get to Josh.

All the same, I made a few notes of the most significant landmarks. I peer at my scrawl, wringing extra details from my broiling brain and adding them in.

"What are you doing?" Josh eyes me suspiciously.

"Just updating these trail notes." I try to sound casual.

"Just follow the river, right?"

"It's gonna split twice, going back upstream. We, uh, we want the left-hand fork, each time. I got some landmarks written down, er...here, so you...so we know we're on the right tributary."

"Great." Josh speaks so flatly I know I ain't fooling him. "Well, if you ain't gonna eat no more, we'd better move."

I can't stop myself from bending busily over the trail pad, though I really can't remember nothing else to add. "Lemme...lemme finish this, first."

How can I get up and walk all afternoon? I just wanna lie down...

JOSHUA

I catch a whiff of familiar Dakotaraptor scent about when I begin to hear not-very-stealthy noises coming up the slope behind us. I look around and chirp to give Dad a head's up, but he just sits there on the boulder beside me and don't react.

Fortunately, Momma shows no interest in him as she comes straight to me and sniffs me all over. As far as she's concerned, I'm sitting beside nothing but a droopy bush. The combination of scentBlock cream and natural scentCam is working—good.

Momma tilts her head to the side and gives an anxious cry, not especially loud, but from such a large creature, loud enough.

Dad's head jerks up, like he's only just noticed her, and with an unstealthy lurch, he kinda topple-rolls right over the boulder we're sitting on, landing hard lower down the slope with a pained grunt. Fortunately, Momma don't react. Too blind and too tired to hunt a shrub, even a moving one?

He lies there breathing in agonized wheezes for a while.

"Darn...huge...raptor..." he pants at last. "No, thank you..."

The boulder leans out a little, making a slight overhang, under which Dad crawls. Under which Dad *almost* crawls. He stops with some of his legs still sticking out and just lies there.

"Dad?" I chirp in my raptor-ish way. "What are y'doing? We gotta get moving."

"Need…need a nap. Try not to let her…eat me… would'ya?"

Fear tightens my throat. "We gotta get to the 'Vi, Dad. I don't think that's a good idea."

"Just gimme…few minutes…"

I swallow. What can I do? Ain't like I can carry him.

Momma settles against the boulder Dad just fell off. She reaches out a wing-arm in a weary attempt to snag me—I dodge easily enough.

"No, Momma. We don't have time to nap. Soon as Dad's on his feet, we gotta go."

When she tucks her wing-arms safely under her, I sit beside her again, stroking her neck. She plonks her great head in my lap to capture me a little and closes her eyes.

Ugh, *no one* is listening to me!

I scan the surrounding landscape, rechecking the terrain carefully. The grown-ups want their nap-time, so I gotta keep guard.

The exhausted, half-dead grown-ups. I try not to let that thought take shape, but it does anyway. My insides wibble-wobble like jello. Momma's just tired, but Dad…

If I can't get him up again, what do I do? Should I

take those trail notes and try to make it to the 'Vi as fast as I can, and bring help back to him? No, it would take hours, even by myself. A whole day, even. And then some more hours to drive back, assuming the vehicle is even out of the mud yet. Dad ain't safe to be left where he is. Even Momma could put her head under there and grab him, even if he'd managed to crawl all the way in. I'd have to get him some place safer—and I ain't sure I'm strong enough to move him.

If he could move himself just far enough, mebbe I could go. Otherwise…what can I do other than keep watch and hope Uncle Z comes before it's too late?

Momma's breathing is a little whistly, a polite almost-snore brought on by all this walking. Dad's breathing more heavily, and kinda rough.

I scan the landscape again, searching desperately for a glint of metal or glass, for movement, watching for danger. But the question keeps running through my head.

Is it flu?

Or is he dying before my eyes?

My throat feels real tight, my eyes hot, but I refuse to let the tears take hold. I ain't safe here, so I can't cry.

I really, *really* ain't safe. None of us are.

Saint Des, what the heck should I do?

ISAIAH

"Dad?" Someone's shaking my arm, hard. Someone cruel and horrible. My ribs stab me with every movement. "Dad? You've *had* a nap. We gotta go. Come on."

Hang on... *Josh?* Sounding awfully bossy. With difficulty, I yank my sleep-caked eyes open. The light impales my eyeballs, making them flinch closed again. Have I ever had such a bad headache? The morning after Josh were conceived, mebbe.

"Dad? Get up!" Josh's firm voice wavers. Turns pleading. "*Please* wake up this time? *Please, Dad!*"

He sounds ready to cry. The quaver in his voice does some'at vicious to my heart. I drag my eyes open again, more slowly, letting them adjust. The sun is a lot further down in the sky than I vaguely remember it were when we stopped.

"How long...sleep?" I mumble.

"Hours, Dad. We can't wait no longer."

Hours? How could I waste so much daylight, so much traveling time? Darn it!

"You gotta move somewhere safer so I can go get Uncle Z, or you gotta get up, Dad."

What? Josh is talking about just wandering off into the wilderness by himself? Well, him and the decrepit raptor, no doubt. No way. I gotta go with him.

Either the sleep's done me good, or the adrenalin

from hearing what Josh is proposing is giving me a boost, 'cause I feel clearer-headed than when I crawled under here.

"Just...gimme a few minutes to get myself together, and...and we'll be off," I tell him.

His huff hovers between skeptical and relieved.

I blink a few more times until I'm sure my eyes will stay open in the light, then ease myself slowly out from under the boulder. *Hang on*...belatedly, I look around for the raptor. Clear-headed, huh?

"She's asleep," says Josh. "Top side of the boulder."

Right. Feeling like I'm stuck in slow motion, I ease my backpack to me, slowly unfasten it. Josh is watching, and I don't wanna worry him, but I don't know how else I can get up and walk, neither. So I take almost a whole syringe of morphine, a whole handful of caffeine tablets, and a double dose of stimulants.

Here's hoping it don't finish me off.

JOSHUA

I'm sure Dad shouldn't be taking all that stuff together, but mebbe it's safer than him staying put here. I sure hope he knows.

He's fastening his pack, anyway, in painful slow motion. His hand rises, patting vaguely at his greenery, checking...

He seems a little puzzled how much of it is still on him, but he slept through me adding new sprigs anywhere I could get to.

Finally, he uses the boulder to pull himself to his feet, leaning hard on the spear-walking stick. He bends stiffly toward his backpack, so I grab it and heft it, helping him get it on.

"Should we stash some of this stuff, Dad? Lighten the pack?"

He leans against the boulder, his eyes half closed, obviously struggling with the weight.

"If your Uncle Z ain't got the 'Vi out yet," he says at last, "then we're still too far away to wanna do that. I'll be fine."

Sure you will. But I don't say it out loud.

"Let's go, then." I wait until Dad is down the slope a little ways before calling back to Momma, in raptor and then in raptor-English. "Come on, Momma. Time to go."

By the time she's got herself up and moving, hopefully we'll be a little way ahead. Safer for Dad.

As we move on, though, Dad does seem better than this morning. Whether the sleep helped, or whether it's totally artificial from the drugs, I dunno. We need to really try to cover some ground while he's up to it. He can't keep taking doses like that. I'm sure I remember him telling me that stimulants and morphine don't mix.

ISAIAH

Saint Des only knows how much I wish we were closer to the 'Vi. I dread to think what state I'm gonna be in when the combination of drugs and adrenaline wears off. No chance we can make it all the way to where I left Zech by then. The speed we're moving, later tomorrow is the earliest we could hope for. Will I still be up to walking anywhere, by then?

Mebbe we *should* dump the non-essentials. Cache them, just in case we have to come back for them.

Non-essentials? What non-essentials? Ain't like I packed for a party.

From the litter of wrappers beside that boulder where we stopped for lunch and a nap, Josh has taken it upon himself to lighten the pack slightly by feeding several cakes of expensive high energy trail rations to the raptor. Well, he probably ate one himself, but I don't believe he ate four.

It's hard to feel annoyed with him—I can't even feel the difference in weight.

JOSHUA

I scan the far horizon again. *Uncle Z? Where are you?*

My heart aches. I realized some'at, during those long hours guarding Dad when I had nothing to do but watch, stroke Momma, and think.

I ain't told Uncle Z I love him since I were six years old. Not since he shot Rudy.

Not since I yelled at him that I'd hate him forever.

I don't hate him.

I hated him for mebbe an hour, then I loved him again. But I ain't never told him. What if he still thinks I hate him?

What if Dad and I get et out here, and he never knows?

What if he's got et, and I can't ever tell him?

Saint Des, if he's gone, please tell him for me, would'ya?

But it ain't the same. I wanna tell him myself. I wanna see his stubbly face smiling as he helps me with some'at, I wanna hear him bantering with Dad. I wanna...

"Here, Josh." Dad's voice is tight. "Help me get this off again, would'ya?"

His brown skin really don't have enough color, kinda gray around the edges.

"You okay?" I grab the pack and support it as he eases his arms out of the straps with slight gasps of pain.

"Yeah. Yeah, fine. I just think you were right about leaving some stuff behind."

I stuff my pockets with ration packs and other useful things. The flare gun and some cartridges I put in my most accessible pocket, since Dad's pockets are all full of bullets.

We keep the thermal blanket and the remains of the survival blanket, plus the roll of grass clothes, since they're so light, and my rabbit fur cape. Everything else we shove into a crack between two rocks and quickly pile some stones on top for a makeshift cache. The backpack is definitely much lighter afterward. I offer to carry it, but Dad heaves it back on. He either wants to leave me free to better fire the oversized rifle, or free to run fast if necessary. Either way, I don't bother arguing 'cause I know I won't win.

Momma catches up just as we're ready to move again. She glances once in Dad's direction, as though she's figuring out that there may be more to the bush that's always hanging around me than her nose tells her. But she thrusts her muzzle against me straight away, sniffing in what seems to be a mixture of anxiety and relief. Too tired to worry about the Dad-bush when I'm clearly not bothered by it. Poor Momma. She's far too old a lady for long-distance hiking.

I give her a quick bit of attention, then follow Dad. How long will those drugs last?

No time to waste.

ISAIAH

I slide from exhaustion to dizzying hyper-alertness to dangerous absent-mindedness over and over again, as though the drugs are fighting it out inside me. Josh stays sharp, thank Saint Des, performing careful terrain inspections each time before hurrying us on our way.

We're making better progress. But what do I do when the drugs wear off?

If necessary, take more. What else?

I stumble into Josh, who's stopped dead in front of me, staring straight ahead, his shoulders rigid.

My heart lurches, even as I clutch Josh's shoulders to stop him falling—or mebbe me from falling.

What does he see?

JOSHUA

I scan the horizon, squinting slightly in the sun, searching desperately...

Was it? Or was it imagination? Sun on water, perhaps?

No. *There...* I let out my long-held breath in a gasp of relief.

"Dad!" My voice comes out strangled. "I saw a glint. Twice. Eleven o'clock. Gotta be a windshield!"

Dad peers intently with his blurry, dilated eyes, hope plain on his face.

"All the way out here, it must be the 'Vi," I add.

"I sure hope so," Dad says, "but any vehicle will do, right now."

"Yeah, they can take us to Uncle Z." I glance over my shoulder. Momma's fallen back out of sight again. "It has to be a 'Vi, though, or they won't have a pen for Momma."

Oh yeah... I need to make sure…

"Dad? You will try to persuade Uncle Z, won't you? Please?"

He don't stop peering at the horizon, and nor do I. "I were, uh, thinking about that."

"Yeah?" I sound wary, 'cause I am. Why don't he just say yes?

"I've decided I'll take your side...on one condition."

Huh? "What?"

"That you promise me that once she is secured in the 'Vi, you will never go into a pen with her again."

I stare at him, my heart unsure whether to lift or sink. I open my mouth, but he adds quickly, "Unless she's muzzled and claw-capped, and me or your Uncle

Z give you permission. Okay? You promise me that, or nothing doing."

It makes me sad to think of only interacting with her with a muzzle in the way—she won't be able to preen me or pick me up—but I don't even have to think for one moment. "I promise, Dad."

She ain't imprinted on me. They ain't neither of them gonna help with it any other way.

He nods. "Okay. I'll do my best with your Uncle Z, then. Just..." he makes a face and glances at me at last, his eyes worried... "please know that if he shoots her anyways, it's because he loves you, okay?"

My heart lurches at the thought of Uncle Z shooting Momma. But... "I know that."

"Good."

Saint Des, please let him listen!

"Should we fire a flare, or wait for him here, or keep going?" Standard procedure says we wait until he gets closer before doing anything that might attract attention. But...

"I think mebbe we'd better fire one," says Dad, echoing my thoughts as he goes on, "He's a long ways away, and if he checks every area as he goes, it'll take him an awful long time to get to us."

Time Dad mebbe don't have.

ISAIAH

I guess I should get the backpack off and get the flare gun, then. The thought makes my heart sink.

BANG!

I start violently, smothering a groan as my ribs complain. Josh has the flare gun out and pointed to the sky. Oh yeah, he took it when we—supposedly—lightened this darn pack. Right.

I watch the flare streak skyward, glowing brightly. Let's hope Zech's looking the right way.

"Should we keep going?" suggests Josh. "Every time we reach high ground and get a glimpse of the 'Vi, we can let off another one."

I'm not sure if he's simply desperate to get me there as fast as he possibly can, or if he desperately wants Momma to be trailing well behind when we arrive so he has time to talk Uncle Z around. Mebbe both.

"Yeah." I belatedly check the nearby area. "Ain't nowhere to hide here, anyways."

Are the drugs wearing off, or am I just spinning through another tired phase?

One foot in front of the other, Isaiah. One foot in front of the other. You're nearly home.

Hmm. "Keep twice as sharp a lookout," I tell Josh. "Don't relax."

"I know that!" comes the indignant response. "Come on, keep up."

JOSHUA

It has to be the 'Vi. My body fizzes with hope and excitement. And if it's the 'Vi, then Uncle Z's okay.

Unless it's someone else's 'Vi. This is a real wild area, so it ain't likely, but it ain't impossible, neither.

Gotta be a 'Vi, though, out here, right?

Dunno how I'll persuade total strangers to put my live Dakotaraptor in their pen when I ain't even sure I can persuade my own uncle.

Pass that rex nest when you come to it, Josh.

I force myself to focus on the terrain, trying to stop thinking about anything else. Despite what I told Dad, it's real hard to concentrate.

When we reach the next higher point, I can't spot the 'Vi, so I don't waste the flare, just check the terrain ahead and hurry Dad on. If we can at least get into the 'Vi before Momma catches up, Uncle Z won't have no reason to shoot her, even if he won't bring her with us.

Kinder to shoot her, than just leave her out here...

I push that cold whisper away.

Terrain, Josh. Terrain! Focus!

ISAIAH

We climb several more of the undulations that come right up to the water's edge here without spotting another glint. We may as well keep moving, though. I glance at the river flowing beside us. We ain't gonna miss Zech, not so long as we're close beside that.

Ahead, the river is trickling over a real shallow area of rock. If we needed to cross it, this would be a perfect place to do it. But we're already on the correct bank.

Beside me, Josh tenses. He drops down behind a boulder and begins a particularly careful scan of the area. "I remember this spot," he murmurs to me. "I got washed up on the rocks and a pack of velociraptors almost et me."

He still ain't had a chance to tell me all about what happened to him, how he ended up with Momma. That must be quite a story. Who got confused first, her or him? Well, gotta be her. I guess he did it deliberately, right? But did he...

Hang on. I should be...I should be looking around for danger...

I try to yank my mind to the landscape around me, but without the distraction of my thoughts, my eyelids begin to sag as though they each weigh as much as a bull triceratops.

"Okay," Josh whispers. "I think it's all clear. Let's go."

JOSHUA

We cross the flat rocky area where I almost became a velociraptor dinner without seeing anything larger than a hawk hovering overhead. Then the riverbank grows craggy again, forcing us to pick our way between boulders and outcrops. Occasionally, I scoot up to the top of one and take a good look, but there's nothing moving out there.

My ears strain for the sound of an engine, but the wind is the wrong way. Good if it carried the sound of the flare to Uncle Z, but bad for us.

I keep climbing boulders and rock pillars, looking out at the flatter ground some distance from the river. That's where Uncle Z will be driving. We could go over there, except without a NavConsole it would be far too easy to wander away from the river without even realizing we'd lost it. We gotta stick close.

How long will it take Uncle Z to get to us? Depends on the terrain, I guess. I doubt we'll be meeting him for a while yet, even if we are closing the distance slightly.

"Come on, Dad." I draw him on again. Apart from not wanting Momma dangerously close to us when we find Uncle Z, I'm also afraid that if we stop to wait somewhere, Dad's gonna pass out or some'at. I reckon it's best to keep him awake and moving until we're actually safe.

Which we ain't, yet.

No, we ain't. I go motionless, waving Dad into stillness too, as a velociraptor call echoes between the rock channel we're walking along.

Where are they? Have they heard us or smelled us? Dad's well scentCammed, and I've gone back to using a little of Momma's dung for scentCam, since there are only a few predators that will actively hunt a Dakotaraptor.

Unless they realize it's old, half-blind, and alone, anyways.

Or a very small human.

Hopefully if we just stay still and quiet, the pack will move on.

ISAIAH

I'm feeling so out of it, it takes me a moment to hear what Josh is reacting to.

Velociraptors.

The rush of adrenaline sharpens my mind some. I hold out my hand to Josh for the gun, offering him the spear. He can defend himself better with the boy-sized spear than with the man-sized chunk of metal.

This confined space means they can only come at us two at a time—one from each direction. So mebbe it ain't a bad place to meet them. Unless...

Josh is looking up at the top of the rocks. Faint

clicking sounds come from up there. Claws.

Yeah, if they can get up there, they can spring down onto us. Not good. We'd be safer out in the open than here.

I poke Josh, and point onwards, then put a finger to my lips. He nods and tip-toes forward, holding his spear clear of the rock walls.

I follow, doing the same with my rifle tip.

Quietly, quietly. We gotta get away without them realizing we're here.

Or...do they already know? The tapping claws are following us...I think.

I tighten my grip on my rifle, finger on the safety catch. One shot, and it's a glorified club, unless I actually have a chance to reload.

Surely this rock passage will open out soon? We need a cave, ideally, or failing that, a rock wall at our back that they can't get on top of. We've passed plenty of smooth-sided rock pillars and outcrops over the last day or two that woulda worked, and plenty of trees, too, but now...

Ahead, the narrow walls widen until they enclose a much larger space. If we get to one side or the other, that's at least one less direction they can come at us from. But if we head out there, we'll probably be visible to anything up on top of the rocks. We can't be absolutely sure they know we're here. They might just be travelling the same way.

It's gotta be harder to get up there than to just walk along down here, though, so it don't look good. I wanna ask Josh how large the pack were, but I don't wanna make noise. Raptors can hear a leaf fall in the forest a mile away, if the wind and atmospheric conditions are right, just like the wolves that were apex predators before them. After them. However you wanna view it. Before and after... No, after and before?

No, no, no, Isaiah, don't get distracted. With an effort of will, I try to concentrate again.

We've come to a halt by the mouth of the open area.

The claw-clicks slow.

They know.

JOSHUA

The pack are stalking us, no question. So we may as well get a move on. I beckon to Dad and jog lightly across the wider area. We gotta get out of these rocks and find somewhere more defensible.

I ease the flare gun from my pocket, point it upward and pull the trigger. They already know we're here. Mebbe the unfamiliar loud noise will make them hesitate, even scare them off entirely. And we need Uncle Z here *now*.

Even as the flare soars upward I'm reloading. I can

shoot a raptor with a flare, if I have to. Ain't kind, but neither's being et alive.

We hurry across the clearing. Back into a narrower gap, but it's the only way outta here. We need to get to the open ground where Uncle Z can drive up to us, find somewhere defensible there.

We weave frantically through the high rocks. Claws are clicking behind us again. The flare only shook them up briefly. I break into a full-out run, frantic to get outta the enclosing rocks before mean toothy things with three-inch killing claws start raining from the sky. Dad's breathing raggedly as he follows, choking off grunts of pain as he scrambles over rough terrain.

How long can he keep up this pace?

There! I can see what looks like the end of the crags ahead. We're almost out! In fact, the rock walls have just widened quite a lot into another rock-bound clearing.

A snarl... I look right, just in time to see a velo leap from the high rock. It's gotta be almost fifteen feet away, but I whip my spear around, lodging the butt against my hip and bracing myself, the flare gun wrecking the grip of my top hand.

The raptor—a juvenile—spots the danger at the last moment, twisting in mid-air but failing to avoid the spear point, which rams right up under its ribcage, knocking the spear from my hands and me to the ground. It shrieks and thrashes. I scoot backward to avoid the lashing claws, then lean to grab my spear as I scramble to my feet. Trying to free it, I yank back as hard as I can but only succeed in dragging the dying raptor along the ground.

Dad's gun tip is suddenly there, pinning the raptor, and I manage to pull my spear loose, looking around frantically, but there are no other velos in sight yet. This were an impatient youngster, attacking without permission. The grown-ups are probably wary of this strange prey.

But not for much longer. We just killed one of their chicks. Now we're not just prey—we're predators too.

And Dad and I both know how raptors react to those.

ISAIAH

Josh turns and heads flat-out toward the open ground again, still clutching his gory spear. It feels totally counter-intuitive to be heading for the open, but the fact the critters can get up on top of these rocks makes it our only option. As we approach the far side of the clearing, shapes suddenly appear in the gap ahead. Two snarling velos, clearly severely peeved about their skewered chick.

Can't blame them for that, but they ain't eating *my* chick. I bring my rifle up to the aim and shoot the larger of the two, the female. Here's hoping she's the matriarch and the rest will scatter with her gone.

I begin to reload even as the velo drops to the ground. The male screeches worriedly and paws at her—a mated pair, definitely—temporarily distracted, thank Saint Des. But blocking our escape route.

The round slides into the chamber. I bring the rifle up again, aiming for the male. But a scuff from behind me makes me spin around just in time to see another male in mid-air, claws forward, coming right at me.

I can't raise the rifle in time...but the flare gun in Josh's hand spits, and the male drops, shrieking, as the flare enters its chest. I spin around again, sighting on the grieving mate just as he looks up and rushes us, snarling fury. He leaps as I fire, and my precious shot misses.

Swearing, I fumble to reload as Josh levels his spear again. The velo veers off as though dodging a triceratops' horns, circling as Josh makes little jabs to keep him at bay. On the ground, the flare-shot raptor shrieks hideously, thrashing in agony, but I can't spare a shot—I can hear the rest of the pack coming. In seconds, we're gonna be encircled.

"Keep your back to mine, Josh," I say, "until we take enough of them down to make another run for it, 'kay?"

"Got'ya." Josh sounds tense, but not panicked.

Brave boy.

JOSHUA

We are *so* dead and devoured. I fumble with the flare-gun, reloading as quickly as I can. There are far too many raptors for just the two of us. They're leaping down into the clearing, surrounding us. The flare-shot raptor is making such terrible noises as the flare burns it from the inside out, I wanna ask Dad to shoot it but I know he can't waste the shot.

No. He takes down another female instead, clearly hoping it might be the matriarch. But I think the matriarch is the one coming toward me—I recognize her from before.

I snap the flare gun shut and take aim at her, but another raptor leaps for me, teeth sinking into my outstretched arm and jolting the gun from my grip. Just barely, I manage to catch it in my left hand, shove it in the raptor's ribs and pull the trigger.

Thank God, I musta hit this one's heart because it simply drops to the ground, twitches slightly, and lies still.

Then I hafta drop the flare gun and bring the spear up as the matriarch springs for me. She twists to the side at the last minute, snarling and circling, trying to get behind me. I keep my back against Dad's backside, waving the spear from side to side.

A juvenile comes at me—I swing the spear, connecting hard with his small head. He drops like a sack of flour and lies still, dead or unconscious.

I wanna look to see how Dad is doing but—

A raptor leaps for me—I point the spear and it twists aside. But a movement from the other side...the matriarch springs, her legs extended in strike position. I twist away, but one killing claw slashes across my thigh—a screech escapes me at the sudden pain, though I try to make it more angry and aggressive than pained—by the time I've swung the spear around, she's gone.

Blood flows hotly down my thigh. Thank Saint Des, the cut were glancing and ain't deep, like the small tooth marks on my arm. But the velos will just keep slicing away at us until we collapse from blood loss, and dinner is served.

The scent of blood is driving them into a kill frenzy. They circle in tighter—I don't know where to point the spear. Then they're rushing us. I swing the spear again, knocking two aside, but small teeth sink into my upper arm, yanking at me.

I try to swing the spear again but the matriarch is

hurtling straight for my chest. I jerk back and the raptor hanging from my arm pulls me off-balance. I hit the ground, trying to land on the darn thing, and coil into a protective ball, my knees clamped up against my stomach, one arm rammed across my neck to protect my throat. Another shriek escapes me. Furious, defiant...but I'm down, and unless I can get up, it's over...

ISAIAH

Josh is down!

I swing the rifle ferociously, twice as hard, trying to take out as many raptors as I can. But the momentum overbalances me and the next minute I'm thudding down on one knee. I push up frantically, punching a raptor with my fist as it leaps at me, but another one's got hold of my wrist with its small jaws—nothing small about the pain from its needle-sharp teeth. I try to shake it off—I gotta help Josh—but a claw scores my back, then another...

Josh is shrieking and screaming like a very peeved something. Dakotaraptor or human, I can't tell.

I gotta help him!

But I can't even help myself.

JOSHUA

Rolling onto my knees, I risk taking my arm from my throat to grab my spear in a double-handed grip. I swing it around me as hard as I can, sending velos flying, and surge back to my feet. I kick a couple away and stab at another one, pinning it to the ground through one wing-arm. It shrieks and struggles to get free.

I snarl and growl like an angry Dakotaraptor, trying to intimidate them. They hang back a little, wary of my come-back. Or perhaps waiting. They've sliced me up a little already. If they're patient enough, even these few small wounds will gradually sap my strength. S'not like I can lower my guard to try to stop the bleeding or nothing.

But they're already drawing in close again. Yeah, they don't reckon they need to wait. Reckon they can eat immediately.

I ready my spear, but I can't fend off another rush like the last one. It were a miracle I made it back to my feet.

A raptor springs, grabbing my spear arm again, weighing it down. A male rushes toward me, eyes on my throat. I struggle to move the spear, but the first velo clings on, too heavy...

I snarl even more ferociously, trying to spook the attacker, but he's still coming. I move my left arm across my throat...if I drop to shield my stomach, I'm on the ground again, but what choice do I have? My knees begin to dip—

With an ear-splitting roar, a brown shape slams into the midst of the velos, sending them tumbling and screeching and fleeing as Momma's teeth close around the raptor that were about to get me. She bites down—*crunch*—and tosses the limp body aside, swinging around, snapping for more.

Dad yanks the raptor from my arm and lobs it away, then pulls me with him as he makes a hasty retreat from the snarling chaos of large raptor and small raptors.

Yeah, half-blind Momma could easily grab one of *us* by accident.

ISAIAH

I've never been so glad to see that old matriarch, but right now we need to get as far away from the whole mob of claws and teeth as we can and find somewhere defensible where we can—

The thought breaks off, unfinished, as a flare soars up ahead of us, the bang echoing between the rock walls.

Zech! I track the path of the flare downward. He's so close!

I push Josh forward. "Josh, run to the 'Vi. Don't stop for nothing, that's an order. I'm right behind you."

I hope. But Josh can make it, even if I can't.

JOSHUA

A juvenile velo's crushed body flies past me, bouncing off the crag and almost taking me out as I sprint for the gap in the rocks. But when I shoot a glance over my shoulder at Momma, my heart sinks.

It's clear the velos are already figuring out that she can't see them properly, that she's frail and old and tired. They're leaping in, slashing at her haunches, avoiding her deadly jaws. The older and more experienced ones are, anyway.

She raises her head and sniffs, screeching to me as she realizes I'm moving away from her.

I screech back to let her know I'm okay, to encourage her to follow me.

Although...

"Josh," moans Dad from behind me. "Don't!"

Yeah, I'm gonna draw them all after us, ain't I? Darn it, Momma needs help! But there ain't nothing I can do with my little spear. It's a miracle I stayed alive as long as I did.

I can't help shooting another look over my shoulder just before entering the rock gully and passing out of sight.

Momma's following us, velos hanging off her here and there, but she's powering onward after her chick.

Yeah, I gotta run to the 'Vi, absolutely as fast as I can, and get my rifle. Then I can pick them off and save her. It's her only chance—and mebbe Dad's too, 'cause he ain't keeping up.

My feet pound the stony ground as I *sprint*.

ISAIAH

Misfire, but Josh is moving now. Good. I can't keep up, so he's getting ahead of me. Normally splitting up would be a terrible idea, but right now his best odds are to reach the 'Vi.

"Keep...going," I pant. "Don't...look back. Just...run."

JOSHUA

Dad's getting so far behind that I'm worried the velos may catch up to him. I've *gotta* get to my rifle! The moment Dad's in sight of Uncle Z, Uncle Z can provide him cover while I get my gun, then I can help.

I scramble over one last rough patch, my eyes sweeping the open ground.

There!

Mebbe eight hundred feet away, a familiar steel grey vehicle is moving toward us at mach speed, mud and turf flying up from under the mighty wheels.

"Come on, Dad!" I yell, and I sprint.

ISAIAH

There's the 'Vi! Thank God! Looking decidedly worse for the wear, but who cares. If we can just get there... I throw a glance over my shoulder. The Dakotaraptor is still distracting the velos, their pack hunting instinct locked onto her. She's plowing determinedly after us, dear old thing, but it ain't looking good.

Josh is halfway to the 'Vi already, streaking across the grassland like a pedigree racing orni. The 'Vi skids to a halt and a moment later the side door opens and Zech's there, raising his rifle, taking aim.

I don't look back again, but I guess the raptors have made it into sight!

I'm too far away to try and warn him off shooting Momma, and I can't spare the breath, neither. My legs shake under me. My head spins. The 'Vi looks a thousand miles away. A thousand miles of swamp or quicksand.

Am I gonna pass out?

JOSHUA

There's Uncle Z! But he's raising his rifle, and he'll shoot the largest and most dangerous predator first. I heave in extra-massive breaths and begin screaming as I run, "Do NOT shoot the Dakota! Shoot the velos! NOT the Dakota! Do NOT shoot the Dakota! Only shoot the velos!"

Uncle Z's rifle tip wavers for a moment as he takes in what I'm shouting, then his aim firms and his gun fires. A pained velo screech reassures me that he heard me okay, so I don't waste time looking around as I power up a slight rise. Dad and Momma need my help *now!*

Dad's so far behind, I can't even hear him no more. I cannot stop! Where did I leave my rifle? Unless Uncle Z moved it, I put it out of the way on a wall rack in the living area before going out-'Vi with Dad a million years ago.

My chest is burning from running this fast and shouting and being so afraid for everyone, but I don't slow down even the tiniest bit until I'm hurling myself up into the 'Vi doorway.

"Josh—"

I ignore Uncle Z, snatching my rifle from the wall rack and spinning around. There's Dad, stumbling along like he's about to fall down and stay down. Uncle Z can cover him, but Momma and the pack are behind that slight rise, and I can't see more than her head and back.

"Do *not* shoot the Dakota," I pant as I spring onto the ladder and scoot up into the turret at top speed. From here I'll have line of sight on the velos. I can shoot them all, get them away from them both!

I yank the lever to open the windows and slide my rifle tip through the bars. They're up the slope now, anyway, and I've got a clear shot!

I get my eye to the sights at once. The velos are all around her, clawing, biting. Her brown plumage is red and matted with blood as she totters onward, struggling to carry their weight as they slash and gnaw at her.

I shoot one—then another. Dad's just stumbling up to the 'Vi at last, *thank you, God.*

My breath catches, my stomach going cold as the velo matriarch's claw drives deep into the softest part of Momma's belly, ripping it open. Momma screeches and snaps blindly, then tries to stumble onward, but she's dragging her guts along the ground behind her. Her legs buckle and she goes down, still snarling and snapping in feeble defiance.

Avoiding her teeth, the velos close in.

I screech to her, a reassuring call that tells her I'm safe, and I guess she hears, 'cause for just a moment she calls back, distracted from her agony.

The velos dip their heads to feed.

I line up the crosshairs on her forehead.

And pull the trigger.

ISAIAH

Zech hauls me up by the scruff of my jacket, dragging me inside the 'Vi. Through a white fog of pain and exhaustion I hear the familiar hiss of the side-door closing just as a shot echoes from the turret. My last glimpse of the outside world is of Momma's head flopping to the ground.

Misfiring rifles and short-circuiting fences and total outages and tarnation and...

Somehow, I drag myself to my feet despite the pain in my ribs from Zech's manhandling and all that running.

"Isaiah?"

I stumble to the ladder, grip the rungs, and begin to climb. After I've climbed the height of a city sky-scraper, I'm finally crawling out into the turret. Josh sits with his arms locked around his knees, face pressed to them, sobbing in a way that makes my chest hurt worse than anything yet. His rifle lies there on the floor beside him.

I drag myself into a sitting position and reach for him, draw him close. He latches on like a baby possum, face buried in my shoulder, his too-strong young arms wrapping around my chest.

I bite back the pain and hold him tight.

JOSHUA

I cling to Dad and I cry and cry and cry.

Why did it have to end like this?

"Why didn't I run faster?" I sob at last. "I shoulda run faster!"

"Aw, Josh." Dad sounds kinda wheezy, and belatedly I ease my grip a little. "If you'd run any faster, we'd be saddling you and entering you in the Under-eleven's Orni Open. You did everything you possibly could."

"Weren't enough," I sniff.

"Sometimes it ain't. At least she went down defending her chick. Proud old matriarch like her, I'm sure she'd prefer that."

"Don't rom...roman...romanticize it," I remember the word at last. "She woulda liked a nice heat lamp, regular meals, and nothing trying to eat her, is what she woulda liked!"

"Yeah, sure, okay," Dad sounds uncomfortable at being called out. "But," his voice goes firmer than I've heard it since he began overdosing himself so badly, "not at the expense of her chick. Trust me, no good parent would trade their child for a comfortable retirement."

He holds me a little tighter again. The hand that's stroking my head shakes against my scalp. Emotion, or exhaustion? Both, though I guess he's putting himself in Momma's shoes.

Momma...

Again, I see those crosshairs in position, I feel myself pull the trigger...

My heart feels like a Utahraptor is tearing it clean open. Sobs swallow me again, and I bury myself against Dad.

"He hurt?" Uncle Z's anxious voice finally penetrates my misery.

"Just a few cuts and bites. Nothing super serious."

"Here, Josh, little man," says Uncle Z, "it's okay. You're safe now." His hand strokes my head too. "That were real smart of you, telling me to leave the Dakota. She totally distracted the velos from you and Dad."

Dad tenses, and I can feel him making 'shut up' gestures at Uncle Z, who tails off into a puzzled silence.

I keep my face pressed to Dad and say nothing.

"Well, we'd better get those cuts taken care of," Uncle Z says after a moment.

Hang on! Uncle Z's worrying about *me*?

I push away from Dad and sit up, swiping my filthy hands over my damp, slimy face.

"Dad needs to go to the hospital," I tell Uncle Z, my voice rough from all that crying.

"What?" A frown appears on Uncle Z's face as he peers at Dad. "Isaiah? Yeah, you look lousy. What's the matter with you?"

Dad opens his mouth, but I jump in. "*Don't* let him tell you he's fine! He wouldn't tell me what the heck happened, so it musta been bad. Earlier he took full morphine, double-stimulants, and a stupid number of caffeine pills. He must be about ready to keel over."

Uncle Z catches his breath. "Isaiah! What happened?"

ISAIAH

I don't wanna say it in front of Josh, but I'm getting real light-headed, and Zech needs to know the facts.

"Angry armadillion caught me a glancing blow in the chest with its tail club, but I really don't think it's too bad."

Yeah, Josh's eyes open wide, exactly the look of terror and horror on his face that I didn't wanna see. Zech's face tightens, but his eyes reflect a similar level of near-panic. He kneels beside me at once and fumbles with my layers.

"An *armadillion*? Isaiah!"

"*Dad!*" Josh almost wails. "Why didn't you *tell*

me?"

"What could you do? *Ow!*" Zech is ruthlessly stripping off everything in the way as he tries to get eyes on what he clearly assumes is my caved-in chest. "Easy, Zech."

"How long ago?" he demands.

"About five days."

"*Isaiah!*"

"Well, what were I supposed to do?" I snap. "I still had to get Josh, didn't I?"

That shuts him up, at least until he finally peels up my underlayer and gets a look at my chest. It's been days since I saw it and, boy, does it look bad now, the bruises blackened and spread.

"Right. Hospital," says Zech, though he looks real relieved it ain't worse.

My head is swimming. Or mebbe I'm in an aquarium, and I'm hearing him through the water. Sounds like. "Sure…" I mutter. "Wake me up when we get there…"

"Nah-ah," Zech cruelly squeezes my shoulder. "Stay awake. We gotta get you downstairs."

JOSHUA

Dad's barely conscious as Uncle Z supports him down the ladder, with me clinging onto his collar from above to stabilize him, but finally we have him lying down on the folded out seat-bed in the cab.

"Can you reach all of those wounds, Josh?" asks Uncle Z.

"Not the two on the back of my arm."

Uncle Z sits me down and quickly cleans the hard-to-get-to bites, filling them with clotting crystals, injecting anti-sepsis serum around them and then sealing them carefully with artificial skin.

"Clean the others out good, Josh," he tells me, heading into the cab with more medical supplies. "But as soon as I've dealt with Dad's cuts, we gotta move."

"Yeah."

Sooner Dad's in the hospital the better.

ISAIAH

"What's the deal with the Dakota?" asks Zech before we've been moving long, dragging me up from sleep that would be a welcome respite from the motion of the vehicle over the rough terrain. He speaks in an undertone, as though Josh—curled up beside me—can't hear him just fine.

Zech may simply be trying to keep me awake and talking, and I don't wanna upset Josh, but if I'm gonna be unconscious or stuck in the hospital for the next little while, it's best Zech knows what's gone down.

"Well, you ain't gonna believe this, but they'd kinda adopted each other. Josh were living with her in her cave. She were almost blind, so he were fishing for her, and she were keeping him warm and protecting him—preening him, treating him just like her chick. Quite the happy little family."

Josh cuddles slightly closer. No, he ain't asleep.

Zech takes his eyes from the terrain ahead to give me a long, long look, trying to figure out if I'm pulling his leg.

"No kidding, Zech. I couldn't believe my eyes when I saw them. Downright terrifying, the whole thing. But it were working. Kept Josh alive and in very good shape the whole time until I found him." I decide not to mention the winter supplies I saw in the cave, or Zech will hound us about Josh's city-phobia twice as much. Josh had no intention of ever hiking to the city, did he?

"He were hoping we could take her to a zoo for a comfortable retirement," I add. "Which woulda had my vote after the way she'd looked after Josh. So, obviously, uh, it's real disappointing how it ended up. We were about to be torn apart by the velos when she intervened and saved us. Well, saved Josh. She weren't interested in the bush."

Zech drives in silence for a while.

"But…why'd she adopt him instead of eating

him?" he asks at last. At least he ain't calling me a liar!

"I dunno." My head is swimming again. "We ain't had much time for chit-chat. Mebbe he asked nicely."

"She were an old matriarch," Josh pipes up at last. "Raised loads of chicks. She were gonna eat me, but I triggered her maternal instincts and persuaded her I were her nestling. I tried to sneak off as soon as I could, but she were such a good momma she just kept fetching me back 'til I figured it were better to stay. She saved me from hypothermia and a deinon and the velos. I couldn't have had a better Momma. And now she's gone." His voice catches. After a moment, he asks in a very small voice, "Do animals go to heaven?"

"No," says Zech automatically—then winces.

"But…" Josh's voice quivers, "I remember some'at from a Midsummer Fair. Around a campfire… Some'at about 'no, but yes.'"

I remember that conversation. There were a priest at the fair for once when Josh were quite small, and Ed asked him about animals going to heaven. Well, it would be Ed, never without some furry companion. And the priest gave a very long and detailed reply that involved a few firm facts and several theories, but basically boiled down to…

"Well, that priest said that probably no animals in heaven, 'cause they don't have the same kinda soul as humans, but God remembers everything all the time, so when God makes heaven and earth all over again, which he's gonna do one day, he could make our animals again too, no problem. So, 'no, but mebbe later,' would be a more accurate answer."

Josh nods, making my chest twinge as his chin presses it. "And that's where lions and lambs play together, right? So she won't eat you or Uncle Z. It'll all be good."

Uncle Z's eyebrow goes up at that, and he looks bemused as he drives. Picturing a huge Dakotaraptor as part of our little family? But Josh seems calmer and happier after that weird conversation.

Until his face falls again. "But you said animals can't love like humans do?"

Oh, shoot. "Well, they can't, not *exactly*," I admit. "But what she *could*, she gave you. She really, really did. She were a fantastic mother, weren't she?"

Josh's face relaxes again, a slight smile making it onto his face. "She sure were."

Increasingly emotionally exhausted on top of everything else, I let my eyes half-close, hoping Josh don't need to talk about this no more right now.

"What happened to you, Uncle Z?" I hear Josh ask, as my head goes increasingly echoey. "What happened to the 'Vi? Looks like it rolled down a hill or some'at."

Zech snorts. "Some'at like that. I tried everything you can imagine to get it out. I dug, I lashed poles to the wheels, but the sand were too soupy for them to get enough traction to walk it free. Oh yeah, I met a pack of Dakotas while hunting for the poles, but they weren't as friendly as your one. I were out of my mind with worry for you guys by then, so I just kinda lost it. Ran straight at them screaming at the top of my lungs and shooting at them. And they thought I must be crazy-dangerous and bolted, and I ran just as hard the other way and got back in the 'Vi. And then I dug some more and…

"Anyways, to cut a long story short, eventually I got so desperate I drilled bolts into the cliffs right at the top of the slope. Hauled the 'Vi clear over onto its side—drastic—but it got the wheels outta the mud. Then dragged it all the way up the slope and stood it up again once it were on firm ground. None of which did it any good, as you can imagine. But it were out, and basically in one piece."

"Why'd you dump the meat?" Josh asks. Their voices are getting real dim now.

"How the heck d'you know about that? I tossed it out to lighten the load, but I were careless and ripped a few packets. That drew some velos, so I chucked the whole lot in the river to get rid of it quick. Hey, is Dad still awake?"

"Dad? Dad, come on, stay awake!"

Yeah, right.

Sorry…

I drift into wonderfully pain-free blackness.

JOSHUA

"Josh? Wake up." I open my eyes to find Uncle Z peering blearily down at me. "Can you drive for just an hour or two? I can't keep my eyes open. It's dead flat and level. I plotted the route to the nearest city in the NavConsole. It's a small one, but of course they have a hospital."

"Sure." I glance at Dad, but he's still asleep or unconscious, like he's been for hours. As I push myself into a sitting position, a yawn forces my jaws wide, though it ain't night yet. After showering to wash the blood off, I've already had a few hours' sleep. I scramble to the end of the bed.

"Wake me if you have a problem," Uncle Z tells me. "Or if you see anything dangerous. Or if you ain't sure of the route. Or the terrain. Or—"

"Or if a single piranaha'saur looks at us funny. Sure, I got it."

I climb into the driver's seat, fasten my roll harness—since however flat the terrain, we're still off-road—then set the cruise control. The huge vehicle moves forward. Uncle Z hovers unhappily for a while, then gets the thermometer and other medical kit and checks Dad's vitals again. He frowns, but don't look totally panicked, then lies down in the space beside Dad, which is barely large enough. But he clearly wants to be on hand in case a piranha'saur does give us the evil eye. Or Dad gets worse?

I heave a sigh of relief as he begins to snore. I were afraid he'd change his mind, since I've never driven unsupervised before. But that wouldn't get Dad to the hospital. To think I really wanna go in-city for once, quick as possible!

I shoot Dad a look now and then as I drive. His skin's usually darker than mine, but now it's the same shade, only with a nasty grayish tinge.

He ain't okay.

God? If Dad could be okay, that's the only thing I want for my birthday. The only thing.

Any birthday. I don't need nothing else, never. For the rest of my life...

Please?

ISAIAH

Josh's matriarch momma tucks me into her nest, drawing a feather blanket over me and crooning softly. I'm so warm and cozy...

Mom smiles sweetly and strokes my hair with a gentle hand.

Mom… It's so good to see her…

No, it's a claw that's stroking me. A very, very sharp claw. My cheek rests on a warm feathery breast. I'm so sleepy…

DAY 13

JOSHUA

Uncle Z's voice jerks me awake, but he's not speaking to me.

"Fangfree Heights City Traffic Control, this is the Wilson HabVi, inbound toward the hospital with an emergency. Entering the restricted zone now."

We're here! I sit up, blinking. It's dark, and city lights surround us with their eerie glow. Immediately, I feel the city pressing hard around me, just waiting to devour me...

"Wilson HabVi," comes a voice from the interCar, "you are clear to proceed to the hospital. No deviation."

"Got it. Out."

City-folk don't like huge HabVis driving around anywhere but the outskirts. At least, they say it's because of the size, but it may be more that they're full of "rough" hunters.

Dad's *still* unconscious, still gray and sick-looking. Thank Saint Des, we're soon pulling up outside the city hospital. I check my arms and legs carefully, making sure none of my wounds are seeping through my clean clothes. God knows what they'd do if they saw my bites.

As soon as we pull up, paramedics rush from a set of double-doors, pushing a gurney. Traffic control alerted them already. Uncle Z's already unhooking the cot sides, opening the door. The paramedics climb up, slide a board under Dad, and lift him out and down.

Uncle Z lifts me down like a little kid, closes the 'Vi, and hurries me after as they wheel Dad inside. I cling to Uncle Z's hand as we enter a strange world of sharp beeping, nose-searing odors, rattling gurneys, glaring lights...

I will not lose it. I will not. We have to be here with Dad...

Uncle Z explains in a few words, and Dad is wheeled away at once for "scans." We have to wait. Uncle Z sits me on his lap and pulls his jacket over my head as though shielding me from everything. It helps a little. I put my head on his shoulder and try to hide in sleep, but I can't sleep when I keep remembering the doctors' serious faces, the way they rushed Dad away so quickly... My throat keeps going tight and painful in a way that has nothing to do with the city...

"Zech?" Unexpectedly, Uncle West's voice booms around the waiting room. "Got your message. How's Isaiah?"

I feel Uncle Z let out a deep breath that shudders

slightly, like he's *real* relieved to see Uncle West, who stoops to give Uncle Z a quick half-hug.

"Hey, is this our little Josh'osaur under here?" West's big hand rests on my head for a moment, and his voice lowers. "Is he asleep?"

"Just working up to a city freak-out, I reckon. I wanna get him out of here, but not before we know how Isaiah is."

"Thiago and Ed are in the outer waiting area, but they'd only let me in here. If there's gonna be much delay, one of us can move your 'Vi before it gets towed, and come back by bus again. Ed's gonna get thrown out, anyways, if they spot that baby groundhog he's got inside his coat. But it'll take the city-folk a while to find a large enough tow truck, I reckon."

Ah. That'll be the main reason Uncle Z contacted Technicolor, I guess. So they could move the 'Vi and we could stay with Dad. And I guess he just wanted them around if Dad…if Dad's hurt bad.

West fetches some city-candy from some'at called a "vending machine" and plays a 'feeding' game with me, poking tasty tidbits under Uncle Z's coat one by one. I ain't hungry for them—and I ain't five, neither!—but I play along for the distraction 'cause I really, really, really don't wanna lose it and have to leave before I know how Dad is.

"Zechariah Wilson?" A calm, professional female

voice…

I throw back the coat and look around. A white-coated doctor stands there, smiling down at us—then across at us as Uncle Z pops to his feet, still holding me like I'm about six.

"Yeah?" Uncle Z sounds strangled.

"The scans show considerable trauma to the rib cage consisting of multiple breaks and extensive bruising. Some minor lung contusions as well, which seem to be healing on their own. We're giving him some oxygen anyway, to provide his lungs with a little help. One break needs monitoring. He might need minor surgery to straighten and set it properly. He's in generally poor condition from exposure and the over-use of the medications, but his cuts and bites aren't serious. Basically, none of it is life-threatening, and he's going to be just fine."

I clutch Uncle Z as horrible quivers take control of my insides. But I can't cry. I'm in-city, and I don't feel safe. Uncle Z's chest vibrates against mine as he breathes very fast for a few moments. When he finally speaks, his voice is very strained, like he really wants to cry too.

"That's great news. Thank you. Is he awake?"

"No. And it's best to let him sleep."

"Right. Right."

We're ushered to a side room where Dad lies in a

strange hospital bed. He's got tubes going into his arm, and a tube under his nose, and a horrible beeping monitor sits by the bed, but his color's better than it has been for days.

Uncle Z clasps Dad's hand for a while, his head bowed like he might be praying. *Yeah, thank you, God, thank you, Saint Des. Thank you, thank you, thank you!*

Thank you, Momma...

"Come on, Zech," West says at last. "Get Josh back to the 'Vi, get him to bed. Get some sleep yourself; you look beat. We'll stay with Isaiah, okay? Oh, and get Ed to give Josh that critter to look after on your way out, why don't ya?"

"I don't want it," I mutter. Like Momma can be replaced by some baby rodent!

West's brow crinkles in surprise. He must guess he's stepped into some'at unawares, because he adds smoothly, "So *he* don't get thrown outta here, I mean."

Nice save, Uncle West. I don't say no more, though. S'not like Uncle Z will want it in the 'Vi.

But...

"Ed," says Uncle Z, striding up to the tallest, thinnest, palest, and blondest of my almost-uncles as we enter the main waiting room. "West says you're to give that thing to Josh for now, 'kay?"

Ed raises an eyebrow, looking as surprised as I feel, but scoops a furry bundle out of his coat and holds it out to me. I open my mouth to refuse—but I get a look at the little face, tiny beady eyes peering innocently at me—and the next moment I find I've held my hands out.

Guess it *does* need looking after. And Ed *is* gonna get chucked outta here if it stays.

"For now" though, Uncle Z said. I'd better not get too attached.

Once we're parked in the 'Vi-park and Uncle Z has made me swallow some disgusting de-worming tablets, I set up a little critter cage with a heat lamp, and feed the baby groundhog, then tuck it in there. Ed will have to have it back when we go to see Dad again tomorrow, anyways. And if I let it sleep with me, I'm just gonna keep wishing it were Momma. Worse, feeling like I've replaced her.

Even though I slept most of the way here, I feel so exhausted that as soon as the little mammal's settled, I creep straight up into my berth, nestle down into my sleeping bag, and try to sleep. But I keep waking up wondering why I'm alone. Where's Momma?

And then I remember.

Momma's gone. My gut clenches.

But Dad...Dad's gonna be okay.

I lie listening to Uncle Z puttering around below for a while, wishing I could be with Dad without freaking out. Wishing Momma could swaddle me. Guiltily tempted to fetch the baby groundhog…

Nope. Not doing that.

Finally, a tap on my door makes me jump. Uncle Z slides it open. "Josh? You wanna sleep in with me tonight?"

"Yeah," I whisper.

"Come on, then, my little caterpillar." He eases me out, sleeping bag and all, and carries me into the cab. Puts me down in the sheltered inside position, and lays out his own sleeping bag.

"Ah, hang on." He heads back into the living area, speaking over his shoulder. "Isaiah wanted me to give you some'at from his pack, but I've been too busy driving to do it." He's back again, sliding into his sleeping bag at last. "Here."

I open my eyes and find myself looking at a large blue feather. A rather tired, faded blue, but the most beautiful blue all the same. "Thanks, Uncle Z," I whisper.

Thanks, Dad.

I close my fingers around Momma's feather and hold it tight. This time, when I rest my head on Uncle Z's chest, my eyelids start to get heavy.

"Uncle Z?" I murmur.

"Yeah?"

"I love you."

His chest shudders. He really is crying this time. "I

love you too, little Josh'osaur." His voice squeaks slightly as he rubs my back, drawing me close. "I love you too."

My eyes close, and then I'm sitting by a fire, and Momma's preening me, and Dad's cooking a real big fish over the flames, and Uncle Z's playing fetch with a velo, and then Dad brings out a real nice cake and they all sing Happy Birthday. To me.

And it's the best birthday ever.

==+==

JOSHUA

JOSHUA

"Tell that hunter-boy to hurry up. I haven't got all day," snaps the man in the suit.

I glance out at the welcome party that stands on the obsoDeck. Ned Greyson, stocky and light-skinned, is Exception City Zoo's Head Raptor Keeper. I know him moderately well—the Wilson HabVi has supplied quite a few critters to this zoo over the years. The young Hispanic man—older than me but with that wet-behind-the-ears air most city-boys have—is an eager young underling, or intern, or some-such. The pretty lady—of Cheyenne heritage, I think—is the zoo vet. And there's the thin, pale man in a suit, looking down his nose at everyone, but especially at me in my camo-jacket and heavy boots. He hasn't even spoken to me. Keeps passing things through Ned.

Ned doesn't 'tell me' anything, he just screws up his face in apology and opens his hand in a 'let it go' gesture. He needn't worry. The guy's getting my goat but it takes more than that to blow my fuse.

"There we go." As Silky the velociraptor finally steps off my Habitat Vehicle's ramp into the zoo's holding pen, I press the button to lift the ramp and seal the rear door. He skitters away nervously, but by the time I've dropped out of the HabVi and climbed up to the obsoDeck to join the group standing looking down into the pen, he's run back up to the rear of the large grey vehicle where it's parked flush with the gateway, begging to be let back in, peeping plaintively like he's a juvenile again. "Sorry, Silky," I tell him, raising my voice. "This is your new home, now."

I ignore Suit-man and speak to Ned. "Yep, one velociraptor, male, adult, and zoo-tame."

Silky scratches at the 'Vi with one wing-arm claw, shoots a nervous look around at the strange pen, then calls pathetically.

"Ready to mate?" queries Ned, a twinkle in his eye.

I grin. "Yep. Though he ain't cutting a very manly figure this moment, is he? Too much new."

Ned grins too, but he looks pleased. Silky is young and healthy, virtually adult size—as tall as a wolf and several times longer from nose to tail tip—and into his adult plumage, his unusually soft, sleek charcoal grey feathers set off nicely by his dark blue ruff. A real beauty, and a perfect zoo animal.

But Suit-man steps up to the edge of the obsoDeck and peers down, making Silky start and bolt into the farthest corner of the pen. Suit-man frowns. "Well, this raptor doesn't seem very zoo-tame to me. It's terrified of everything."

"What d'you expect? He's never been in a place like this."

"We're paying extra for a raptor that isn't going to cower away from people and make the visitors think we're mistreating it. I've heard of you hunters' tricks. If you're trying to pass off some sub-standard creature on us, you won't get paid at all."

Ned winces and holds up a hand. "Now, Mr. Grundvick—"

But I don't care what Ned plans to say. Suit-man's suspicion is just one slur too many. He's gonna get punched if he keeps treating hunters like this—this guy could try even a hunter's self-restraint. But there are better ways to make a point.

"Not tame, huh?" I take two steps to the edge of the obsoDeck.

"Aw, heck, Joshua, don't you—"

I ignore Ned—and drop lightly down into the pen.

DARRYL

After knocking back my last swig of coffee, I slip on my denim jacket and pause on my way to the gun locker, checking my reflection in the hall mirror. Shoulder-length brown hair brushed—and loose, for once—face clean, blue eyes...glum. But this has happened, whether I like it or not, so I might as well make a good first impression.

"Harry, get down here, we're going to be late!"

The volume of Dad's latest bellow up the stairs shows that he means business. Well, *I'm* ready, at least.

I thought my younger brother had come around to the 'might as well make a good impression' viewpoint as well, but there's still no noise from upstairs. The fact is, when your dad comes back from a routine weekend market and supply trip to the city and announces that he's got honest-to-God *married* and that the woman — sorry, step-mom — will be coming to live with you, three weeks really isn't enough time to deal with it.

Harry totally lost it. Screamed Lord knows what at Dad, then ran off to the nearest barn. I managed not to do any screaming, but I had to go up and shut myself in the farmhouse's observation turret for almost an hour, and talk to myself *a lot*. You know: *Dad's been alone a long time, Darryl; if he's fallen in love that's wonderful, isn't it, Darryl; you want your father to be happy, don't you, Darryl?*

He totally sprung it on us, though. I guess he was so scared Potential Step-Mom — sorry, Carol — would come to her senses and decide that no handsome, propertied man of her own age was worth going and living unSPARKed on some farm. Carol's a city girl, all right.

When I finally managed to go back down and say something about being happy for Dad and try to show some interest in his new bride, he showed me a photo on his phone, and my heart didn't lift. Just sank even further. Manicured Carol looked like she'd never got within a mile of the city fence in her life, let alone stepped outside it. A less likely farmer's wife I had never seen.

Dad could tell what I was thinking, of course. Brain not completely scrambled by love. "I know Carol's no farmer, Darryl my girl," he told me, "but really, it doesn't matter, does it? We've run the farm by ourselves all this time. She can run her fashion design and consultancy business from the house—I'm getting a faster Net connection put in. And *we'll* run the farm, just as before. And you and Harry will inherit it, Darryl, no question. Carol has her own money."

I reach the gun locker and place my hand on the scanner. Much as I hated to hear Dad talking about *his will*, it's a relief to know the farm is safe. I could put up with a harem of step-moms if I had to, but if someone took the farm from me...

As I take my rifle from the rack I can't help smiling at the thought of Dad with a *harem* of Carols. No, not Dad. We're Catholic, you know. One spouse at a time. Carol's 'not religious,' apparently. I hope that won't matter. Dad did say he thinks she's 'open to it' so that's something.

I throw my ammunition sash on and check the pouches. Three hold full mags, but since we'll be traveling unSPARKed...I'll add the fourth pouch. I put my hand on the scanner to open the ammo box and take a handful of HiPiRs, or Hide Piercing Rounds. Penetrate any hide up to T. rex, these will. Though for T. rex, I really would prefer a bigger gun. *Much* bigger.

"HARRY!" roars Dad, then heads over to me. "Whoa, girl, wait up. Come on, put the rifle away."

"What?" I turn an incredulous look on him. "We're travelling unSPARKed, Dad."

"Carol's nervous enough about the trip as it is, let alone living out here. If we turn up looking like Rambo-family, she's going to freak out. I'll have my rifle. Leave yours here. Just this once."

"But why have one rifle when you can have three?" I demand.

"Most people don't take *any* weapons when they travel, Darryl."

"*City* people. And sometimes when they break down or crash, they get eaten."

"Come on, Darryl, just this once. It will make Carol feel so much better."

Dad's pleading tone is too much. I unsling my rifle from my shoulder and put it back in its place. "All right. But we'd better not end up Raptor Food."

"Of course we won't." He sounds downright cheerful with relief.

JOSHUA

"Hey, Silky-boy." I move out into the middle of the small space and drop into a crouch, making myself smaller and non-threatening as I pull a training treat from my pocket. One knee I keep bent, blocking access to my stomach, while I tuck my left wrist under my chin, palm inwards, shielding my neck. Zoo-tame ain't all the way tame, not by a long shot. "Hey, Silky-boy, Mr. Suit thinks you ain't tame enough for his liking. Poor Silky-boy. Come on, then..."

"Joshua, just come out of there," urges Ned, in a low voice.

I ignore him, too busy saying friendly things in velociraptor-speak, though I need hardly bother. Silky is already running eagerly towards me, drawn as much by my familiarity as by the treat. When he pauses a few feet away, his head on the same level as mine since I'm crouched down, I toss him the meaty drop and pull out another one. He advances again, more confidently. When he's almost close enough to grab for it, I toss it into his mouth. "Good boy. Not scared of humans, are you? Just scared of new."

He takes the last few steps and rubs his head against me, like a hatchling begging a parent for food. Yes, he's very nervous of the strange place, and it's making him even friendlier than usual.

Crooning reassuringly like an adult to a chick—but

keeping my knee and left wrist firmly in place—I stroke his charcoal grey back, healthy young velociraptor scent filling my nostrils. When he just carries on nudging me with his head and peeping anxiously, I slide an arm around him in a hug and ruffle his breast feathers, then glance at Mr. Suit.

"So, mister," I ask him, Silky's teeth inches from my face, "is this raptor tame enough for your liking?"

Get PLEASE DON'T FEED THE DINOSAURS from your favorite retailer today!

ABOUT THE AUTHOR

Corinna Turner has been writing since she was fourteen and likes strong protagonists with plenty of integrity. Although she spends as much time as possible writing, she cannot keep up with the flow of ideas, for which she offers thanks—and occasional grumbles!—to the Holy Spirit. She is the author of over thirty books, including the Carnegie Medal Nominated I Am Margaret series, and her work has been translated into four languages. She was awarded the St. Katherine Drexel award in 2022.

She is a Lay Dominican with an MA in English from Oxford University and lives in the UK. She is a member of a number of organizations, including the Society of Authors, Catholic Teen Books, Catholic Reads, the Angelic Warfare Confraternity, and the Sodality of the Blessed Sacrament. She used to have a Giant African Land Snail, Peter, with a 6½" long shell, but now makes do with a cactus and a campervan.

Get in touch with Corinna...

Facebook: Corinna Turner

Don't forget to sign up for

NEWS

&

FREE SHORT STORIES

at:

www.UnSeenBooks.com

All Free/Exclusive content subject to availability.